CHARLES D HALE

Heaven's Gate

Sheriff Harrison Saga Vol 1

SGM

This book is dedicated to my sister, Diane Griego, in loving memory.

Contents

CHAPTER ONE

I had been driving for a long time, but I had no idea where I was nor how long it had been since my journey began. I felt like I was caught in a time warp with no sense of a beginning, purpose or destination. The gentle humming of the car's engine and the staccato thumping of the tires on the highway drew me into a trance-like state. A thousand ragged shreds of thought fluttered wildly through my mind, and I felt like I was looking through a kaleidoscope, trying to make sense out of meaningless snatches of blurred and jumbled shapes.

The painful memory besieged me and I struggled desperately to push it away, trying to escape the pain and torment that came with it. Regardless of how hard I tried, though, I couldn't elude the agony of those horrible few minutes – a mere sliver of time that had changed my life forever. Now, weeks later, I was on a journey to nowhere, trying to put the past behind me, but knowing that I'd never be able to forget the day my whole world had come to an end.

Janet had packed the picnic basket with loving care and little Jason had assembled all of his favorite toys to take with him to the park. We were looking forward to a relaxing day at our favorite getaway place, a quiet wooded area high in the rolling, verdant hills overlooking Santa Monica Bay. We would bask in sunny skies and smog-free air, away from the hectic pace to which we had both become too accustomed since I had taken my last promotion in the District Attorney Office and Janet had gone back to teaching.

I would be spending an idyllic day with the two loves of my life – I couldn't have imagined a more perfect outing. The toil and stress of weeks of hard work, jumbled schedules, missed meals, hurried phone calls and infrequent love-making was finally about to give way to a few hours of peaceful relaxation and enjoyment for our small family of three.

" Clint, love, I need to run down to the market and pick up some sodas for Jason and myself and a six-pack of Coors for you," Janet called out cheerfully. "I thought we had enough but we're running low. While you finish packing the van I'll take your car, if that's okay."

Somewhere deep inside me a faint warning signal sounded, but I ignored it, determined that nothing would interrupt our special day.

"Sure, hon, but don't wreck it," I joked weakly. "The county will make me pay for it. You've got Jason, right?"

"Yes, darling. He's with me. Not to worry."

Seconds later, she turned the key in the ignition, and the alarm that had sounded earlier in my head rose to a high, piercing shriek as the powerful force of the explosion shattered the windows of our house, shook the walls with the severity of a major earthquake and threw me violently to the floor. My family disintegrated in a whoosh of searing heat and raging flame.

Now, weeks later, after taking a leave of absence from the D.A.'s office, I was desperately trying to escape the suffocating emptiness and loneliness that held me in its grip. In the dim recesses of my mind, I knew that I'd one day have to return to L.A. to relive that horrible day – the man who'd planted the bomb in my car had been caught and would eventually stand trial, and I would be there for the whole, painful ordeal. For the time being, I just wanted to escape from the past and I wasn't particularly interested in where I ended up or when.

Eventually, my thoughts drifted back to the reality of the moment and I became aware that I was on a winding mountain road with sheer cliffs and steep drop-offs on either side. In the distance, majestic spires of lofty mountains thrust themselves into a cloudless, azure sky. Far below, dense forests of ponderosa pine, Douglas fir, aspen and blue spruce towered above a rolling sea of red, white, yellow and gold flowers of all descriptions.

Overhead, a hawk soared gracefully on invisible currents, eyeing the ground below for prey. Several miles ahead, signs of civilization were nestled in a broad valley where the mountains abruptly parted. There was something peaceful and inviting about the place.

The town was called Climax, five miles ahead. The faded letters were hardly visible on an aged wooden sign that clung precariously to a tired- looking post on the side of the road. The name intrigued me, creating visions of dusty streets adorned with hitching posts, ancient miners lounging on wooden sidewalks, overloaded pack mules, rowdy saloons, drunken cowboys, the tinkling sound of a player piano, lusty women with painted lips and wandering eyes, and mean-looking desperados. I wondered what I might discover in this town with the curious name.

I was suddenly jolted back to reality when I saw an aging Ford sedan rushing toward me from the opposite direction at great speed. It rocked crazily from side to side, and I instinctively knew that it was out of control. To my right, the narrow shoulder of the road dropped off into a deep canyon, hundreds of feet below. To the left, a sheer rock wall was separated from the roadway by only a few feet. I was directly in the sedan's path, and I didn't think there was enough room to maneuver out of its way. The driver's face was contorted in horror, and he desperately tried to gain control of the car as it hurtled toward me. There was no time to think, and I knew that certain death was only seconds away. I felt the only chance either of us had was to go into the wall, but the odds of us surviving the impact were dubious.

The oncoming car was smaller and lighter than my powerful town car, so I knew that I had the advantage of weight and mass. I might survive a head-on collision between the two cars, but the other driver would not fare as well. It was obvious that I needed as much speed as possible to turn my car into a sledgehammer that would be able to stop the other car from careening off the roadway and hurtling into the canyon below. I mashed the accelerator to the floor to gain maximum velocity and the engine screamed in protest. It was going to be very close.

Just before impact, I spun the wheel into a hard left turn, aiming to hit the other car with a glancing blow that would force it into the cliff wall. The bone-jarring impact threw me into the dashboard and a searing hot pain stabbed into my side. My thoughts slowed to quarter-speed and my vision was blurred as a choking cloud of dust, dirt, rock, burnt rubber and hissing steam showered both cars as they collided angrily in a thunderous cacophony of ripping metal, shredded rubber and shattered glass. For a brief instant the two vehicles appeared to be locked in mortal combat and then careened wildly out of control, traversing the jagged face of the cliff before coming mercifully to a grinding halt.

The force of the impact threw me out of my car like a rag doll and a lightning bolt of pain shot through my shoulder as my body was slammed savagely to the ground. Much too late I regretted my stubborn resistance to seat belts as I confirmed that all my major body parts appeared to be intact.

I tried to ignore my own injuries and turned my attention to the other driver. He was still strapped in his seat belt in a car that was a jumbled mass of twisted steel and metal. I struggled to my feet, and I could smell the

4

distinctive odor of gasoline. Fear gripped me as I realized that the fuel tank of his car must have ruptured. I could see a steady stream of fuel pouring out onto the ground and it was headed directly toward the burning engine of the Ford. In just a few seconds the fire would ignite the gasoline. If the other driver was not dead already, the resulting explosion would surely kill him.

I half-crawled, half-ran to the driver's door and struggled to free him from the shoulder harnesses that had trapped him. He was an old man – in his sixties perhaps – and small in stature. His body was limp and there was no sign of life, but I knew I had to get him away from that car before it became a searing ball of fire. I was able to unlatch the restraint, and he fell into my arms. Blood poured from an ugly gash on his forehead; his eyes were glazed over as if the life was slowly ebbing from his body.

I knew that there was not a second to waste. I grabbed one arm and dragged him to the side of the road where a large pile of rocks afforded scant protection. Just as I threw myself on top of him, our bodies were hammered by a powerful explosion that sucked the air from my lungs and smothered us with a searing blanket of heat. The last thing I remember was wondering whether either of us would live or die.

CHAPTER TWO

The large, round face stared coolly down at me with no hint of emotion. She had a mass of short, curly hair that was blonde turning to grey and her face was punctuated by a large, round nose that perched atop a wide mouth framed by thick red lips that were twisted into an unpleasant frown. Her deep-set eyes were small and dark and were overshadowed by large dark eyebrows that nearly joined in the middle of her forehead. The name tag mounted above her large bosom identified her as "M. Snyder". The sight of her jolted me awake.

"Well, Mr. Harrison, it's nice to see you back among the living!"

In stark contrast to her menacing countenance, her voice was cheerful, soft and soothing. Her abrupt intrusion into my consciousness confused me and I stared at her without saying anything, but the compassion in her voice was reassuring.

She put large hands on her wide hips and looked at me warmly. "Considering what you've been through, I'd say you're a purty tough hombre. We thought you had at least a concussion, but nothing showed up on the MRI. "Other than a few bruised ribs, and that nasty cut on your arm that took seventeen stitches to close—by the way—you're in better shape than one would expect!"

I made a move to sit up, and a hot arrow of pain jabbed deep into my side. down.

"Not so fast, mister," the nurse said, leaning forward to gently push me back.

Words tumbled from my mouth and sounded something like "Where am I?"

She chucked warmly and said, "Why, Mr. Harrison, you're in the Climax Medical Center – the finest little urgent care clinic west of Durango!" The grin on her face grew even wider.

Before her words could register in my jumbled thoughts she continued.

"The doctors on his rounds now and he needs to see you before you go making any long-range plans," she said, straightening the sheet over me. "I'll let him know you're awake and he'll be in shortly. I expect he'll have you out of here in a jiffy, 'cause we need all the beds we've got for really sick folks." She winked cheerfully at me.

Before I could reply, she was gone, and I was left alone to contemplate my situation. I felt like I had been trampled over by a pack of mules, but my injuries could have been considerably worse. My head throbbed and I reached across my body and felt a large gauze bandage that covered most of my forearm. I turned onto my left side and the burning pain returned. From my days in varsity football, I knew that time was the only remedy to heal bruised ribs.

My thoughts drifted back to the awful collision; an image of the driver of the other car flashed into my mind and I wondered if he had survived. The impact of the crash had been severe, and I began to have second thoughts about the logic of my actions. By forcing my car into his, I had caused a collision that could very well have killed us both. But what was the alternative?

If I had somehow evaded him, would he have gone over the cliff? Then again, maybe he could have gotten his car under control without my intervention. Had I caused the death of an innocent person? The idea was too horrible to contemplate, and I mumbled a prayer for God to spare the man's life.

"Mr. Harrison, you're looking much better than you did a few hours ago!" The booming male voice with a slight British accent startled me. He was tall and angular with a long, narrow, deeply tanned face. A large black mustache framed a wide smile that was highlighted by two rows of sparkling white teeth. The gentle brown eyes looking intently at me conveyed sincerity and warmth.

"I've felt better." I managed a grin.

The doctor's name tag told me that he was "J. Bradford". He appeared to be in his forties, and he carried himself like a man who was used to being in charge, but his reassuring bedside manner suggested that he did not take himself too seriously.

"I understand that you were in quite a crash. It's amazing that anyone survived. You certainly have a great deal to be thankful for." He spoke as he consulted the chart next to my bed, checked my pulse, inspected the pupils of my eyes and made a few additional notations on the chart.

"I'm releasing you now, Mr. Harrison," he said, "but you need to take it easy for a few days. I'll be giving the nurse a prescription for a pain killer and an antibiotic to keep your wound from getting infected. I'd like to see you back in a few days to remove those stitches and to check on your condition. Is that possible?" I thought to myself, *I have no immediate plans – this place is as good as any to recoup.*

"Sure," I said, "I can check back. When would be good?"

He looked up from the chipboard and said, "Check with Nurse Snyder. She will make an appointment for you. She'll be by shortly to get you checked out. In the meantime, you can get what's left of your clothes on. They are in somewhat worse shape than you."

The doctor was on his way out when I remembered the old man and, almost fearing the answer, I asked, "Doctor . . . the driver of the other car. Was he . . . that is, how is he . . . ?"

Part of me wasn't sure that I really wanted to know, but I knew that I'd have no peace until I learned of the other driver's fate.

Dr. Bradford turned back toward me and hesitated for a moment, the large smile replaced by a frown, as if to confirm my fear. "Ben Griffin's in real bad shape, Mr. Harrison."

Ben Griffin? Now, at least, the old man had a name

"He had severe internal injuries," Dr. Bradford continued, "along with a concussion and several broken bones. He's very lucky that the paramedics were able to get him here as quickly as they did. We almost lost him in the operating room and he's still not out of it yet. Right now, he's in a comatose state and I expect it may be several days before we can make any better prognosis of his condition."

A wave of relief rushed over me, and I felt as if a huge weight had been lifted from my shoulders. Knowing that the old man – Mr. Griffin – had survived the crash was welcome news notwithstanding the severity of his injuries.

"I understand that we have you to thank for saving Ben's life." I didn't know what to say so I said nothing.

Doctor Bradford folded his arms across his chest and looked at me squarely in the eyes. "Another motorist arrived on the scene moments after the wreck. He observed you pulling Ben Griffin from his car just seconds before the gas tank ignited and the entire car went up in a ball of fire. Ben would have been a goner if you hadn't reacted so quickly."

I was embarrassed by his praise, and I felt my cheeks grow warm. "To tell you the truth, Doc, I don't remember much about what happened after the crash, but I'm relieved to hear the old fellow – this Mr. Griffin – didn't die."

"You probably have short-term amnesia associated with the trauma of the accident. You'll regain your memory in due time. But there's no mistake about what you did. Harry Barber, one of the first emergency responders to arrive on the scene, got the story straight from the eyewitness and by now everyone in town knows you're a hero!" The doctor's eyes twinkled as he told me the story, and my cheeks grew even warmer.

The doctor left to continue his rounds, and I was once again alone with my thoughts. I said another prayer for Mr. Griffin, but I was uncomfortable with the idea of being called a hero. I had merely reacted to the circumstances of the moment as anyone would have done, and I deserved no credit for that. I waited for a while for Nurse Snyder to return but I began to get restless and decided to take matters into my own hands and get dressed. I crawled slowly from the bed and tried to ignore the pain that continued to jab sharply into my side. I managed to get to the floor and was struggling to pull what was left of my jeans up my legs when Nurse Snyder abruptly strode into the room, took one look at my bare buttocks and smiled broadly.

"Well, if you don't beat all," she chuckled. "I've seen many a perfect behind in my day, but you've got one of the cutest!"

I blushed the color of burgundy wine and hurriedly pulled my jeans up over my hips and dropped the hospital gown to the floor.

"Here you go," she said, and handed me my shirt, which was torn and bloody. I took one look at it and tossed it into the trash receptacle next to the bed. "Here, try this instead." She handed me a plastic wrapped package.

I tore it open and found a gaily decorated T-shirt celebrating the town's centennial anniversary two years previously.

"We had a bunch of these left over from the centennial celebration," she explained. "This one looks to be about your size."

"Thanks," I said, slipping it on, trying not to show the pain that raced through every muscle of my body at the slightest move.

As if reading my mind, she said, "The doctor gave me some painkillers and antibiotics for you." She handed me a small paper bag. "Be sure to follow the directions." I took the bag from her and promised to do as the doctor ordered.

She handed me her clipboard with several forms attached to it. "Here, sign the bottom of these two and the third one's yours. Come back here Thursday at 1:00 PM sharp so the doc can remove these stitches and check you over." Now she was sounding like my mom, and it made me feel warm inside.

I signed where she had indicated, accepted the third form, and started for the door, but she grabbed me gently by the arm to stop me and said, "Before you go, there's someone outside who would like to see you. Are you up for a visitor?"

I was taken off guard. "I don't know a soul in this town. Who'd want to see me?"

"Her name is Melanie Griffin," Nurse Snyder replied. "Her father is Ben Griffin, the man you saved in the crash. She insists on seeing you, if you don't mind."

CHAPTER THREE

Melanie Griffin was a petite, trim woman who appeared to be in her mid-thirties. She had large blue eyes, blonde hair that fell neatly to her shoulders and a wide mouth that framed a perfect set of white teeth. I noticed immediately that she was one of those women who looked their best with little or no cosmetic's. She wore a sleeveless sweater that clung firmly to her full bosom and white shorts that covered only a portion of shapely tan legs. Her feet were encased in white sandals that revealed pink-painted toenails.

"Mr. Harrison? I'm Melanie Griffin. I don't know how to thank you for saving my father's life!" Her voice was strained, and the impact of her father's situation had taken its toll. I could tell that she was struggling with her emotions.

"I'm relieved to know that your father survived the crash," I said, "but I simply did what anyone in that same situation would have done." As I said these words, I wondered how many more times I would have to repeat them in the next several days. The burning returned to my cheeks and made me even more uncomfortable.

Her eyes filled with tears, and she appeared to momentarily lose control, slumping into a chair next to the hospital bed. "I don't know what I would do without him." She choked back sobs, and I tried to think of something to say to comfort her.

Finally, I managed, "You need to get yourself under control. I think your father would want that."

Her body shuddered; then she abruptly stood up, having regained her composure.

I offered her my handkerchief, and she took it and began dabbing at her eyes. "Thanks so much, Mr. Harrison. I apologize for getting so worked up, but I'm very attached to my father. He's all I have in this world."

"I understand," I said. "I was pretty attached to my dad too before ... before he passed away."

Not exactly the best way to reassure her, I thought.

She steadied her voice and said, "I heard what happened out there at the crash and I know that my father would not be alive right now if it were not for your quick actions. You have my eternal gratitude."

I wanted to protest but I knew it would be a wasted effort so I said nothing.

"And now, Mr. Harrison," she said in a very businesslike manner, "let's get you out of here. Do you have a place to stay in town?"

I was impressed at how quickly she had regained her composure and had assumed a "take charge" attitude. I could tell that she was accustomed to having her way, so I did not protest.

"No," I replied casually, "I hadn't planned on staying, but the doctor ..."

"Well," she jumped in, most likely learning of my agenda – or lack of one, from Nurse Snyder, "you'll need a place to stay for a few days while you recuperate, and I know just the place." I started to object when she said with an inquisitive look, "I'm sure someone will want to know where you are and why they haven't heard from you."

Her words caused a tightness in my chest. I shifted my eyes to avoid looking at her and it probably telegraphed more than I wanted her to know.

"Well, at any rate," she said, as if acknowledging my own discomfort, "let's get you checked out."

While I completed the paperwork required for my release, Melanie went to make a telephone call. When she returned, she informed the bewildered and somewhat intimidated insurance clerk that all charges relating to my brief stay should be forwarded to her at the *Climax Gazette*. I started to protest but she would not hear of it. She was clearly in charge of the situation and I suspected that it would be pointless to argue.

We emerged from the medical center to see a bronze sun melting into the grey-blue rim of mountains on the southwestern horizon. The air was cool and refreshing and saturated with the pungent odor of pine, spruce and juniper. It was a stimulating spectacle, and I felt more alive than I had in a long time.

"Well, Mr. Harrison," Melanie said jokingly, "your chariot awaits you!"

She pointed to an army surplus jeep that looked like it had been through more than its share of combat. She referred to it as "Baby" as if it were a member of the family. Baby was badly banged up from nearly every angle, and the left rear fender appeared to be attached to the chassis with a coat hanger. The windshield had a large crack that divided it into two pieces and I couldn't tell what was holding them together. One headlight dangled precariously from its socket and half of the front bumper was missing.

Despite the dilapidated look of the jeep, when she turned the key in the ignition, the engine came alive with a throaty roar. The ride was bumpy and uncomfortable, but I was impressed with her driving skill. Even with its broken-down appearance, the jeep seemed to be in remarkably good mechanical condition and was ideally suited to the rugged terrain.

"I think you'll find the Summit Inn to your liking. It's the nicest place in town," she shouted over the noisy roar of the engine. "I called ahead and booked a room for you. I hope you don't mind."

It was kind of her to take the trouble and I told her so.

"It's no trouble, really, Mr. Harrison. It's the least I could do for you after all . . ." Her voice trailed off and worry lines etched her forehead. I figured that she must be thinking about her father. I was thinking of him too. It was also very important to me that he pull through his ordeal.

The jeep rocketed at breakneck speed on a series of twisting secondary roads. I held on to what little support I could find and had flashbacks to some of the wildest pursuits I had been involved in long ago during my time as a uniformed police officer. We hurtled up a steep, winding road surrounded on both sides by thick stands of ponderosa pine and juniper trees. My ears popped as the altitude increased with each wrenching turn of the road, and I wondered if the Summit Inn was a magic castle perched high on a lofty mountaintop. We rounded a sharp turn in the road and came upon a clearing that provided a majestic view of the valley below.

The jeep came to a screeching halt beneath an expansive portico supported by wide Grecian columns. We were in front of a large, wonderfully ornate building of Victorian design, with a peculiar mixture of corniced eaves, angular bay windows, spiraling towers, large cupolas and railed balconies that spilled out onto several levels. Delicate wainscoting and gingerbread molding edged every angle and shapely curve. It appeared that each room had a porch or balcony offering a breathtaking view of the valley.

The Summit Inn was the color of putty with green and white trim on the windows, shutters, balcony railings and doors. The grounds surrounding the inn were neatly manicured with perfectly sculpted hedgerows, dazzling flower gardens and a large pond with a geyser-like fountain. It was the kind of place you'd expect to see on the front cover of a brochure from some expensive resort – definitely not what I would have imagined in this little town with such an unlikely name.

"The Summit Inn is an excellent place to stay," Melanie said, jumping effortlessly from the jeep. "Amos and Martha Greer are the innkeepers and they like to pamper their guests." She came around to my side of the jeep to assist me, and I was surprised at how weak I felt as I stood, trying to control a trembling in my legs.

She must have read my thoughts. "You look exhausted. A good night's rest will do you a world of good."

I did feel a bit drowsy and I realized that I was still feeling the effect of the medication Nurse Snyder had given me in the hospital.

Melanie led me into a tastefully decorated lobby that resembled the interior of a 19th century Victorian mansion. It featured several large stuffed chairs, a divan, a circular coffee table and a large china cabinet with a beautifully delicate china service. A large vase of fresh cut red, white and pink roses sat atop a matching end table. The floors were gleaming hardwood decorated with several small throw rugs that perfectly matched the mauve and cream tones of wallpaper and trim. Just as we entered, a full-length grandfather clock began chiming somberly and I instinctively checked my watch to discover that it was precisely four o'clock. Nothing if not punctual, I thought.

A tall, stoop-shouldered man who appeared to be in his late sixties stood behind a counter. He wore a friendly smile and had wire-rimmed spectacles perched on the tip of a large, angular nose. His soft, clear-blue eyes twinkled as he watched us enter.

He walked around the counter, gathered Melanie up in his arms, and said, "Sorry to hear about your dad. But don't you worry none, child. He'll pull through this in fine shape." He spoke to her like she was family and there was genuine concern in his voice.

Melanie pulled herself away from him and turned to me. "Amos, this is Mr. Harrison. He's the man who saved Daddy's life and I would like you to put him up at least until Thursday – or when he's ready to travel again. Mr. Harrison, this is Amos Greer."

Amos turned to me for the first time and peered at me through thick lenses. He extended a large hand, and I took it, impressed at his strong grip. "How do you do, Mr. Harrison! We owe you a debt of gratitude," he said cheerfully. "You are most welcome in our humble hostelry." He bowed slightly and I was warmed by his effusive manner and friendly greeting.

He turned to Melanie and said, "Now, honey, I'll take good care of Mr. Harrison. You go on and check on your dad. Let us know if the missus and I can do anything." With that he pushed her gently toward the door. She turned and gave him a loving peck on the cheek and waved to me. Moments later I heard Baby's throaty roar as she sped away.

Amos turned back to me and said, "Let's get you settled, Mr. Harrison. You look like you could use some rest."

I didn't argue. I probably looked about as bad as I felt and bed rest sounded like a very good idea.

Amos retrieved a key from a row of hooks on the wall and motioned for me to follow him. He walked quickly down a long hallway, then up a stairway and down another hallway. He stopped in front of room 231 and pushed the key into the lock. He opened the door and stepped aside, allowing me to enter.

The room was spacious and tastefully appointed. It had a large, four- poster bed, a love seat and a rocking chair that sat in front of a large bay window through which the bright rays of the sun washed over craggy, snow-capped mountain peaks. A large fireplace with a marble mantle and an ornate gold metal grill adorned the wall opposite the bed.

Amos pointed out the bathtub and shower and a small closet and a large oak dresser. There was a large-screen HD television that Amos informed me proudly was equipped with a satellite receiver. All in all, it was a charming and comfortable room and the bed looked especially inviting.

Amos smiled broadly and must have sensed my growing fatigue. He handed me the key and said, "You get some rest. Breakfast is served from six until nine.

"I'll see if Martha can't rustle up some clothes for you to wear until you can get some of your own."

I realized that I must look like a street urchin but I was too tired to care.

"If there's anything else we can do for you, just call," he said, pointing to the telephone on the bedside table.

With that, he closed the door behind himself, and I was alone. I quickly stripped off my clothes and stepped into the shower. The hot water washed over me and massaged my aching muscles. I let the water run until the fatigue was more than I could bear. I toweled myself dry, and opened the window to allow the cool, mountain air to breathe life into the room.

I lay down on the bed and reflected back on the events of the day, wondering what might lie ahead in this place called Climax. Despite my fatigue, sleep would not come. I was plagued by flashbacks of the fateful day I lost my precious wife and son. I could not think about the evil men who did this. That would come later . . . after the mourning period my wife and son deserved.

I wondered if I would ever find peace again. Would the emptiness I felt ever be filled? How could I ever regain the happiness I had once known? Despite these nagging and worrisome thoughts, somewhere deep inside I sensed a small glimmer of hope. A faint voice seemed to be whispering to me that my life was about to change dramatically. But would that change be for the best?

CHAPTER FOUR

Golden rays of sunlight cascaded through the large bay window of my room and I struggled to remember where I was. Slowly, painfully, I sat up and tried to clear the haze from my brain. I glanced at my watch and was surprised to find that it was nearly noon. I found it hard to believe because it was long after the time that I usually started my day. I could only guess that the trauma of my injuries and the general rundown condition I had been in had taken their toll, but the long rest had done me a lot of good, and I felt refreshed and anxious to face the new day.

I swung my feet onto the hardwood floor, and I felt a sharp pang of hunger as my stomach grumbled its displeasure. I tried to remember when I had last eaten. My thoughts were interrupted by the shrill ring of the telephone next to my bed and I wondered who could possibly be calling me.

I reached for the receiver. "Hello?" The curiosity in my voice must have been obvious.

"Good morning, Mr. Harrison." It was a female voice that I recognized as Melanie Griffin.

"Morning, Melanie." I was surprised to hear from her.

"I'm terribly sorry, Mr. Harrison," she apologized. "I woke you up, didn't I? Please forgive me."

"No, that's quite all right," I said, "I was just getting up when you called – and please call me Clint. We've known each other long enough to forgo the formalities."

She hesitated for a moment, then said, "Well, all right . . . Clint, if you like. I just called to see how you are feeling and if there's anything you need."

"That's very nice of you, Melanie, but you've already done much more than ..." My voice trailed as I searched for the right words and came up short.

"I am eternally indebted to you, Clint," she said warmly. "If there is anything else you need, please let me know."

I remembered how hungry I was. "I'm starved and you must know a good place to eat here in town. How about letting me buy you lunch?"

She laughed and said, "That's quite all right, Clint, you don't need to do that."

"I insist," I replied firmly. "I'm feeling much better, and I need to get out. Besides, there is some kind of creature making terrible sounds from deep in my stomach, so you would be doing me a favor."

She laughed again and said, "Oh, very well, Clint. There are a few nice little places in town where we can quell your hunger pains, and I haven't eaten since yesterday myself. How soon will you be ready?"

I looked at my watch: 11:45 AM. "How about 12:45 – will that work for you?"

She said that it would, and she'd meet me in front of the inn.

I washed up and found a pair of pants and a short-sleeved shirt on a hanger by the door and a small plastic bag with some men's underclothes. Amos Greer was good to his word. I put them on and was impressed to discover that they were just about a perfect fit. I looked in the full-length mirror on the closet door and was relieved to see that, despite my 40 years, the midline bulge had not yet overtaken me and the 190 pounds I'd weighed six months ago was still well-proportioned over my six foot frame.

When I was ready to see what the day would hold, I stood for a moment at the window and admired the beauty of the spectacle before me. It was early summer and the trees were full and alive with their foliage. The sky was blue with a few thin clouds overhead. In the distance, rugged snow-capped mountains stood like watchful centurions.

The peaceful setting was in stark contrast to the painful memories of my personal tragedy that could have been avoided if I had not pushed my professional career and self-interests ahead my family's well-being. The fact that the car bomb was meant for me and that my beloved wife and son paid the ultimate price for my own ambition and prosecutorial zeal would haunt me forever.

I walked down to the office, trying to push the horrible knowledge of my own guilt out of my mind. I wanted to think of this day as a new beginning. I desperately needed something – I was not sure what – to heal the raw wound in my soul. Perhaps I would find that something here in Climax. That thought gave me comfort as I looked forward to having lunch with Melanie.

CHAPTER FIVE

The Farmhouse restaurant was a sprawling, ramshackle edifice, located about a mile from town. It appeared rundown and in general disrepair from the outside, but the large unpaved parking lot was filled to capacity and attested to its popularity.

We alighted from the jeep and Melanie said apologetically, "It's a lot nicer inside. I think you'll like it if you're a big eater."

The growling in my stomach was growing louder and I admitted that it had been a while since I had eaten a good meal.

A long, expansive porch ran the width of the building. We entered the restaurant and the delicious aromas that greeted us promised that this was going to be a culinary treat. Just inside the front door was a spacious parlor that served as a lobby and waiting area. Off to one side was a large room housing a long, ornate bar and several tables, all of them occupied. Down a long hallway was a spacious dining room which was also very crowded. Several waitresses dressed in calico skirts, white blouses and gaily-colored aprons bustled about carrying trays heaped high with steaming platters of food. It smelled delicious and I began to involuntarily salivate. I was anxious to find out for myself just how good the food was.

A smiling, buxom hostess greeted us warmly when we entered. She wrapped Melanie in a bear hug and said, "Melanie, you sweet dear, how are you?" She held Melanie at arm's length and examined her. "I heard about your daddy! Is he doing all right? How are you holding up?"

Melanie smiled sweetly and said, "Thanks, Helen. Daddy's condition is still critical, but they are doing everything they can for him, and we're all praying he'll pull through." There was a tightness in her voice, but she managed to maintain her composure.

"Well, you know he's in our prayers, too, honey," the woman said, finally releasing Melanie from her grasp, then eying me curiously.

"Helen, this is Clint Harrison, the man who pulled Daddy from the wreck and saved his life."

My cheeks once again burned with embarrassment as I offered her my hand, which she accepted eagerly. Her grip was firm but warm and she rewarded me with a wide smile. "Mr. Harrison, you are an honored guest in our establishment. I hope you brought your appetite!"

I admitted that I was famished, and she picked up two oversize menus from a table and, motioning us to follow her, marched down the hallway. She led us to a small room with a half dozen tables, only two of which were occupied. She directed us to one next to a huge bay window that looked out over a small lake nestled in a grove of spruce trees and ponderosa pine. Far above, the purple rim of the mountains faded into a clear blue sky. It was a spectacular view, and I understood another reason why this place was so popular.

"Just about anything on the menu is good," Melanie said, studying the listing of offerings and daily specials carefully. "I always have trouble making up my mind because there's so much to choose from."

I scanned the menu and saw that she was not exaggerating. The selection was extensive, but I settled on the meatloaf special with mashed potatoes, gravy, corn on the cob, coleslaw and applesauce. Melanie ordered the hot roast beef sandwich with mashed potatoes, mixed vegetables and a green salad. A pretty, dark-haired waitress took our orders and brought me black coffee and Melanie a tall glass of iced tea.

"Do you eat here often?" I asked.

"Not a lot," she said. "I'm usually too busy working at the newspaper and taking care of the house and volunteering at the senior citizen center."

She paused to sip her iced tea and take in the marvelous view. "I often don't eat lunch at all. Other times I just have fruit or a salad, which is just as well anyway."

"It's beautiful here. Have you lived here all your life?"

"Almost," she said, smiling faintly. "We moved here when I was just eight. Daddy had worked on a newspaper back in St. Louis when Mom was diagnosed with a rare, acute form of asthma which was aggravated by the high heat and humidity typical of the St. Louis area. The doctors said that a change in climate might do her good and suggested Colorado or Arizona due to the low humidity and clean air."

She looked directly at me and I noted that her eyes were as blue as the cloudless sky. "Daddy learned that the fellow who owned the newspaper here in town was looking for a buyer, so he took what little pension money he had, borrowed the rest and put up enough for a down payment."

"So the move out west was just what the doctor ordered!"

A shadow passed over her face, and she gazed out the window at nothing in particular. "Not really. Mom died the year after we arrived. It turns out the move here only prolonged her life a few months."

"I'm sorry," I said, feeling terrible and wishing I had not brought up the subject.

"It's all right, Clint," she said, her smile returning. "Mom loved it out here and she's buried on a small hill overlooking the valley she loved so much. The move was good for her and for us, even if it didn't save her life."

Before I could think of anything else to say, our food arrived. Eating was a welcome diversion from the conversation, and we said very little for the next several minutes. The portions were generous, and the food was delicious.

I managed to finish the meal and felt a tightening around my waist when Melanie said with a twinkle in her eye, "You look as though the food was to your liking."

"It's been a while since I've had a meal like that one," I admitted.

Melanie fell quiet as the waitress returned to refill our drinks and take away the platters. She looked lost in thought, and I wondered what she was thinking but didn't want to intrude. Finally, she said, "I cannot understand where Daddy was going yesterday when the accident occurred."

"What do you mean?" I asked, somewhat intrigued.

She shrugged her shoulders. "We were supposed to be meeting for lunch. He said he had something very important to tell me about a big story he was working on, but he wouldn't say what it was. He acted very strange, but I didn't think anything of it at the time. Now, I . . ." Her voice trailed off and she seemed lost in thought.

"It sounds mysterious," I said, joining her in contemplation.

She looked at me intently and replied, "Yes, well, the interesting thing is that he called me just before we were supposed to meet and said that he had to run out for a while and we'd have to do lunch later." She shook her head. "That's not like my daddy. He's about the most predictable man I know. I can't imagine what in the world could have made him rush out like that."

I found myself wondering the same thing. "Any idea what this big story was that he was working on?"

"Not a clue. Daddy can be very secretive when he wants to be." She let out a little laugh. "I'm afraid he still has some of that old newspaperman's investigator's blood running through his veins."

I nodded knowingly. As a former investigator and Assistant District Attorney, I understood what she meant probably more than she realized. Cops and newspaper reporters sometimes share a common interest even though they often use different methods to pursue their leads.

I asked the waitress for the check, but she informed me that Helen said it was already taken care of. I knew better than to protest but I thanked Helen on the way out and she assured me that it had been her pleasure.

Neither of us spoke on the ride back to the inn. When we pulled up to the Summit, there were a lot of questions running through my mind, so I tried to think of a way to prolong the conversation.

"I imagine you'll be quite busy running things at the newspaper until your dad gets back on his feet."

She frowned and said, "Yes, it's going to be very difficult, at least for the first few weeks or so."

I sensed that she was holding something back. "I don't doubt it," I replied. "I spent one high school summer helping my uncle with a weekly newspaper in Northern California. It was interesting work but I never worked harder in my life!"

Something flashed in her eyes and she said, "Well, then, you know what I'm facing. I've been after Daddy for more than a year now to get someone to help him out, but he's too mule-headed to admit he can't do it all by himself anymore." Her voice had a distressed tone, and I sensed that this was a sensitive subject.

She paused for a moment, then said, "That newspaper is his whole life, and he won't even consider slowing down or letting anyone help him with it. He's sixty-two years old and he just won't accept the fact that he needs assistance."

It sounded as if Ben Griffin was a very proud man and I could respect that, but his stubbornness was clearly causing a problem for Melanie that he probably had never intended.

"Surely there must be someone else who can help out," I said. "Doesn't he even have an assistant or someone else other than you?"

She shook her head slowly and stared at the far horizon. "No, there's really no one else. Daddy is very particular about who he allows around his newspaper, and sometimes I'm not sure he even trusts me," she said with annoyance. "The only other person in town who knows anything about running the paper is Sam Dooley. My dad fired him two years ago after they had a big falling out. They haven't talked to each other since."

She looked directly into my eyes, and I had the impression that she wanted to ask me something but was holding back.

I began to feel very uncomfortable and searched for something to say. Finally, I suggested, "Maybe this Dooley character might be willing to . . ."

She unleashed a bitter laugh and said, "I'm sure old Sam will be in no mood to help, even with Daddy in the hospital."

I couldn't understand why anyone would not want to help this nice young woman in her time of need. What was I missing?

"It might be worth talking to him. It sounds like he may be your only chance."

She shook her head firmly. "You don't know Sam. Next to my father, he's the most stubborn man I know. He swore he'd never set foot inside *The Gazette* office again until my dad was dead and buried." She covered her eyes to hide the tears, and I could feel her heartache. I wanted desperately to help her, but I had problems of my tears...to deal with.

I gently patted her hand. "You need to keep positive thoughts in your head right now." I told her, not knowing what else to say. She took a tissue from her purse and wiped the tears from her eyes. "I know, you're right," she replied, her voice trembling. "It's just that I rely so much on Daddy, and I don't know what I would do without . . ." She paused, unable to finish.

"I'd be happy to help . . ." I said tentatively, having no real idea what I could do that would be of any real assistance.

She dabbed at her eyes again and looked hopefully at me. "I hate to ask you, Clint. You've done so much already . . ." She paused for a moment. "Besides, I know you'll be anxious to be on your way just as soon as you're feeling up to it."

Before I realized what I was saying, I blurted out, "I really have no plans at this time but . . ." I caught myself before saying anything else, but it may have been too late. Melanie gave me a strange look as if trying to read my thoughts. Before she could say anything, I patted her hand again and simply said, "If there's anything I can do for you, Melanie, just tell me what it is."

She looked at me thoughtfully for a moment. "Well Clint, if you're sure you don't mind, there is something . . ."

She hesitated as if trying to collect her thoughts and I began to wonder what I was getting myself into. Had I promised something I couldn't deliver? Uncertainty began gnawing at my insides, but there was no turning back now.

CHAPTER SIX

The truth is, Clint, I desperately need someone to help me at the newspaper . . . just until Daddy gets back on his feet. And there's simply no one else other than Sam Dooley, who can do what needs to be done, and Sam just won't do it."

I could hear the strain in her voice, and I felt myself wanting to help her out, but what she was asking for was far beyond anything I knew how to do, or cared to do, and I tried to tell her so, but she just waved off my protests.

"You said yourself that you worked on your uncle's newspaper when you were younger."

I tried to explain to her that it had been a long time ago and I had forgotten most of what I'd learned, but she would have nothing of it.

Her voice transitioned from insistence to pleading, then back to insistence, and I felt my resistance weakening. She seemed to sense this and said, "Clint, you said you were willing to help me out, and you just said you had no immediate plans. There's only so much sightseeing you can do around here, so what's the point of talking about it anymore?"

I immediately regretted my blundering statement about not having any plans but there was no retreating at this point so I simply nodded in agreement as I asked myself, *How bad could it possibly be?* I had nowhere else to go and nothing else to do and spending a few days working in her company actually didn't seem like such a bad idea after all. After assessing my limited options, I resigned myself to the inevitable. "I guess I can give it a try, but . . ."

Her eyes grew large with relief, and she said excitedly, "I promise you, Clint. You won't regret it!"

When I asked her exactly what she expected me to do I discovered she had a plan all worked out. Why was I not surprised!

"It's simple, really," she assured me. "I need you to work on those presses and keep them running. I can handle the office work and business end of things, at least for a while. But those presses are . . . that is . . . were, Daddy's job after Sam Dooley quit and that's really a man's job anyway."

She was right. From my limited experience I knew that running the presses was hard work and I wasn't sure that I was the man for the job, but by now I knew better than to raise any doubts about my ability. She was convinced I could do what needed to be done and that was pretty much all there was to it!

"Working in a newspaper is like riding a bicycle. Once you've learned how, you don't forget. I've no doubt that anything you've forgotten will come back to you in a flash." Her positive attitude and indefatigable spirit were beginning to have an effect on me. The more she talked the more she had me believing that her plan was workable.

The sun was high and bright in the sky and the air was fresh and invigorating. It was such a beautiful day and I was enjoying the wonders of nature. So much that I eagerly agreed when she suggested that we take a stroll around the inn.

We walked until we found a lovely gazebo overlooking a pond at the rear of the inn. Several mallard ducks were enjoying themselves on the water. We sat and admired the view while Melanie filled me in on some of the problems that had befallen the newspaper in recent months. I listened with growing interest. It was obvious that the accident that had nearly taken Ben Griffin's life was just the most recent setback the newspaper had suffered lately.

"To tell you the truth, Clint," she said with a slight quiver in her voice, "the newspaper is struggling to survive. I've tried to get Daddy to sell out and retire but he will not even discuss it."

She went on to relate that most of their problems had started earlier in the year when her dad had run a series of stinging editorials against a large land developer, the A. B. Donovan Development Corporation, that was trying to acquire and develop a 5,000-acre section of land several miles northwest of the town. The company was hoping to open a coal mining operation, which likely would be an economic boom for the region.

"Geological surveys have apparently revealed a rich deposit of coal two thousand feet below the surface. There's enough coal there to keep Donovan in the mining business for fifty years or more," Melanie explained.

"But why was your father opposed to the plan? I'd think that the town would benefit a great deal by that kind of development."

"Because" she grimaced, "the land in question intrudes upon the Sequoia Indian Reservation, which claims to have historical title to the entire northern section of the valley, including that section that Donovan has planned to develop."

"Well," I said, "If the Indians have title to that land . . ."

"It's not that simple, Clint," she said patiently, as though explaining the

ABCs to a three-year-old child. "While the Indians lay claim to the land, they have no official title and there is no record of it ever being deeded to them. They claim that there was a deed issued more than 100 years ago but that the deed was later destroyed by an unscrupulous Indian agent who'd been trying to blackmail the Indians in return for the deed. The Indians say that all the records were destroyed when the Indian agent was fired by the federal government for dereliction of duty."

"Well," I replied, "without a deed or any supporting documents, it doesn't seem that the Indians have much to support their claim."

"Actually," she responded, "they have quite a bit going for them." "How is that possible?" My interest was growing by the minute.

"First, they have my father, who is a champion of Native American rights, partly because he is one-sixteenth Kiowa Indian himself, and partly because he has always been a defender of the underdog. And in this case, the Indian is clearly the underdog."

Her pride in her father was obvious. *He's lucky to have such a daughter*, I thought.

"Second," she continued, her voice trembling slightly, "there is B. J. Tall Horse, who is the son of James Tall Horse, the aging tribal chief at the reservation. B. J., which stands for Byron James, is Harvard educated and an outspoken proponent of Indian rights. He is to the Sequoia Indians what Martin Luther King was to the African-American people during the civil rights protests of the seventies. He is their spiritual leader, their knight in shining armor, and their chief spokesman. He has managed to keep the Donovan Corporation at bay for more than a year with public hearings, legal maneuvers and personal heroics."

"He sounds like quite a man," I said. But I also knew the power of the law and the ability of high-priced lawyers to use the legal system to their clients' advantage. So far, my money was on the Donovan Corporation, but I didn't say that to Melanie.

"The Indians also have Uncle Henry in their corner," she said, looking like she had just bitten into a sour lemon.

"Uncle Henry? Is he *your* uncle?"

"God no," she said derisively. "That would be U. S. Senator Henry Horner, who is your typical self-centered, egotistic politician and who'll use anyone or anything to further his political career. The folks around here nicknamed him 'uncle' years ago . . . I'm not sure why."

She clearly had a low opinion of this man, and I wondered what was behind it.

"It's no secret that he plans on running for the presidency four years from now," she continued, "and he's using the controversy at the reservation to gain as much political clout as he can."

He indeed sounds like a typical politician, I thought, but I did not comment. "But I'd think that he could get just as much political capital out of backing the Donovan Corporation. It would seem that they have the law on their side and backing a major development like that would seem to be the popular thing to do."

"You're right about that," she replied, "but Horner's nobody's fool. He's a master at playing both sides against each other."

The bitterness in her voice underlined her dislike for Senator Horner, and I was beginning to have a very dim view of him myself. My own career as a cop and later as an Assistant DA had given me a strong dislike for politicians in general so it didn't take much for me to imagine Senator Horner in the worst possible light.

"He claims to support Indian rights and has backed every legal maneuver B.J. Tall Horse has made, but he's also promised to aid the Donovan Corporation in getting federal legislation passed to open lands currently protected from development or mining exploration. Whether he has the political clout to keep his promise is doubtful, but at least he can appear to favor both sides on this issue. It's a classic case of backing whichever side wins. One way or another, Horner comes out on top."

I thought about this for a moment, then said, "You mentioned that there have been other problems at the newspaper. What did you mean?"

She told me that some of the merchants in town had dropped their advertisements to protest her father's support of the Indians' land claims. "They feel that the Donovan Corporation development would be good for the town's economy and therefore in their own interests."

I could understand why they might feel that way.

"We've also had thefts of paper and supplies from our warehouse as well as apparent sabotage when the valve of a large oil tank at the rear of the shop was forced open causing more than 500 gallons of diesel fuel to spill onto the ground. We were lucky it didn't catch fire and burn down the entire building. Fortunately, a passing patrol car from the Sheriff's Department noticed it and called the volunteer fire department."

I had to admit that they were having a run of very bad luck. It was easy to understand why she would feel so stressed.

"We can't say for sure that any of these things have any direct connection with my father's backing of the Indian land claims, but it seems awfully odd that it all started soon after his editorials against the Donovan Corporation began appearing in the newspaper."

We walked a while longer and Melanie abruptly shifted the conversation. "You haven't told me much about yourself. Are you harboring a deep dark secret?" There was a lilting laugh in her voice, and I knew that she was teasing me, but her curiosity made me uncomfortable and I tried not to show it.

When I said nothing, she asked softly, "What about family? Surely you must have someone." Her questions caught me by surprise and made me uncomfortable. I tried without success to think of a suitable answer. My hesitation was obvious and may have been mistaken for evasion, but I wasn't ready to discuss the tragedy of my personal life. The wounds were still too raw and painful. She seemed to sense my reluctance to talk about myself and deftly changed the subject.

"I'd like to get an early start tomorrow. There's so much to show you, and I have plenty to do myself. Would 8:00 AM be too early to pick you up?"

I assured her that I would be ready to go by then. We returned to the jeep, and she climbed in. Her spirit brightened and she looked as if a burden had been lifted from her shoulders. I was happy that I had decided to help her.

She waved at me and without another word she was speeding down the hill in a cloud of dust. The last thing I saw was her blonde hair dancing gaily in the wind and I had to laugh. I watched her disappear in a cloud of dust and I began to wonder what the next few days would hold for me. For the first time since I had lost the best part of my life, I was beginning to look forward to something, but I was not sure what that might be.

I returned to my room where I found myself experiencing eager anticipation about what the future might hold as well as a lingering doubt about my ability to be of any real assistance to Melanie. I began to feel as if the weight that had been lifted from her shoulders was now on my own. The more I thought about it, the more determined I was to find some way of approaching this Sam Dooley fellow with an appeal to help Melanie, at least until her father was back on his feet. While this sounded like a tall order, I made up my mind that it was worth a try.

CHAPTER SEVEN

White jagged streaks of lightning split the black curtain of night accompanied by roaring claps of thunder. I felt as if I were being unmercifully thrown about by something I could not see, but whose presence was both frightening and overpowering. I was terrified and struggled to free myself, but was powerless against the strange, overwhelming forces that seemed to hold me prisoner. Then, all was eerily still, and I stared in horror as a diaphanous form began to materialize in the dark shadow around me. A hideous, inhuman face began to materialize; its eyes glowing like red balls of fire, its mouth twisted into an evil snarl that sent cold chills down my spine.

I knew it was the face of the devil, and I cursed myself for my own helplessness. I felt as if the evil spirit was sucking the breath from my lungs, and I gasped frantically for air.

Its shrieks were then replaced by a terrifying wailing sound of someone being savagely tortured. The evil visage faded slowly into a vapor-like mist from which slowly emerged the tormented face of my wife, Janet. There was terror in her eyes as she cried out to me, her mournful pleas piercing my soul with unrelenting pain. I tried to reach out to her, to somehow save her from the death that awaited her. But I was paralyzed by fear and by my own guilt.

She disappeared into a hot, flaming ball of fire as her agonizing cries faded slowly, pitifully away. I desperately cried out to her to come back to me, but it was useless. Once again, she was gone, only to return in these terrible, agonizing dreams. With one last booming clap of thunder and a blinding flash of lightning, I woke to find myself gasping for breath and bathed in sweat, my pulse racing like an out of control jet engine. I was lying naked on the bed staring out the window at the grey clouds that still hung like a shroud over the eastern horizon. Lace curtains swirled silently in the cool breeze and ushered in the sweet smell of rain. I lay motionless for several minutes while I tried to erase the haunting nightmare from my mind, but the frightening images and terrifying cries were so real that it was impossible to escape from them.

The awful images came often. While no two were alike, they all ended the same, horrific way, with me trying in vain to save my wife and son from the terrible death that had taken them from me. Each succeeding failure brought greater remorse: I was unable to help them when they needed me most.

I could not escape from the realization that I was responsible for the death of my wife and son. Three years earlier I had been promoted to the post of Deputy District Attorney in Los Angeles County and had been appointed to head up a special local-state-federal task force aimed at tracking down, capturing and prosecuting members of the Ortega drug cartel, one of the largest and most lucrative illicit drug operations in Southern California.

I had previously spent a dozen years on the street as a patrol officer and detective in Manhattan Beach and had taken a personal oath to wage war on drug traffickers after my best friend and football teammate, Mike Harmon, overdosed on heroin at the tender age of 19. Knowing that I would have limited impact as a uniformed police officer, I went to night school for six years and finally earned my JD degree from the University of Southern California. I applied immediately for a job with the L. A. County District Attorney's Office and continued my personal crusade against drug traffickers with growing vengeance and success. My tireless efforts were rewarded by a series of rapid-fire promotions and my appointment as head of the drug task force was, to my way of thinking, the crowning jewel of my career.

Due in large part to a powerful team of undercover operatives, investigators, and prosecutors, we had dealt the Ortega Cartel a near-fatal blow by successfully prosecuting Manuel Ortega, the drug czar's number one son, and several of his trusted lieutenants. We worked relentlessly, nights and weekends, and whenever necessary to get the goods on the top echelons of the Ortega organization. Each member of the carefully chosen task force had the same burning desire to put the Ortega family out of business, and to send a loud warning to anyone who might be foolish enough to think about following in their footsteps.

But we paid a heavy toll for our successes. Two of my undercover operatives were murdered by members of the Ortega family, two of my best investigators were divorced by their wives due to the endless hours spent away from their families, and one of my best prosecutors, who had received a number of death threats, decided to accept a well-paying job in a high-profile law firm in San Diego. The long hours and countless weekends away from home undermined the stability of my own marriage and it was only our mutual love and respect for each other and an abiding commitment to the vows we had taken, along with monumental patience and understanding by my wife that held us together. A weaker marriage would not have endured the strain. I received my own share of death threats but I shrugged them off as an acceptable cost of pursuing my chosen line of work. In the end though, it was my family who paid the ultimate price and that fact would forever torment me.

At 6:30 AM my alarm clock buzzed me back to reality and I grudgingly pulled myself out of bed and did my best to focus on what this new day might bring. I found another neatly stacked pile of cloths on the dresser and made a mental note to thank Amos Greer or his wife, if I saw her, for their thoughtfulness.

After I showered, shaved and dressed, growling sounds of protest from my stomach reminded me that I had not eaten since lunch the day before.

It was nearly seven when I made my way down to the dining room, large and cheerfully decorated in country style. Bright sunlight poured in through a series of large windows and provided a breathtaking view of the verdant forests that covered the distant foothills. Above them, snow-capped mountains looked down upon the valley with majestic splendor.

A small woman wearing a wide smile and a colorful calico dress greeted me and led me to a table near the window. "I'm Martha Greer," she said warmly, handed me a menu and filled my cup with steaming black coffee. "You must be Mr. Harrison."

I admitted that I was, and she told me that Estelle would be with me shortly.

Before she left, I thanked her for the clothes.

She took a good look at me and congratulated herself on getting the size right. "Don't you think nothin' of it, Mr. Harrison. They're just a few old things I had in the closet. I been meanin' to take 'em to the church raffle but I keep forgettin'. You're welcome to 'em and more if you need." With that, she turned and walked briskly to the kitchen.

In less than a minute, Estelle arrived to take my order. I had expected an older woman, and I was surprised to see a very attractive young woman who could not have been more than sixteen. She had beautiful dark eyes, a wide, full mouth and high cheekbones. From her copper-toned skin and ebony hair that trailed down her back in long braids, I guessed she was from the Sequoia Indian Reservation that Melanie had told me about. She moved about gracefully as if she wore wings while she placed a glass of ice water on the table and asked me for my order. She took it without writing it down and turned to go into the kitchen.

Then I remembered something and called after her, "And some OJ, please."

She turned back to me with a questioning look.

"OJ," I said again. "You know, orange juice. A large glass please."

She nodded and mouthed the letters "OJ," then disappeared into the kitchen.

I had apparently just helped expand her English vocabulary.

I watched her go, thinking how shy she must be, having spoken very little and avoided making eye contact with me. But there was something about her – some kind of inner beauty – that was both interesting and mysterious.

While I waited, I looked over a copy of *The Climax Gazette* that someone had left on the table. It was typical of most small-town weeklies and contained a lot of local news as well as limited national coverage of politics, finances and sports. I found to my dismay that my Dodgers were in no better shape since the All Star break than they were before it, and I found myself looking ahead to next year, as many Dodger fans were accustomed to doing.

I read with interest an article about the latest round of legal skirmishes between the Sequoia Indians and the Donovan Corporation, reflecting on what Melanie had told me the day before about her father's position on that issue. While I could admire him for having the courage to stand up for what he thought was right, it was easy to see why his views were not popular among many local people and businesses that saw the Donovan project as a means of revitalizing the small town. It was a tough call either way and I wondered how it would all turn out, and what impact it would have on Ben Griffin – if he lived – and on Melanie and the newspaper.

Estelle brought my food, and my orange juice, and set them before me. "OJ," she said proudly, as if she'd just learned something very important.

I took the chilled glass from her and raised it to her in salutation. "OJ," I said, and took a sip of the delicious liquid, then placed the glass back down on the table.

I tried to strike up a conversation with her, but she didn't linger and moved on to another customer before I could think of something to say, but her shyness didn't affect her efficiency. In addition, the food was hot, tasty and plentiful and for the second time in as many days I could feel a tightening around my waist as I devoured the last morsel. Just as I finished, I spotted Amos Greer walking by, nursing a cup of coffee, and I waved him over to join me.

"Good morning, Amos," I said. He slid into the chair opposite mine. Estelle appeared as if on cue and silently refilled our coffee cups.

"Well, Mr. Harrison," he said jovially, "you seem to be healing nicely!" "I'm feeling much better," I said, flashing him a thumbs-up. "Have you heard anything about Ben Griffin's condition?"

"No change I'm told." He shook his head sadly. "But at least he's holdin' his own."

"Well, that's better than the alternative," I said, and Amos nodded.

"I hear tell that you've agreed to help Melanie out down at the newspaper until her dad can get back on his feet," Amos said with enthusiasm.

I remembered how news travels fast in a small town, so I was not surprised that just about every move I made would be telegraphed with amazing efficiency.

"Well, for a while anyway," I admitted. "But I'm not sure how much help I'll be."

"Nonsense, my boy," he retorted emphatically. "I expect you can do a world of good for Melanie, and I'm pleased you'll be stayin' round for a spell. We need good men like you in these parts!" His eyes twinkled brightly adding emphasis to his words, and I was encouraged by his expression of confidence. "I just wish there was someone a lot more capable than myself . . ." I hesitated for a moment, then asked, "What do you know about this fellow, Sam Dooley?"

A shadow fell over his face and he was slow to respond. Finally, he exhaled and said, his voice no more than a whisper, "Dooley's one heckuva newspaper man, Clint, but I . . ." His voice trailed off, and he seemed hesitant to say more.

"You know, Clint," Amos said painfully, "Ben Griffin and Sam Dooley had a fallin' out a coupla years ago and they've had nothin' to do with one 'nother since."

"Yes, I know," I said, nodding my head. "Melanie told me, but she also said that Sam Dooley was probably the most capable press man in these parts."

Estelle appeared out of nowhere to offer more coffee but both Amos and I waved her off.

Amos appeared to be deep in thought. I continued tentatively, "I'm wondering if there is any chance that he might be willing to forget about the past and do what he can to help Melanie . . ."

Amos shook his head doubtfully. "You don't know Sam, Clint." I started to say something, but he waved me off. "Sam's got a mean streak in him a mile wide, and when he's drinkin', which is most of the time, there's just no way to talk sense to him."

Amos shook his head again. "I've known the man for twenty-five years and he can be the most contrary soul who ever walked this earth!"

Amos spat these words out angrily and I was beginning to get the picture: Sam Dooley was not going to be any help. But still, in the back of my mind, I felt he was Melanie's only real chance, and I had to at least try and see if he would agree to help out. Even if it did turn out to be a waste of time, I figured it was worth a shot. Amos looked me squarely in the eyes and said, "I can see you're not convinced."

I looked helplessly at him, and he shrugged his shoulders in resignation. "Well, you can try to talk some sense into ol' Dooley, but don't say I didn't warn you!" With that, he gave me a pat on the arm and rose to leave.

"Amos, before you go, can you tell me where I might find Sam Dooley?"

He snorted and said without hesitation, "The nearest bar stool, I reckon, if the bars are open. If not, he's got a place over behind Charley Riggs' Building Supply on Depot Street. He works there off and on . . . when he's sober, and like I said, that ain't often."

He started to leave, then turned back as if he had forgotten something.

"By the way," he said, "they brought some-a your things up from Ralph's Auto Salvage where they towed your car. I'm afraid there's not much left of that Town Car, though." "It was a rental," I shrugged, "and I had full coverage, but I'd better contact the rental car agency in L.A. and let them know about the crash."

It then occurred to me that I had no transportation, and I didn't want to rely on Melanie to drive me around. I asked Amos if there was a car rental place in town.

"Not really," he said, shaking his head slowly, "but Ralph does rent out a few clunkers from time to time." He laughed and said, "He's the original 'Rent-a-Wreck Ralph.' But if you need somethin' to drive for a few days, I've got just the thing."

Amos pulled a ring of keys from his pocket, detached one, and handed it to me. "You're welcome to use the ol' station wagon out back. We used to use it to pick up supplies and whatnot, but since we bought the new van, we don't need it all that much."

It was a very generous offer, and I suggested that he let me pay him something for the use of the car, but he wouldn't hear of it, so I finally agreed to accept his generosity.

"As I said, Clint, we need good men like you in these here parts and loanin' you that ol' wagon is little enough for what yer doin' for Melanie."

I thanked him again, then looked at my watch. It was nearly 8:00 AM. Melanie would be picking me up in a few minutes. I returned to my room to wash up and arrived in the lobby just as Melanie pulled up in front. She waved at me, and I climbed in with a smile on my face and a growing sense of anticipation. The sky was a blue sea of tranquility, the air was filled with the pungent scent of pine and juniper, I was seated next to a lovely young woman whose indomitable spirit could conquer Mount Everest, and it felt good to be alive.

CHAPTER EIGHT

I got into the jeep and hung on while Melanie negotiated the twisting, bumpy road down the hill at a speed that seemed to allow only two wheels on the road at one time. I was holding on with both hands while she looked totally oblivious to what I considered a near-death experience. She was wearing a wide-brimmed straw hat with a large ribbon that flapped madly in the wind. I expected it to fly off her head at any second. After what felt like a bone-jarring ride on the Tilt-A-Whirl at a carnival, the road gradually leveled off. She slowed just a little and, other than "hello," spoke to me for the first time.

"I hope you're ready to get to work," she said, practically brimming over with excitement. "We're on deadline in two days and we're two days behind! We have a lot of catching up to do!"

Her bright smile and enthusiasm buoyed my confidence. "I'm all yours," I said, hoping not to disappoint her.

On level streets she slowed a bit, and I managed to catch my breath while she explained what she had in mind. "I need you to look at the presses and make sure all of the maintenance has been kept up on them. That was Daddy's job, and he wouldn't let anyone else around them, except Sam Dooley, when they were talking to each other. I've got a girl who helps me in the office and most of the line setting is done by computer now, but the presses are what I'm most concerned about."

I remembered some of what I had learned from working with my uncle and I've always been mechanically inclined, but I wasn't convinced that it was going to be as easy as she made it sound. I hadn't given up on the idea of trying to coax Sam Dooley out of "retirement" if I could find him, and if he was sober, but I didn't feel like sharing that with Melanie. Instead, I listened and tried to display the same level of confidence that she seemed to have in me.

Downtown Climax was a picture postcard of Americana, with neat and well-maintained buildings, clean streets and sidewalks, and stately shade trees lining the boulevards. A rotary drive, reminiscent of towns I had visited in New England, circled a two-story brick and masonry courthouse that was the centerpiece of a beautifully manicured lawn. In front of the courthouse, a tall, elegant war memorial loomed above a squat Civil War cannon.

The Climax Gazette building was located on Third Street, just two blocks from the center of town. It was an attractive, two-story, Colonial style red brick structure with white trim. Melanie parked in a small dirt lot next to the building, jumped out, and headed for a side door marked "Private - No Entrance" and I scrambled to catch up. She held the door open and ushered me inside. We were in a storeroom piled high with paper rolls, large oil drums and high racks of shelves containing reams of paper and an assortment of office supplies. My senses were assaulted with the caustic odor of solvents, oils, degreasers and other chemicals used to lubricate and clean the machinery.

"The presses are in the back," she said, pointing to the rear of the building. "You can check them out in a few minutes but first let me give you the nickel tour."

She turned right into a short hallway that led to the business office. I counted either three or four unoccupied workstations – I couldn't be sure due to the clutter of books, paper, file folders, coffee cups, soda cans, candy wrappers, and miscellaneous debris piled high on every available surface.

She pointed to an elderly woman who was barely visible behind a formidable stack of papers and file folders. "This is Ellie, our faithful bookkeeper."

Ellie had a wild mane of fiery red hair, a ruddy complexion, squinting eyes and a beak-like nose perched above a thin-lipped mouth that twisted into an unnatural smile when she spoke. "Pleased ta meetcha," she squealed and then disappeared behind the pile of paper on her desk. I could only wonder how she could find anything in that mess, but I had more important concerns of my own.

Melanie laughed gaily, as if reading my mind. "Ellie is our class clown. She can be hilarious when she wants to, but she's as good a bookkeeper as you'll ever find. We'd be lost without her."

I smiled and decided to take her word on that.

Melanie led me back down the hallway to several offices, one of which she told me was hers. It was a sharp contrast to the front office, with modern furniture neatly arranged around a rectangular oak table that served as both desk and workstation. A state-of-the-art computer, display screen, and combination fax machine and printer were neatly arranged on the table. She was obviously a neat and orderly person, and I guessed that, while Ben Griffin might be the boss of the operation, it was probably Melanie who kept the business on an even keel. "And this is Daddy's office," Melanie said with just a hint of disgust in her voice, as she led me to the office directly across from hers. This office was even more littered and untidy than the one in front. A disorderly and confusing assortment of papers, boxes, file folders and ledgers covered nearly every square inch of the large desk and two wooden chairs that faced it. Empty and near-empty Styrofoam cups were everywhere. A large metal ash tray was overflowing with cigar butts and the stench of stale cigars hung like a dense cloud in the room. A patina of dust covered nearly everything, and I wondered how anyone could work in such squalor.

My own revulsion must have registered with Melanie, for she said, "You're probably wondering how he gets anything done, aren't you?"

I didn't reply but my eyes said it all.

She nodded her head in agreement. "I would offer to let you use Daddy's desk but I'm afraid it's beyond hope. We have another office in back that should do well enough for now."

She led me to a small cubicle next to the storeroom. It was clean and neat, containing just the basic necessities: a small desk, a chair, a telephone, a file cabinet and, to my delight, a small coffee maker and sink.

Melanie followed my eyes and said, "Help yourself, Clint. There're coffee and filters in the cabinet over the sink. Daddy is the only coffee drinker here, so you can have this all to yourself."

I thanked her and assured her I would take advantage of the offer.

She turned to me and said, "Well, that's about it. I've got several calls to make, so why don't you go on back to the press area and see what there is to see."

"I'll be glad to," I said, "but I have one or two personal errands to run before I can get started. Do you mind if I borrow your jeep? I promise to bring it back in one piece."

She laughed at my attempt at humor and said, "Well, sure, that's fine.

Can I help you with anything?"

"No," I said, taking the car keys from her. "I won't be long, and I'll work till whatever time it takes to get those presses in shape."

She returned to her own office, and I left through the side door, got into the jeep and fired Baby up. I felt guilty for misleading her, but I knew what her reaction would be if I told her what I really had in mind. After taking one quick glance at those huge presses, I knew that I was no match for them. Melanie was counting on me, and I didn't want to let her down. The only chance – slim as it might be – was to locate Sam Dooley and somehow talk him into giving us a hand.

CHAPTER NINE

I stopped by the courthouse to get directions to Depot Street and found it easily enough. The C. Riggs Building Supply was a large, two-story wood frame structure that occupied the better half of an entire city block. I entered a cluttered but clean office to find a small, gnome-like man sitting at a desk. He was busily making entries in a large ledger and did not appear to notice me. He spoke in a harsh whisper, apparently to himself, and I waited patiently for him to notice me.

"Just a minute – just a minute, please, and I'll be with you," he said finally, in an exasperated tone of voice. "I'm missing an invoice, and I need to find it before it drives me crazy."

Not wanting to add to his distress, I said nothing and sat quietly in one of the wooden chairs next to his desk, studying the little man. He appeared to be in his mid-to-late fifties but he could have been much older. A few willowy wisps of white gossamer hair clung to the sides of a head that was too large for the shoulders upon which it rested. He was slight of build and stature, probably not more than five feet tall. His legs were so short that his feet did not touch the floor as he sat in the chair. He was, despite his size, a handsome man with a naturally pleasant smile. He wore wire-rimmed spectacles that perched precariously on his small nose and, from time to time, he reached up to push them back in place.

Suddenly, he slammed his fist down on the desktop and exclaimed, "There! Gads! That is annoying. It was right there all the time!" I had no idea what he meant but I was glad for him, and I smiled to let him know.

"I knew it was there, but I'll be dad gummed if I could find it." His voice had a high soprano pitch, and I imagined him soloing in a church choir.

He deftly made a notation in the ledger, closed it triumphantly and turned to me with a beaming smile. "And now, sir, forgive me for keeping you waiting. I'm Abe Feldman. What can I do for you?" He extended a small, pudgy hand and I took it, finding his grip surprisingly firm.

I smiled back at the quaint little man, gave him my name, then got right to the point. "I'm looking for Sam Dooley. I was told that I might find him here."

The smile faded from Abe's face, and he looked at me questioningly, probably wondering what business a total stranger might have with Sam Dooley. "Yes . . . ," he said cautiously, "Sam can usually be found around here. May I ask why you need to see him?"

"It's a personal matter," I said, hoping that my explanation would suffice. He looked inquisitively at me again as if expecting me to elaborate, but I remained silent.

After a moment, he must have concluded that I had said all I intended to because he hopped off his chair, motioned me to follow him and scampered toward the rear of the store.

Despite his diminutive size, he was quite agile, and I hurried to keep up.

"Sam is usually out back this time of the day," he explained. "Is he expecting you?" "No," I replied, "he's not expecting me. But I do have some important business to discuss with him."

Abe raised his eyebrows and looked at me quizzically, but he didn't ask another question even though he was brimming over with curiosity. The last thing I needed was another person telling me that I was on a mission impossible.

He led me though a large warehouse stacked high with packing crates and boxes of every size and shape and smelling of freshly cut lumber. Two men were working on a loading dock, unloading large crates from a tractor trailer. Abe pointed to a corner of the warehouse. "Those go over there, next to the shingles," he said authoritatively. The two laborers nodded and obeyed without comment.

We walked down some stairs at the side of the loading dock and approached a small, ramshackle shed at the rear of the warehouse. It was constructed of an odd assortment of sheets of galvanized metal, plywood and heavy plastic sheeting. It had a slanted roof made of tar paper covered plywood that looked as if it might fly off in a strong wind. There was a door on the side facing the alley and one window which was covered with cardboard, plastic and tar paper. I stood in awe wondering how someone could actually live in such a place.

Abe saw the look on my face and grinned, saying, "He should be in there."

He pounded his closed fist on the door and shouted, "Sam, you got company!"

There was no response from inside and Abe repeated his assault on the door and shouted even louder to get Sam's attention, but there was still no sign of life from inside.

Abe lost his patience, kicked the door violently, and shouted in a shrill voice, "Sam, you got company! Get your miserable behind out here!"

He turned to me with a grin on his face and a twinkle in his eye. "I think that'll get his attention."

With that, he was gone, and I was left alone to make my own introduction to Sam Dooley.

CHAPTER TEN

I began to wonder if there really was anyone inside the dilapidated shack and was about ready to leave when an explosive tirade of guttural grunts, groans, and shouts erupted from inside the odd dwelling. It sounded like the savage snarling of a wild animal and the hair on the back of my neck stood erect. I panicked and looked about for a quick escape route. My instincts told me to flee but my legs were paralyzed and I stood frozen in place, unable to do anything but fear for my life.

I eventually recognized the sounds as human, but they were no less vicious in tone. "Gol durn sonavabuck, confounded . . . (unintelligible), no account . . . (unintelligible) . . . little geezer . . . (unintelligible)... "

By this time, I decided that it would probably be best to leave quietly and come again another time, but my curiosity to see what kind of person was responsible for such a terrible commotion kept me from moving. My pulse was racing at twice its normal speed. I waited fearfully to see what would happen next. I didn't have long to wait.

Without warning the door flew open so fast that I thought it would fly off the rusty hinges that held it in place. Then, like some strange apparition, a tall, gaunt, rail-thin man emerged from the darkness. He towered over me several inches but could not have weighed more than 150 pounds. His arms and legs were bony and angular and he moved with a stooped, awkward gait, reminding me of a drunken sailor on his first shore leave. A shaggy mane of snow-white hair covered his head and face. Beneath the beard I could see a small, angry- looking mouth and a large, bulbous nose perched beneath two large eyes that blazed with fury as he glared at me. I was fearful of what he might do next, but I stood my ground, transfixed by the eerie spectacle walking toward me.

The old man was dressed in a dingy, torn pair of overalls that had been patched several times and hung loosely on his small frame. They were held in place by a pair of worn, frayed suspenders. He wore a soiled, long-sleeved V- neck undershirt that exposed a coarse mass of white hair that covered his upper chest.

"Who'n the tarnation, are you?" he bellowed at me angrily. "And why in blazes did you roust me out of a sound sleep?" His wild eyes were red-rimmed and bloodshot, and he reeked of alcohol and perspiration. I tensed myself for the worse, expecting him to attack me but he only stood there, swaying slightly, glaring fiercely at me.

I was so startled by his appearance that I groped for words. I eventually recovered my composure enough to say, "Mr. Dooley, I'm Clint Harrison and I've come to talk to you about a job that might interest you."

He continued to stare at me and blinked his eyes repeatedly, as if trying to grasp the meaning of my words. Finally, he bellowed in a high-pitched voice that sounded like the braying of a mule. "What on God's green earth makes ya think I need a job?"

He punctuated his words by throwing his scrawny arms wildly in the air and spat a mouthful of nasty-looking liquid on the ground. The foul brown mess spattered near my feet and I instinctively jumped to the side.

He wasn't done with me yet. He spat again, this time right between my feet and said, "And why in hell do ya think I'd be interested in any freakin' job you got?"

I quickly realized that my initial strategy was not paying off, and I desperately tried to think of a different tactic, but I knew I was no match for this mean old codger. Amos had been right on target.

"Look here, Mr. Dooley, I'm in trouble and I need your help."

Summoning up all the courage I could muster, I looked directly into his eyes, and I thought I saw just a flicker of interest – just enough to make me want to stay the course.

He continued to glare at me with malice in his eyes, but he made no move to attack me, so I plunged recklessly ahead.

"You see, Mr. Dooley, you may be the only man around who can help me."

I paused to let him think about what I'd said, but suspicion and distrust were still evident in the way he looked at me and in the tone of his voice.

"And just how do ya reckon I can help ya, seein' that I don't have the slightest idea who ya are or why you'd come lookin' fer me."

The angry glow in his eyes had dimmed a bit and his voice had dropped a decibel or two. I sensed that I was making some progress and began to regain my confidence. I decided to plunge ahead and tell him the rest of my story and see how he reacted.

I took a deep breath, gathered up all the confidence I could muster and said as calmly as possible, "The truth is, Mr. Dooley, I've agreed to help out Melanie Griffin at the newspaper while her dad is laid up." He reacted visibly when I said Melanie's name but remained quiet.

"I need someone to give me a hand. I've been told that you . . ."

His eyes flashed with anger when what I was asking him to do dawned on him, and he spat out a bitter "Not interested!"

Without another word, he turned and walked rapidly down the alley, his shoulders hunched forward, and his hands buried in the pockets of his tattered jeans. I trailed after him, my brain working in overdrive, trying to think of some way to convince him to change his mind.

By now I knew that logic alone would not move him, but I suspected that he was a man who respected someone who was not afraid to stand up to him and decided to give it a shot.

"Mr. Dooley," I said, with more authority than I felt, "you need to hear me out."

It was not exactly a command, but it was a darn good imitation, and it appeared to work.

Sam Dooley stopped abruptly as if I had challenged his manhood, and I wondered if I had crossed the line. Slowly he turned to face me and stared at me with dark, piercing eyes. His jaw jumped up and down as he savagely chewed a large, messy wad of tobacco. I could see that the few teeth he had left were heavily stained from the stuff. A small stream of dark tobacco juice dribbled from his lips.

He put his hands on his hips as a sign of defiance and said, "You'n me have nothin' to discuss, sonny." He spoke with finality, and I knew that his mind was made up, but his tone was no longer menacing, and I took some comfort in that.

I started to say something to him, but he wasn't through yet. "If yer loco enough to work for that jackass, Ben Griffin, it's no concern-a mine."

He turned to walk away but I caught up with him and kept pace, determined to make him hear me out.

"Mr. Dooley," I said with as much force as I could summon, "I know that you and Ben Griffin had a falling out, and that's none of my business, but I don't see why you should take your anger out on Melanie. She's doing her best to keep the paper running and I've agreed to help her but . . ."

Once again, I sensed a change in his attitude when I mentioned Melanie. Her name had struck a soft spot somewhere deep inside that ornery old man. We reached the street, and he turned left and stopped in front of a place called The Shanghai Lounge. Sam paused as if debating his next move, then snorted, "I could use a drink, sonny."

He looked at me and for the first time the anger was gone from his eyes. I could see what I thought was a twinkle peeking out from somewhere deep under those bushy eyebrows. "Did I hear ya say yer buyin'?"

CHAPTER ELEVEN

The Shanghai Lounge was dimly lit with an assortment of multi-colored neon beer signs and the mournful crooning of an unknown country/western singer, coming from a jukebox, could be heard above the sound of scattered conversations. We sat on stools at one end of a large oval bar that dominated the room. There were booths on either wall and several small tables at the rear, but none were occupied. Two old men seated at the opposite end of the bar were engaged in an animated conversation about national politics, and the bartender, a fat, balding man with a large handlebar mustache and dark, doleful eyes, appeared to be serving as the moderator. He approached us as we sat down.

"Howdy, Sam. The usual?"

Without waiting for an answer, the bartender eyed me curiously and said, "How 'bout you, stranger?"

It was too early in the day for me. I ordered coffee and he poured it from a blackened pot sitting on a warmer behind the bar. With practiced ease, he poured Sam a tall bourbon on the rocks. He waited as I counted out several bills and placed them on the bar. He rang the register and returned to place a handful of change on the counter.

Sam took a long sip of the amber liquor and grunted with pleasure. Some of the anger I had observed earlier seemed to drain from him and he appeared to relax just a little. He said nothing and I sensed that he was running something through his mind, so I let him think. I sipped my coffee and was pleasantly surprised to discover that it was freshly brewed.

Finally, after taking another long sip of his whiskey, Sam Dooley said somberly, "So ya know 'bout Ben Griffin 'n' me, do ya?"

Without waiting for me to answer, he snorted and said, "Ya get that from Melanie, did ya?"

As he spoke, he stared at his own reflection in the large mirror behind the bar. After a long, silent moment, he turned to look at me as if waiting for me to reply. I shrugged and said, "I agreed to help Melanie out after she learned I had once worked on a small newspaper years ago."

He nodded slowly and I continued.

"But I don't have the kind of experience or ability she needs. She told me that there was only one other man in town, besides her father, who could do what needs to be done, so I . . ."

He turned and locked me with a cold, baleful stare and I feared that I may have unleashed his wrath again.

"So she sent ya here lookin' fer me, did she?" he said bitterly, then drained the amber liquid from his glass and nodded to the bartender for another.

"No, Sam, she didn't ask me to find you," I said firmly. "It was my idea. She doesn't know I'm here. In fact, she probably wouldn't approve of me coming to see you. She has a lot of pride, and she knows how you feel about her father." I locked him in my gaze and didn't blink. It seemed to work.

While the bartender brought him another drink and refilled my coffee, Sam Dooley looked back at me quizzically while he thought over what I had just said. I was encouraged – maybe there was hope yet.

Sam snarled scornfully, "She tell you what caused the fuss 'tween her ol' man 'n' me in the first place?"

He took another drink and stared into space, perhaps reliving the event in question.

"No, we didn't discuss it," I replied. "She just said something about how stubborn her father was and that . . ."

"Stubborn?!" A loud, high-pitched horse laugh exploded from his lips, and he slammed his open palm on the counter, nearly spilling my coffee and temporarily interrupting the heated debate at the other end of the bar.

"Yer damn right he's stubborn, only stubborn ain't the name fer it. Mules 're stubborn but I seen Missouri mules with more common sense than that man!"

He took another long sip from his drink, and I waited for him to get the anger and frustration out of his system.

Sam looked at me; his large, bushy eyebrows arched like sagging tents over his fiery, bloodshot eyes. "You wanna know the real problem with Ben Griffin, sonny?"

He was not looking for an answer, so I said nothing and let him tell me. "The real problem with Ben Griffin," he continued, his speech slightly slurred from the whiskey, "is that there's only one way ta do somethin' and that's Ben Griffin's way – and if that ain't good enough fer ya, then there's the highway."

He finished his drink and slammed the glass down on the bar with a dramatic flourish. Then he turned to me and jabbed his stubby finger into my chest to emphasize his point. "He can be the most contrary person, I tell ya, and mean ta boot! As far as me 'n' him not getting 'long, it wasn't jist one thing that come 'tween us," he said as he continued to poke his finger into my chest, as if punishing me for bringing up Ben Griffin's name, "I was sick 'n' tired-a havin' that man nitpick everythin' I said or did and never give credit for nuthin' I did, which was plenty!"

The anger in his voice turned into pain as he filled me in on his bitter relationship with Ben Griffin. I could almost feel his anguish and I could not help but empathize with him.

"I give him fair warnin' that I'd walk out if'n he didn't lighten up – and walk I did when I had as much as I could take of that spiteful, contrary cuss!"

The bartender approached and silently offered Sam another drink, but he pushed his empty glass away in finality. He remained silent for a while and I sensed that he might be willing to listen to what I had to say, so I screwed up my courage and hoped for the best.

"I can understand your frustration, Sam, but I've got a newspaper to get out and you're the only man in these parts I can turn to. I need you to put your feelings about Ben Griffin aside for the time being and lend me a hand. Melanie has no one else to turn to."

I looked into his eyes and searched for compassion, for understanding, for some indication that he was softening, but he showed no sign of relenting, so I plunged ahead, unwilling to accept defeat.

"It's not like you would be working for Ben Griffin," I said, trying to reason with him. "You'd be working with me . . . and for Melanie."

I thought I detected a softening in his eyes. Was I getting through to him?

"With her dad unconscious, and not knowing if he's going to make it or not, doesn't she deserve at least that?"

He stared at nothing in particular and seemed to be lost in thought. I wasn't sure what to make of his silence, and I'd run out of things to say. I was beginning to lose hope when finally he spoke.

"So what in tarnation do ya know 'bout runnin' a newspaper, sonny?"

For the first time since I had met him, his tone was almost conciliatory. It was the first real sign that he might agree to accept my offer, and I struggled to contain my enthusiasm.

But before I could answer, he said, "I don't mind tellin' ya, it ain't no easy job 'n' I ain't sure even the two-a us – even if'n I said I'd help out – would be up to it."

"You may be right, Sam, but the way I see it, we're Melanie's only chance." I hoped that his concern for Melanie would help to convince him and I waited for his response.

I sensed that he was weakening, and I needed to close the deal before he could reconsider. "I promise you, Sam, that if things don't work out, why then ... ."

He cut me off in mid-sentence and said with defiance, "If things don't work out, sonny boy, I walk."

He spat the words out and looked at me with fierce determination. He wanted me to know that our arrangement, if there was to be one, would be on his terms and that was fine with me. At this point, nothing was going to dampen my sense of elation, but I suspected that working with Sam Dooley was going to be a challenge and I only hoped I would be up to it.

"Sam," I said confidently, "all I ask is that you give it a chance."

He grunted what I took to be his agreement and rose from his stool to go. I left some more cash on the bar and walked out with him, squinting into the bright morning sun.

"I expect we oughta be gettin' on down ta the office," he said resolutely. "It's the middle-a the day and we got a pile-a work ta git done."

We walked to the jeep, and I drove us back to the newspaper. On the way, I wondered whether convincing Sam Dooley to come back to work for *The Gazette* would prove to be worth the effort. I tried to imagine how Melanie would react to Sam's return and began to wonder if I had made a terrible mistake. But it was too late to turn back now, and we'd know soon enough if I'd made the situation better or worse. We arrived at the *Gazette* office, and I felt my pulse quickening. I prayed that things would work out the way I planned. If not, what was the alternative? I really didn't know.

CHAPTER TWELVE

Once inside, Sam gazed around warily. I could see that he was uneasy about returning – I couldn't really blame him. I looked around for Melanie and tried to think of a way to break the news to her. It might have been better to discuss my plan with her before going off on my own, but the genie was out of the bottle and there was no way to get it back inside.

I invited Sam into my small office, but he was more interested in examining the press room. He promptly marched in there, muttering soft epithets under his breath.

I was still wondering about Melanie's reaction to seeing Sam Dooley when I overheard her talking on the telephone. She sounded quite upset about something. I was worried she had received bad news about her father. I walked toward her office, and it became obvious that the conversation had nothing to do with her father's condition.

"But you've been one of my father's biggest supporters," she was saying. "How can you just . . ."

She paused and I could hear the faint buzzing of someone on the other end of the connection.

"Yes, I know your position on this development, Mr. Pemberton, but you of all people should know that my father is only trying to . . ."

She was interrupted again. Then, speaking in a low, trembling voice, she said, "Yes . . . yes, I understand . . . but I hope you'll reconsider." There was more buzzing on the other end, then a faint click, and the conversation ended. To no one in particular, Melanie said, "Yes, I understand. Thank you . . . for nothing!"

She placed the telephone receiver back on the cradle and began to cry. Her shoulders shook in rhythm to her sobs. I wanted to reach out to her, but I was reluctant to intrude in such an awkward situation.

When I could hold back no longer, I walked into her office and said, "Melanie, what's wrong? Can I help?"

I must have startled her. She jumped out of her chair, turned toward me, and nervously wiped the tears from her eyes while she tried to regain her composure. She managed an awkward smile, but it did not mask her anxiety.

"Well, that was just one more piece of bad news," she said, her voice quivering with emotion. "I received a letter from the bank informing me that they are not going to renew our line of credit due to what they called the newspaper's 'uncertain financial projections.' In other words, they think we're a bad risk!"

She laughed derisively and I thought she might start crying again, but she held herself in check.

"I called Jim Pemberton at home," she explained. "He's the chief loan officer and has been a friend of Daddy's for years. He didn't really want to talk to me,

70

but the bottom line is they are concerned about all the business we are losing because of Daddy's stand on the Donovan Company's development project." She stopped to get some tissue from her desk and dabbed at the tears in her eyes before continuing. "Now, with Daddy in the hospital for who knows how long, they don't expect the newspaper to survive much longer."

She started crying again and her body shook as she sobbed loudly. I shed my reluctance and took her into my arms tentatively – trying to give her my support. She clung to me tightly and I could feel her heart beating frantically against my chest. I didn't know what to say, so I just held her, hoping to calm her down.

Then I asked, "Can the newspaper operate without the bank's help?"

She slowly recovered her composure, and said, "Well, we can get along for a while on our current assets and receivables, but we will need that line of credit by next month when a balloon payment comes up on some presses Dad bought two years ago. We established the line of credit last year to cover some of our capital expenses and there has been no problem until now."

This seemed as good a time as any to break the news about Sam Dooley. I tried to find the right words, but they stuck in my throat. Melanie looked at me curiously, probably wondering if I had more bad news for her.

"What is it, Clint," she implored. "What's wrong now?" She looked as if she would burst into tears again at any moment.

"I . . . uh . . . that is, I . . ." The words still would not come out no matter how hard I tried to force them.

Then she gasped, and for a moment I thought she was going to pass out, just as a familiar high-pitched voice bellowed out from the doorway behind me, "Now what's all this dadburned fuss about?"

I turned to see Sam Dooley poking his head into the room. He stood with his hands on his hips, a grease-stained rag hanging around his neck, smelling of diesel oil and solvent. His tone was harsh, but the hint of a smile peaked out from behind his bushy beard.

I turned back to Melanie and tried to read her thoughts, but her face was frozen in disbelief, shock, or some other emotion – I wasn't sure. Assuming the worst, I began to apologize. "Look, . . . I . . . ah . . ."

Before I could finish, Sam broke in. "'Fore you go gettin' all excited 'n' carryin' on, ya'd better be knowin' that them presses need some serious work! God only knows what kinda treatment they been gettin' since I left."

Without saying a word, Melanie ran to him, and he gathered her up in his arms as a father might welcome a daughter who he had not seen for a very long time. She pressed her face into his dirty denim shirt and said something. Her words were muffled, but the meaning was clear. The tears in her eyes were those of joy and, at least for the moment, all of the bitter hardships and bad news she had dealt with in the last few days were being washed away.

I watched the joyous reunion, feeling a warm glow deep inside me. My gut instincts had served me well. It was good to know that Melanie now had someone in her corner she could trust – and I would be there too, just in case.

CHAPTER THIRTEEN

Melanie and Sam spent a while catching up, then I finished the rest of the day with a crash course in newspaper operations from Sam. I was thoroughly impressed with the depth of his knowledge. Despite his coarse language, gruff appearance, and menacing manner, he knew his way around a printing press, and I quickly realized how totally lost I would have been without him. The longer we worked, the better I felt about our ability to get the newspaper out on time. *The Climax Gazette* was back on track.

It was evening before I knew it, and Melanie was heading out to visit her father. She offered to drop me off at the Summit Inn, but I had promised to have dinner with Sam Dooley. He was an interesting character, and I wanted to get to know him better.

"But how will you get back to the Summit?" She had a worried look on her face.

"I'll probably just call Amos Greer and ask him to pick me up." "Nonsense," she replied. "You call me – I'll be available."

Before I could protest, she wrote down her cell phone number on a slip of paper and pressed it into my hand. Then she was off in Baby, a cloud of dust chasing after her. I watched her go, shaking my head and wondered what it would be like to ride in the jeep with all four wheels on the ground at the same time.

The Main Street Café was a pleasant, airy restaurant, located just across the square from the courthouse. It was nearly eight o'clock when Sam and I arrived, and the place was still alive with customers. I noticed a marked sheriff's car parked in a loading zone in front of the place. *Here on official business*, I supposed.

We waited at the register, observing the "Please Wait to be Seated" sign posted nearby. There were only two waitresses working, and they were both busy. One was a tall, older woman, with a flat, angular face that may have been pretty at one time – but years of hard work had taken their toll. Her legs, arms, and torso were long and skinny, and her lean figure reminded me of a marathon runner.

Despite her wearied, washed-out appearance, her eyes were bright, and she moved briskly about from one table to the next, keeping up a steady, folksy chatter with her customers. "How y'all doin' Marilu? Want a bit more coffee? Hey, Fred, how's Martha an' that yungun? Bobby Jo, y'all ready for suma that blueberry pie?"

The other waitress was young and shapely and had a wholesome smile that made her face glow. She, like her partner, was quite animated and bustled about the room with high energy and efficiency. I was impressed with how well the two of them managed to handle the crowd of diners. Both waitresses appeared to be on a first name basis with just about everyone in the room. I concluded that most of them were regulars.

"Must be a popular place," I said to Sam.

74

He nodded and said simply, "They got suma the best grub in these parts." Sam Dooley was no stranger to many of the customers; he nodded and barked out greetings to several of them as we waited our turn. I ignored the curious stares of those who wondered about the stranger in Sam's company. When the older waitress approached us with menus, Sam's face lit up, and he managed a wide grin through his few remaining tobacco-stained teeth.

"Hi, Sam," the waitress said, flashing a tired smile in his direction.

"Howdy, Mabel," Sam said in a low, gentle voice that surprised me. Was there a warm and tender human being hiding somewhere beneath that gruff exterior? Perhaps there was more to this man that I had yet to learn.

Mabel turned and swiftly led us to a booth in the rear. "Mary Alice will take your order," she said, nodding to the younger waitress, then handed us two worn menus.

Sam's disappointment was obvious. "Why, we're not good 'nough fer ya?" he asked in mock indignation.

"Sorry, Sam, but Mary Alice promised to close up for me. I'm headin' home just as soon as I can finish up my last two tables."

This didn't seem to sit well with Sam, and I wondered if there might be something between the two of them.

I couldn't resist the temptation: "You and Mabel must have something going, eh Sam?"

He wasn't amused.

"Nope, that ain't so," he retorted angrily. "She's jest the best durn waitress they got here, that's what, Mr. Nosey!"

He lowered his voice so no one else could hear. "And, she knows jist how I like my food."

He dropped the menu in disgust and I tried not to laugh, but I couldn't keep the smile from my lips.

Mary Alice arrived with a pitcher of ice water and two mugs of steaming black coffee. With practiced ease, she expertly filled our water glasses and placed the coffee cups and saucers in front of us. The coffee smelled delicious and made me realize just how hungry I was. I had skipped lunch and was famished.

Mary Alice looked at me and asked, "One check or two?"

"One will be fine," I said. Sam nodded his appreciation. It was the least I could do for his agreeing to help Melanie out of a tight spot.

Mary Alice returned a few minutes later to take our orders. "The soup is cream of broccoli or Boston bean. The daily special is pot roast with mashed potatoes and gravy, mixed vegetable, roll and butter."

I ordered the special and Sam followed my lead. He appeared to have forgotten about Mabel, and we exchanged bits and pieces of personal history. I was surprised to learn that he had worked on some of the largest newspapers in the country, including the *Los Angeles Times*, the *St. Louis Post-Dispatch* and the *Chicago Tribune*. He was apparently something of a vagabond and didn't stay in any one place too long. Neither of us said anything about our personal lives and that was just as well. There was still a lot of pain left over from the past, and I was doing my best to put it out of my mind.

Our conversation was interrupted when Mary Alice returned and placed several large platters of food in front of us. The aroma was enticing, and I couldn't wait to dig in. Neither of us spoke for several minutes, and we concentrated instead on tackling the large platters of food before us.

When we had eaten our fill, Mary Alice returned, refilled our coffee mugs, and took away the dishes. She offered us dessert, but we both declined. I was so full that I couldn't have eaten another thing, and Sam grunted that he was in just about the same shape.

Mary Alice returned with the check and placed it down in front of me. "How was everything?" She flashed us both with a wide grin.

"Excellent." I said with enthusiasm. "I don't know when I've had a better meal."

Mary Alice grinned and said, "Well, that's real nice ta hear, Mr. uh ..."

"I'm Clint. Clint Harrison." I said, accepting her hand. "I'm working over at *The Gazette* with Sam," nodding toward him. She ignored Sam, who looked totally bored with this conversation.

Her eyes grew wide in recognition when she heard my name. "Why then, you're that fella who saved old man Griffin's life the other day, aren't you?"

I could feel my face redden again and I hoped that no one else had overheard her. Out of the corner of my eye, I saw Sam Dooley react sharply when she mentioned Ben Griffin's name, and I wondered anxiously what thoughts were going through his mind.

I lowered my voice. "I didn't actually save his life. I just happened to be at the right place and time to help him out of a tough spot."

"Well, that's not the way I heard it," she gushed." At that moment we both realized we were still holding each other's hand. She quickly withdrew hers and reached over and plucked my check from the table.

"Your money's no good here, Mr. Harrison. Lots of folks here in town feel they owe you a debt of gratitude."

I knew better than to argue with her, so I accepted her offer gracefully. "I heard you were from L. A.," she said with obvious interest.

I admitted that I was.

"I grew up in Manhattan Beach, just two blocks up from the ocean. You know where the Strand is?"

I had grown up not too far from there and told her so.

Her face brightened as she related memories of an earlier time. It was as if we were suddenly kindred spirits, and I wanted to share more of our mutual experiences, but by this time Mabel had gone, and Mary Alice was left to deal with the remaining customers. We would just have to pick up the conversation another time. By now, Sam was looking impossibly bored, but I wanted to finish my coffee. I gestured *one more minute* with my forefinger and he grudgingly grunted his acquiescence. Mary Alice went to the register and said something to the cashier, whose eyes grew wide and looked intently at me. Just then, a large, beefy man wearing a County Sheriff's uniform swaggered up to the counter, put his arm around Mary Alice's waist and pulled her close to him. She tried to pull away but she was no match for him.

She responded with a yelp of protest. "Cut it out, J.D. That hurts!"

She didn't say it with much conviction, however, and she looked more annoyed than hurt.

"Well now, Mary Alice," the portly lawman said, his voice dripping with sarcasm. "I've been watching you with the stranger there, and it seems to me you've been given' him the wrong idea."

He shot me with a menacing look and I nonchalantly avoided his glare. I knew his type. I was willing to bet he had been the high school bully.

"What do you mean by that, J.D.?" she said, finally pulling away from him. "I was only taking care of business." She was clearly irritated by his conduct, but he didn't back down.

He said mockingly, "I know what kinda *business* you got in mind, Mary Alice, but you must be forgettin' 'bout our . . . uh . . . relationship."

He turned around to face me with his hands on his ample hips and his thumbs tucked into his gun belt that drooped around his pot belly.

Mary Alice turned to him with fire in her eyes and said angrily, "Look here, J. D. Potter, you don't own me, and you never will. I'm free to do what I want with whom I want, and you had just better get that straight in your head!" With that, she wheeled abruptly and stomped into the kitchen. Some of the diners were amused, but I was annoyed by it. I looked to Sam for support, but he was just as amused as the rest of the crowd.

The chagrined deputy seemed to be debating whether or not he should go after her, but then he must have thought better of it and returned to his seat. On the way, he passed threateningly close to me, and I could smell stale cigars and body odor reeking from him. I had troubled imagining a pretty young woman like Mary Alice having anything to do with this obscene oaf. He impressed me as someone who was used to having his own way, and I formed an immediate dislike for him. As a cop, I had known officers who used the badge and uniform to take advantage of others, and it had never set well with me. I also didn't appreciate the disrepute that such persons brought to our profession.

Sam Dooley tapped me lightly on the arm. "You don't wanna be messin' with J. D. Potter, sonny boy. He's a mean coyote and he's got the law on his side." His voice was a low whisper, and I wondered if he was speaking from personal experience. In any event, I had no wish to get mixed up with the law in this small town.

Sam and I were about to leave when Deputy Potter rose from his seat and strode purposefully to our table. My stomach muscles tightened in anticipation of an ugly confrontation.

Potter placed his large, beefy hands on our table and leaned toward me with his face only inches from mine. His breath had an unpleasant odor, and a scowl twisted his lips. He had small, lifeless eyes, a big, round nose, and huge ears that protruded from the sides of his head. He reminded me of a large bovine creature and I did my best to mask my disgust.

"I don't know what yer plans are here in Climax, stranger, but I sure hope they don't include Mary Alice." Between the fat lips, two rows of jagged, yellow-stained teeth moved as he spoke. "As I just explained, she's already taken."

I could see that Sam was growing tense, like a pit bull straining at its leash. I put my hand on his arm to settle him down. I wasn't looking for trouble, but I wasn't about to let this overweight tough guy think he could intimidate me.

"Why deputy," I said, casually, "I have no idea what you mean. Mr. Dooley and I were just having dinner and we're about to leave. We mean no trouble for you or anyone else."

This stopped the deputy in his tracks. He paused to think about what to say next. Perhaps he misinterpreted my words as a sign of submission. His menacing grimace turned into a wide, sneering grin. I reluctantly elected to let him think he had won the battle, but I suspected that the war was far from over.

He leaned back from the table, placed his hands on his hips in an arrogant display of bravado, and said, "Well, if you know what's good fer ya, buddy boy, you'll stay clear-a Mary Alice. Otherwise," he snarled, "it could get real unpleasant fer ya 'roun' here."

I stared into his eyes, said nothing, and put on my best poker face, despite my anger. Sam was squirming in his seat, but Potter's attention was focused only on me. The deputy thrust out his chest and, in a mock salute, touched the tip of the sweat-stained Stetson perched jauntily on the back of his head. He sauntered away, apparently satisfied that I had been sufficiently warned. He headed for the door and on the way out, he spotted Mary Alice at the register. He stopped long enough to whisper something in her ear and slapped her lightly on the rear end with his open hand. She said something to him that I couldn't hear, but the message I read in her eyes was clear enough.

We left the Main Street Café and Sam said that he was headed back to the newspaper office to do some more work on the presses. I admired his energy, but it was nearly nine o'clock and I was worn out. I needed to get some rest. On the way back to the office, Sam filled his cheek with a load of chew and warned me again to avoid any contact with Deputy Potter, and I assured him that I had no interest in having anything more to do with the ill-mannered lawman.

But I was curious about the "relationship" between the pretty young waitress and the beefy deputy. They clearly were not the All-American Couple and I asked Sam what he knew about them.

"Anythin' 'tween Mary Alice and J. D. Potter is jist in his head," he snorted contemptuously. "I think they mighta gone out wunst in high school or sumpin', but that's 'bout it. If she was of a mind to go out with a man, she could do better'n him, that's fer sure." As if to emphasize his point, he spat out an ugly wad of tobacco juice that splattered in the curb.

Then he turned and eyed me suspiciously. "You got eyes fer her, doncha?" I assured him that I didn't, but I don't think he believed me. He couldn't know the anguish that I continued to suffer from the horrible death of my wife and son, and I was not ready to share that with him, or with anyone else, for that matter. While I found Mary Alice to be a pleasant enough young lady and easy to talk to, there was no room in my life for another woman. Besides, both Sam and I would have plenty to keep us busy for the next several days as we struggled to help Melanie keep the newspaper in business. Maybe, after the hard work in front of us was finished, there would be time to get to know the lady from Manhattan Beach a little better.

CHAPTER FOURTEEN

I woke up rested and rejuvenated just before six o'clock, my spirits lifted by the rising sun breaking over the eastern horizon. For the first time in a very long while, I'd slept through the night, uninterrupted by flashbacks of past horrors. I prayed each day that I would someday be free of the haunting memories that continued to plague me.

I took a hot shower, shaved, dressed and made my way down to the dining room, surprised to find that it was already crowded with guests. An older waitress took my order and delivered my food with the same efficiency that I had received from Estelle. I ate slowly, savoring the delicious food and reflecting on the events of the previous day. I felt good about the progress Sam Dooley, and I had made, and I was anxious to get back to the office to do a little investigating.

Sam certainly didn't need my help, and there were a few things I wanted to check out. The recent setbacks experienced by the newspaper, for example, had me curious – to say nothing about Ben Griffin's accident just as he was on his way to a mysterious appointment – with who? Perhaps I would find the answer somewhere in Ben Griffin's cluttered office.

I also had very pleasant thoughts about reminiscing with Mary Alice and some not-so-pleasant thoughts about my encounter with J. D. Potter, the overweight, overbearing and obnoxious deputy. I hoped that he and I had seen the last of each other, but I had a strange foreboding that we'd likely cross paths again. It wasn't something that I was looking forward to. I was finishing my coffee when Amos Greer stopped by my table. I invited him to join me. I couldn't help but notice the lines etched deep into his forehead as he sat down across from me.

"You looked worried, Amos," I said, bracing myself for bad news "It's Estelle. She and William, her cousin, who's our dishwasher, didn't show up for work today. That's highly unusual,"

I could tell by the look in his eyes that he was deeply concerned. "I'm sure there must be a reasonable explanation," I said.

He shook his head sadly. "Not likely. They're very dependable and have never been late for work or missed a day's work in three years. I'm real concerned about them."

"Have you called their home? Is there some way to reach them?"

Amos shook his head again. "They live on the reservation with an elderly grandmother, and they have no telephone. I've no way to reach them and I'm real worried that somethin' bad may have happened to them, Clint."

I started to suggest that he might want to ask the Sheriff's Department to check on them, then realized that if Deputy J. D. Potter was typical of what their Sheriff's Department had to offer, he might very well be reluctant to turn there for help.

"Surely there must be someone at the reservation who can check on their welfare?"

I felt that he was probably making a lot more out of two people not showing up for work than I would have, but maybe he knew something I didn't. He sighed heavily; the worry lines etched even deeper into his forehead.

"Not really. They have a tribal council which is sorta like their own town government, but they're kinda funny 'bout outsiders and I'm not sure how cooperative they'd be."

He paused, took a deep breath and continued. "'Course, seein' as how they been treated by white folks in the past, I can't say as I blame 'em."

I thought about it for a minute, then shrugged. "Let me make an inquiry or two. Maybe I can find something out."

I almost immediately regretted making the offer, but I couldn't take it back. My lack of familiarity with local law enforcement, along with my utter lack of knowledge about how things are done on an Indian reservation, rendered me useless – something I realized too late.

Amos was visibly relieved at my suggestion and expressed his thanks. Then he reminded me that the car he offered to loan me was still available whenever I needed it. I decided that now would be as good a time as any to take him up on the offer. I thanked him again for his generosity but he brushed my thanks away with a wave of his arm. "I'd rather see it put to some good use than sitting out in back gatherin' dust."

The station wagon was old and big and dirty and took its time moving through the gears but was a surprisingly comfortable ride and I managed to arrive at the office a few minutes after 7:30. Sam Dooley was already at work, growling under his breath at no one in particular. I could see that he needed no help from me and I decided to check out some of the files in Ben Griffin's office. I was curious to learn more about some of the problems *The Gazette* had been having in recent weeks. Maybe it was just a streak of bad luck and maybe it was something much more sinister. Either way, it wouldn't hurt to do some investigating of my own.

I looked around Ben Griffin's office and marveled that anyone could get anything done amid such clutter. Then I noticed that there was a small room located just to the rear of his office. I tried the door, but it was locked. My cop instinct kicked in, and my curiosity revved up to full throttle, and I decided to see what was so important that it had to be kept behind locked doors.

I opened the top drawer of Ben's desk and spotted several keys, each attached to a faded tag. One of these bore the words "file room". I fit it into the door lock and turned it. The door opened easily and revealed a dozen file cabinets. I discovered that each was crammed full of file folders containing correspondence, newspaper clippings, invoices and various other records dating back several years. I felt a little bit like an intruder, but it was just possible that, in all these files, I might find out what it was that Ben Griffin had been so secretive about just before the accident. I just wished I knew where to start looking.

I began by quickly scanning the contents of the file cabinets, trying to deduce any semblance of logic or order, but found none. I did observe that one file cabinet was unlike all the rest – it was equipped with a large keyed padlock and locking bar. None of the other file cabinets were locked and I wondered why its contents warranted such great security. I returned to Ben's desk drawer and searched for a key that might fit the padlock. Finding none, I pulled the drawer all the way out and discovered a key taped to its underside. I tried it and found that it opened the padlock. Anticipation coursed through my veins as I removed the locking bar and began to explore the contents of the file cabinet.

Three of the four drawers contained a few old ledgers while the top drawer held a set of manila file folders which surprisingly were neatly organized and of recent vintage. I thumbed through them and suspected that I had struck pay dirt when I read "A. B. Donovan Development Company" on one of the labels. I withdrew the entire set of files and took them back to my office where I could inspect them closer.

I placed the stack of file folders on the table, made myself a pot of coffee, and set out to see what I could learn about what Ben Griffin had discovered in his investigation of the Donovan Corporation. I was about to discover something that would lead me deeper into a mystery that defied explanation.

CHAPTER FIFTEEN

The first folder I opened contained a series of newspaper clippings from *The Climax Gazette*, describing the controversy surrounding the Donovan Corporation's attempt to develop the land adjacent to the Sequoia Indian Reservation. I looked these over briefly and learned little more than I already knew.

Another folder, much bulkier than the first, contained copies of correspondence and legal documents from both the Donovan Corporation and the Sequoia Tribal Council and various state and federal agencies involving the Donovan Corporation's attempts to develop the land in question. My legal training allowed me to quickly sort out the essential details from the minutia that was of little real interest.

In my haste, I almost missed a small black ledger that was tucked among some of the legal documents. It appeared to be a handwritten account of a series of events involving the Donovan Corporation that had taken place over the preceding 18 months. I read with fascination one man's story of what had transpired since the Donovan Corporation first announced its plans to develop the land near the Sequoia Indian Reservation. The writer described in detail personal contacts and conversations he had with representatives of the Donovan Corporation, the Indian tribe, and state and federal regulatory agencies.

I could only assume that the writer of the journal was Ben Griffin, but without showing it to Melanie, I would not know for sure. Then I remembered that Melanie told me about her father's mistrust of computers and other modern conveniences, and the handwritten journal began to make more sense.

Midway through the pages, I came across an intriguing entry in which the writer described having a conversation with a man called "Pete", (apparently a code name for an informant), who was the source of much of the inside information the writer had obtained about the efforts of The Donovan Corporation to acquire the land in question. If I understood what I was reading, Pete was employed high enough in the hierarchy of the Donovan Corporation to know a great deal about the company's inner workings and corporate strategy.

According to the journal, nearly all of the contacts between Pete and himself had been by telephone, although there had been at least two meetings between them. However, in both cases, the meeting had been during the hours of darkness and in a secluded area where the writer had been unable to obtain a good look at Pete. He could only describe Pete as a white male, tall and slender, probably between forty and fifty years of age, with a slight Southern accent.

As I read on, I found myself wondering about the possible motivation of the man called Pete to subvert the interests of his own employer. I know full well the importance of motivation in explaining human behavior. Realizing why people act the way they do helps them to understand their actions in a way that nothing else does. The question of motive continued to trouble me as I read on.

According to Pete, the Donovan Corporation was attempting to place intense pressure on state and federal regulatory agencies by exerting the power of several influential state and federal legislators who had befriended Donovan in the past and who, Pete alleged, had accepted large cash campaign donations from the Donovan Corporation. If this was true and could be substantiated, it would certainly place a shadow over the credibility of the Donovan Corporation's efforts.

The gravity of these allegations was disturbing. I realized that Ben Griffin could very well have placed himself in great danger if he attempted to make these allegations public. How credible were these allegations? Was it possible that Ben Griffin was being deliberately misled to undermine his opposition to the Donovan Corporation's efforts? Had Ben Griffin's accident anything to do with his investigation? These thoughts continued to race through my mind as I read on.

My naturally suspicious instincts went on high alert when I came across an entry dated just three months earlier, in which Pete reported that the executives of the Donovan Corporation were getting increasingly agitated by the opposition of the newspaper to the proposed development. According to Pete, Ben Griffin had been targeted for "neutralization" by the top-level executives of the Donovan Corporation! Pete reported that there had been a series of secret meetings of the management team in which possible ways to eliminate the newspaper's opposition were discussed.

It was suggested, for example, that it might be possible to bring intense financial pressure on the newspaper by removing advertisements and curtailing financial support from banks and creditors. I immediately thought of the letter Melanie had received from Jim Pemberton informing her of the bank's decision not to renew the newspaper's line of credit. This could be an indication that Donovan Corporation's plan had been launched. The sinister implication of what I was reading made me angry.

I was even more appalled to learn that, at one of those meetings, there had even been suggestions of physical attacks on the newspaper and Ben Griffin personally. Incredibly, there looked to be a consensus among the members of the management team, who weren't identified, that these drastic actions might have to be seriously considered if more subtle tactics to overcome the newspaper's opposition were unsuccessful. As I read, I grew more convinced than ever that the accident that nearly killed Ben Griffin had been no accident at all. I made a mental note to check with the Sheriff's Department to see if their investigation of the crash would lend support to my suspicions.

The journal went on to relate that several alternatives were considered, including setting fire to the newspaper office, making death threats against Ben Griffin and his daughter, and sabotaging the newspaper's offices and presses. These actions, it was believed, would either put the newspaper out of business or seriously cripple its operations. I found it hard to believe that the Donovan Corporation's top management personnel could seriously consider such illegal and underhanded tactics, as if they were discussing options for maximizing profits or increasing productivity.

More recent entries in the journal confirmed that some of these outrageous ideas had been implemented. For example, a later entry described a small fire that had been discovered in a pile of rubbish that had been placed at the rear of the newspaper. While no incendiary device was discovered, the investigation suggested that an accelerant might have been used to start the fire. However, the laboratory report could not exclude the possibility that the ignition source had been a discarded container of cleaning solvent that had been improperly placed in a dumpster at the rear of the building by a clean-up crew who'd been working in an adjacent building.

The fire was discovered by a trash collector at 6:30 AM and had been quickly extinguished by the Climax Fire Department. The journal entry also noted that had the fire burned much longer, it could have ignited several large drums of cleaning fluid that were stored nearby, and the resulting explosion and fire would probably have dealt a fatal blow to the newspaper.

A few pages later, I discovered an entry describing a conversation in which the writer asked Pete if the fire could have been deliberately set by someone from the Donovan Corporation. Pete declined to say, but he did confirm that such an act had been discussed at one of the meetings in which he was present. According to the journal, the writer asked Pete if he knew who, if anyone, at Donovan could have done such a thing. Pete claimed ignorance, but admitted that "There's always someone available to do that kind of work if the price is right."

Another entry revealed that, only two weeks after the fire, another incident occurred that could have considerably disrupted the newspaper's ability to stay in business. A shipment of newsprint from a supplier in Oregon had inadvertently been diverted to another newspaper two states away. By the time the mix up was discovered, it was too late to obtain a replacement shipment from the supplier. Fortunately, Ben Griffin was able to rely upon the good will of a rival publisher, who agreed to send him enough newsprint to last him until the original shipment could be replaced.

The entry went on to say the supplier explained that a simple computer entry had switched the destination for the newsprint delivery. It was unknown how the switch had been made or by whom, nor could it be determined whether the act was accidental or deliberate. In a subsequent conversation with the writer, Pete admitted that disruption of bulk supplies, including paper and ink, was among the tactics discussed by Donovan executives.

When I finished, I was surprised to see that three hours had elapsed since I began reading the journal. I replaced all the files, locked the file cabinet, returned the key to where I'd found it, and locked the door to the file room. Then I sat for a long while and contemplated my next move.

I figured it was a safe bet that someone in the Donovan Corporation was behind the acts of sabotage that had nearly ruined *The Gazette*. If I could identify and locate this fellow Pete, I might be able to convince him to cooperate with me in an investigation. My first step, however, would be to speak with someone at the Sheriff's Department about what I had discovered. If criminal activity was involved, as it certainly appeared to be, this was a matter for the local law enforcement to handle. I just hoped that I could avoid running into Deputy Potter while at the Sheriff's Office. That would be enough to ruin my entire day.

On the way out, I waved to Melanie and told her that I would be leaving for a little while. It was only four blocks to the Sheriff's Department, which was adjacent to the courthouse, and I decided to walk and enjoy the midday sun and refreshing mountain air. I felt a sense of excitement that reminded me of my days as a prosecutor on the eve of a new case. The scent of prey was in the air, and I was on the prowl.

CHAPTER SIXTEEN

I was only two blocks from the courthouse when, as if on cue, a marked sheriff's car pulled up beside me and none other than Deputy J. D. Potter alighted and approached me. He wore mirrored aviator sunglasses, a soiled baseball-style cap and the same mean grin he had the last time I saw him. I wondered if he had been born with it or if he wore it only for special occasions. I expected nothing but the worst from him and was immediately on alert. My body tensed and my stomach muscles tightened involuntarily.

"Afternoon, Mr. Harrison," the plump deputy said, more cordially than I had expected. He appeared out of character. His pleasant greeting did nothing to allay my suspicions, however.

I played it casual and said, "What can I do for you, Deputy?"

"You need to come with me, Mr. Harrison," he said evenly.

The malevolence I'd seen in him in our last encounter was missing, and I wondered why.

I wasn't sure if it was a direct order or an invitation, but I wasn't about to argue the point. After all, the Sheriff's Department was my original destination. Nevertheless, I couldn't control my curiosity.

"With you? Why? Have I done something wrong?"

"No sir, not at all." he replied, doing his best to be polite.

For a second, I wondered if I had misjudged him earlier, but I was pretty sure I hadn't. I know a bully when I see one. "Sheriff Jenkins needs to have a word with you," Deputy Potter said casually. "He sent me to fetch you."

Now I was really confused. What business could the sheriff possibly have with me? *Well,* I thought *there was one sure way to find out.*

"All right," I said, "let's go."

Potter appeared surprised – perhaps disappointed – that I was being so agreeable. He opened the passenger door of his car and motioned me in. With all the clutter of radio equipment, modems, keyboards and other electronic devices, there's not much room in the front seat of a police car for a passenger, but there's a distinct difference between riding in the front seat and riding in the rear seat, which is normally reserved for passengers of a different persuasion. I took his offer as a sign that I wasn't in any trouble with the law, and this helped ease the tension.

The El Dorado County Sheriff's Department was located directly behind the courthouse. It was a squat, two-story stucco building with a Spanish tile roof characteristic of some of the late-nineteenth century buildings typically found in the southwestern United States. Bars on the windows of the second floor of the building were telltale signs that a jail was housed within.

Potter parked his cruiser at the rear of the building, and I followed him through a side entrance marked "Employees Only". We walked down a long hallway to a small reception area. An attractive, middle-aged woman was busy working at a computer but managed to break away from her work long enough to give me an engaging smile. The nameplate on her desk identified her as "Irene Duffy". Potter motioned me to one of the chairs in the room and disappeared behind an unmarked door.

In less than a minute, Deputy Potter emerged and announced that Sheriff Jenkins would see me. I followed him through the door and found myself in a large office attractively paneled in dark oak. Two walls were covered with floor-to-ceiling bookcases. The wall behind the sheriff's desk was adorned with photographs, plaques, framed letters and miscellaneous memorabilia that testified to Sheriff Jenkins' stature and popularity among some of the state's top political figures over a quarter of a century. I was immediately impressed.

The sheriff was a tall, angular man who topped me by several inches, and who bore what was referred to in the military as a strong "command presence". It's a term reserved for those individuals who immediately impress others with their "take change" attitude and the ability to be solidly in control of any situation. General George S. Patton, General Dwight David Eisenhower and General Douglas MacArthur were such men.

I estimated him to be in his mid-sixties, but he had taken good care of himself. His skin was the color of copper and had the texture of leather. He had a pronounced, jutting jaw, a large bushy mustache that bristled over an even set of white teeth, and piercing blue eyes that looked as if they could drill holes in granite. He was the epitome of the old-time western lawman, and I was just a little intimidated by him.

Sheriff Jenkins rose from his cluttered desk and grasped my hand in a strong, firm handshake. "I'm pleased to meet you, Mr. Harrison." He motioned me to a heavy leather chair facing his desk. He offered me coffee, but I declined, having had my fill of caffeine at the office. I settled into the comfortable chair, more curious than ever to know what business he could possibly have with me.

He glanced at Deputy Potter, who had remained standing by the door, and nodded to him to leave. The deputy reluctantly stepped outside and closed the door behind him.

The sheriff said nothing for several seconds, but gazed steadily into my eyes, perhaps sizing me up. I felt a little bit like an insect under a magnifying glass, but I managed to remain nonchalant and kept my discomfort under wraps.

Finally, he said, "You probably wonder why I sent for you." I nodded and waited for him to continue.

He gave me an icy stare and said, "I've been looking into your traffic accident, and I have several concerns."

His words caught me off guard and I wondered if he was about to read me my Miranda Rights, and I went on instant alert.

"But before I get into my investigation into the crash, I should tell you that I have checked into your background, and I know that you were an Assistant District Attorney in L.A. until recently."

I wasn't surprised that he'd checked me out, although it did nothing to ease my apprehension. Strangers in small towns raise many questions, and law enforcement officials have a powerful intelligence network. It doesn't take long to find out more about you than you might want them to know. "Yes, that's right, Sheriff," I said, still wondering where this conversation was headed.

His voice softened and he said, "I also know about your wife and child. I simply can't imagine how you managed to deal with such a tragedy."

He paused for a moment, and I could see real compassion in his eyes that said more than any words could have. I was moved by his obvious empathy, and I thanked him. My earlier apprehension quickly dissolved.

"I understand they got the man who planted the bomb."

"Yes," I replied, trying to control my emotion. "It was meant for me. The hit was ordered by Carlos Ortega, the top man of the Ortega drug cartel. The guy who planted the bomb was captured in a shootout with an FBI task force. After lengthy questioning, he gave the feds enough to indict Ortega. He's in federal custody awaiting trial for contract killing and assorted other crimes."

"You'll be returning to L.A. for the trial, I expect," the sheriff said.

I sighed heavily. "Yes. It's not something I'm looking forward to, but if Carlos gets the death penalty, I want to be there to see his face when they read the verdict, and if he ever gets executed, I want to be there to see them stick the needle in his arm."

My stomach was in an uproar when I thought about the man who'd taken so much from me.

"I don't blame you a bit," Sheriff Jenks said empathetically.

He paused for a moment to put that conversation behind us, then said, "In case you're wondering, I'm not just some hick sheriff who only ran for office because I had nothing better to do."

The hint of a smile played on his lips, but the look in his eyes was strictly business.

"Before coming to Climax, I spent twenty years with the Phoenix Police Department, where I worked my way up the ranks from patrolman to

Assistant Chief. I'm also a graduate of the FBI National Academy and I have a bachelor's degree in criminal justice from Arizona State University."

I glanced at the wall behind him and saw the large, framed seal of the FBI National Academy just above his head. His degree from Arizona State was prominently displayed next to it. They were notable achievements, and I was impressed with his pedigree. This was a man who undeniably knew the job, and I suspected the voters of this county were getting their money's worth from Sheriff Jenkins. But I still didn't know why he had sent for me, and the more we talked, the more my curiosity mounted.

I was still waiting for him to get to the point, so I decided to prime the pump.

"What can I do for you, Sheriff?"

For several seconds he gazed out the window at the majestic mountains in the distance and appeared lost in thought.

Then he turned back, locked me in his steely gaze, and, in a near- whisper, said, "What I'm about to tell you, Mr. Harrison, is extremely confidential and must not be repeated to anyone. I'm telling you this because I believe I can trust you. I think that you may be just the man I need to help me." I felt a tingling sensation on the back of my neck. What could the sheriff possibly want with me and why was he being so secretive? I wasn't sure I wanted to know.

CHAPTER SEVENTEEN

"As you may have noticed, Mr. Harrison, this is a small town, and we have few resources. Climax has no police department and the only regular deputies I have are J.D. Potter, who tries hard but is somewhat limited, and Herb Snyder, the night man. Plus, I have a few part-times who will work on occasion for somethin' less than minimum wage. That's the best I can do on the budget the county commissioners give me."

"What about other law enforcement agencies?" I asked, knowing the close networking that goes on in the law enforcement community.

"Oh, I can sometimes get help from the State Patrol, but that all depends on how busy they are at the time, and they're not much better off than we are. Seems like we're all being asked to do more with less these days. So, when I do get a major investigation, which isn't very often, I usually end up working the case myself, which is exactly what I am doing right now."

He stood up, walked to the window, and stared at nothing in particular, as if sorting through his thoughts. He stood ramrod straight and had a physique that a man half his age would envy.

The sheriff turned back to me and said, "Mr. Harrison, I believe that what happened to Ben Griffin on that mountain road was no accident."

His words struck me with the force of a mule kick, and he now had my full attention.

"I have evidence indicating that Ben's car was sabotaged – the brake lines were cut just before he got into that car."

He let those words hang in the air while I pondered them.

"That's not all," he continued, "I believe the so-called 'accident' was only the latest in a series of deliberate attempts to put him out of business."

I reflected on what I had learned from reading Ben Griffin's journal. The sheriff's words confirmed my own suspicions. I remained silent and waited to hear what else he had to say.

He sat down again and sighed heavily, looking as if he was carrying a heavy burden on his shoulders. I could see the strain of worry in his eyes. He looked at me in dead earnest and said, "What we're dealing with here is serious business, and I desperately need someone like you to assist me."

He paused again, as if waiting for my reaction. I didn't know what to say. The last thing I needed was another job, if that was what he was asking me to do. Besides, I'd already made a commitment to help Melanie with the newspaper, and she was counting on me. How could I let her down? On the other hand, the attacks on Ben Griffin and the newspaper needed to be investigated and the sheriff had made it clear he didn't have the resources to do the job. Sometimes fate comes knocking at the most unexpected time and in the most unlikely way.

My stomach was churning with both excitement and apprehension, but I took the bait anyway. "Just what do you have in mind, Sheriff?"

I wanted to tell him what I'd learned from Ben's journal, but I'd rather hear what he had to say first, and then decide if I should seriously consider his request.

"The fact is, Mr. Harrison, I believe that the sabotage of Ben Griffin's car may have something to do with the feud between the Donovan Corporation and the Sequoia Indians."

"What makes you think that?"

"I received a call from Ben Griffin an hour before the crash," the sheriff said. "He gave me a rundown on some information he'd received from some confidential source who apparently told him that he'd been targeted by a group of executives at the Donovan Corporation who were tired of his editorials attacking them for their legal battles with the Indians."

The sheriff shook his head. "I know it sounds preposterous, but I've known Ben Griffin for as long as he and Melanie have lived in this town. He's as honest as the day is long, and he's not one to make such allegations without good reason. That's why I took his information seriously."

"But what proof do you have that . . ." Before I could finish, he waved me off.

"Ben told me he was on his way to meet with his informant, and he'd call me when he returned. I tried to convince him to let me go with him, but he refused, saying that the informant wouldn't deal with anyone but himself. The next thing I know, Ben Griffin nearly gets himself killed on the side of a mountain, and that's where you came into the picture."

"I can understand your suspicions, Sheriff, but how does that concern me?" He nodded and said, "Truth is, Mr. Harrison, I have no one I can count on to conduct a low-level investigation of the kind that's needed here."

I knew where this was going, but I wanted to know more about what he had in mind, so I allowed him to continue.

"I've talked to my friends at the FBI, but they are all tied up on that *posse comitatus* investigation going on in the southern part of the state, and they can't lend me a single agent. The State Patrol has been faced with budget cuts and can't spare anyone either. I need someone who knows law enforcement, and who can work in an undercover capacity without anyone being the wiser. The way I see it, you're just the man for the job."

I figured this was a good time to tell him about Ben Griffin's journal. As I told him what I'd learned from it, he listened intently, from time to time nodding his head. I sensed that what I was telling him only confirmed his own suspicions.

When I finished, he said, "That's incredible! I had no idea these things had been happening until Ben called me and told me himself. The journal is all the confirmation we need."

"But the journal itself isn't proof," I countered. "You need more than that."

"You're absolutely right, Harrison, and that's where you come in!" Sheriff Jenkins nodded. He'd clearly given this some thought. "Your position at the newspaper fits in perfectly with what I have in mind."

He paused, took a long breath, then continued. "I need someone who can conduct a very sensitive investigation without being noticed. As Ben Griffin's stand-in, you'll be in a perfect position to gather information that I can use to crack this case."

I could see the logic of his plan. As a representative of the newspaper, I'd be able to go just about anywhere, talk to anyone, and surreptitiously obtain information that might help solve the case. I had to admit that what the sheriff had in mind just might work, but was I really the man for the job? I wasn't sure I was ready to take on this kind of challenge, and the sheriff must have fathomed my uncertainty.

"Look, Harrison, I don't know how long you're planning on staying here in Climax, but as long as you've agreed to help Melanie with the newspaper, seems to me there's no reason you can't do both. God knows I need the help, and you've got the background!"

I felt myself weakening and said, "If I do agree to help, where would I start?"

A thin smile broke over the sheriff's face. He reached inside his desk and withdrew a manila folder and handed it to me. "You can start by looking this over. It's a copy of the investigation I conducted following the traffic accident."

I accepted the file and quickly scanned the contents while he watched. It was a standard traffic accident report, but it included a statement from the mechanic who'd inspected Ben's car after the accident. According to the mechanic, the brake line had a small nick in it, resulting in a slow leaking of the brake fluid. This must have accounted for Ben's being unable to control his car just before the crash.

Then I came across a clear plastic evidence bag about four inches wide and six inches long. It contained a page from a small notebook. I recognized it as a page from Ben Griffin's journal.

"What's this?" I asked, holding it out to him.

"Not sure. Melanie found this in her dad's shirt pocket when she was going through his things at the hospital. She thought it might be important and gave it to me."

There were words written on the scrap of paper, but they were badly smudged, making them impossible to read.

"It might be something and then again it might not," I said, squinting as I tried to decipher the words. "Is there some way we can get a crime lab to help us decipher whatever is written on the note?"

The sheriff smiled and said, "You bet! I had Fred Granger down at the state crime lab take a look at this through his high-intensity microscope and he came up with something that may tell us where Ben Griffin was headed before the accident."

My curiosity peaked. "And what did he come up with?"

"The note contains two words and four numbers. The numbers appear to be 1230, which is probably meant as either 12:30 AM or PM."

I nodded. 12:30 PM would be shortly after the accident. "It could mean that he was on his way to meet someone at 12:30 PM," I said.

The sheriff nodded. "Yep, the time fits almost like a glove."

"But what were the words? And what do they have to do his meeting?"

Sheriff Jenkins hesitated for a moment, then said, "I'm not sure, but I think the words on that note may be the key to the mystery behind Ben Griffin's accident."

A tightening sensation gripped my stomach. "What are the words?"

"'Heaven's Gate,'" the sheriff replied coldly. "I think Ben Griffin's accident had something to do with Heaven's Gate."

CHAPTER EIGHTEEN

I had no idea of the significance of what Sheriff Jenkins had just said, but, by the look on his face, it must have been very important.

"I don't understand," I said with mounting interest. "What is Heaven's Gate? And what could that possibly have to do with Ben Griffin's accident?"

The sheriff shook his head slowly in bewilderment. "I don't have the faintest idea. I've checked around and the best I can come up with is that it's some kind of sacred place or a ritual somewhere up in the mountains on the Sequoia Indian Reservation. It's anyone's guess how it ties in with Ben Griffin's investigation or his accident."

If I was hoping for the sheriff to enlighten me, I was disappointed. "Where do you think we should go from here?" I had a few ideas of my own, but this was the sheriff's case, and I wanted to know what he thought should be done.

He nodded and said, "First, I think we need to track down this fellow 'Pete', and see if he'll be willing to share with us the information, he gave Ben Griffin."

"That's not a bad idea, Sheriff, but how do I go about finding him? If he's a member of the Donovan management team, how do we know he'll be willing to talk with me?"

The sheriff shrugged his shoulders. He'd come to the same conclusion. Finding Ben's informant wouldn't be easy. And I'd seen nothing in Ben's journal to suggest where I might start.

"Maybe I should just go out to the Donovan Corporation and see if I can find anyone or anything that might back up some of these allegations."

The sheriff's face grew dark with concern. "Just how do you think you can go about doing that, Harrison? I can't imagine why anyone out there would want to tell you anything, especially if they've something to hide."

I was dismayed at his lack of confidence. I needed encouragement from him, not pessimism. But a plan was taking shape in my mind, and I decided to try it out on him.

Summoning up all the self-assurance I could muster, I said, "I think I'm about to perform my first official act in my capacity as the interim . . . ah, whatever. . . of the *Climax Gazette*. It's time that a representative of the *Gazette* spoke face-to-face with the corporate officials at Donovan and got their side of the story about the dispute with the Sequoia Indians."

The sheriff gazed at me thoughtfully for a moment, trying to weigh the merits of my idea. I had to admit it was a bit shaky, but still worth a try.

"Since I've no connection with Ben Griffin – don't even know him, in fact – I might be able to convince the folks at Donovan that I'm approaching the story from a whole new angle, with no editorial position one way or the other. Maybe a gentler, softer approach will be just what we need to get them to open up and to defend the accusations that have been leveled against them."

The sheriff continued to listen, and I could tell that he was starting to like the idea. "If things go as planned," I continued, "it could have a dual effect. First," I said, holding up my finger for emphasis, "it may get them to pull back on their targeting – if that's what they've been doing – and second, we may just be able to flush out the mole in their company."

I stopped to get the sheriff's reaction. He still wasn't sure. "How so – I mean on that second point?"

"Simple," I said, grinning impishly. "If this 'Pete' thinks I'm going soft on Donovan, he might feel compelled to contact me and arrange for a secret meeting to get me back on track with what's really been going on."

Sheriff Jenkins grinned at me and nodded. "I like your plan, but you need to go easy out there. If the information in Ben's journal is accurate, some of those boys may not welcome your inquiries, regardless of how you play it – and you may find yourself number one on their target list."

His words sent a chill down my spine, and I realized that there was clearly an element of risk in my plan.

"I won't take any unnecessary risks, Sheriff," I promised.

He gave me a skeptical look that said it all. Then he reached into a desk drawer, retrieved a small metallic object that looked like a pregnant cell phone and handed it to me. He explained that it was, in fact, equipped with a paging device.

After he explained how to use it, he said, "I want you to keep me informed of your movements at all times."

"That's not a problem," I said. It was reassuring to know that I could contact him instantly if I smelled trouble.

"If possible, call me at least once a day and let me know of any progress you've made. Otherwise, I don't want to hear from you or see you except in your capacity as a representative of the newspaper. I'll use this to contact you if I need you." He held up a matching phone.

"As far as our little visit today," the sheriff said, "let's just say I had you in here to go over a few details about the crash. That's essentially correct, right?" He gave me a knowing wink and I nodded my understanding. Our arrangement was to be strictly "off the record", at least for the time being.

I looked at the cell phone and asked him if he had a charger to go with it. The last thing I needed was for the phone to go dead just when I needed it most.

He shook his head vigorously. "Shouldn't need one. These were developed for the U. S. military and have a minimum active life of thirty days before they need re-charging."

I looked at the small device in wonder and thought how good it would be to have one of my own.

"It's equipped with a special solar powered microchip that works very much like the small batteries in your watch. Under optimum conditions, they should last for 120 hours or more."

"That should be plenty," *The marvels of modern technology*, I said to myself.

"Plus, it contains a GPS tracking device. If the GPS locator is activated, I can find you, even if the cell phone is turned off."

He showed me a small button on the side of the device I hadn't noticed before.

"When it's on, you'll see a small green light flash in the upper left corner of the face plate."

I turned it on as instructed and saw the tiny green light begin flashing.

"It's amazing what they come up with these days," I said, thinking that the GPS would be of no value to me. As long as I could call the sheriff, I had all the security I needed.

I was about to leave when I remembered what Amos Greer had told me about Estelle and her cousin William. I asked Sheriff Jenkins if he had any contacts out on the reservation that I could call to inquire about their welfare.

"Not really," he said while a frown played on his lips. "They have their own tribal police. But the real power on the reservation is B. J. Tall Horse and I don't know how much help you'll get from him."

"Are you telling me that he's not very cooperative?"

"That would be something of an understatement," the sheriff said with sarcasm dripping from his voice. "I've tried to establish a working relationship with the tribal police for years, but I get nowhere with them. They want to keep everything that goes on at that reservation strictly off-limits to us. And they couldn't care less about anything that happens off the reservation."

"It sounds as if I need to add Mr. Tall Horse to my list of appointments."
"Good luck on that," he replied with a definite lack of enthusiasm.

I appreciated his candor – forewarned is forearmed, as they say, but I owed it to Amos to look into the welfare of Estelle and William. Plus, I needed to get a statement from someone – probably Mr. B. J. Tall Horse himself – on their side of the legal battle with the Donovan Corporation. Pretending to be a representative of the newspaper would be a perfect cover for what I needed to do.

"I'm glad to have you in on this with me, Harrison," the sheriff said while walking me to the door. I could see he was greatly relieved to have me working with him, while I, on the other hand, wondered what I had gotten myself into. We shook hands and I promised to keep him informed of any progress I made.

I left the sheriff's office, and I noticed J. D. Potter leaning against his patrol car eyeing me warily. I could only imagine the questions that were dancing around inside his head. Just now, though, I had other and more important concerns than Deputy Potter, and I was anxious to get started on my new assignment.

CHAPTER NINETEEN

I arrived at the newspaper office to find Melanie engaged in an animated telephone conversation with someone. She appeared to be in a cheerful mood. I hoped it was good news about her father.

I returned to my office and retrieved the file of newspaper clippings I'd scanned earlier. I remembered seeing an article relating that Michael S. Gallagher, the Donovan Corporation's Vice-President in charge of development, had arrived in Climax to personally oversee a series of conferences with state and federal agency representatives to review the proposed development. I found the article and learned that Gallagher was from the firm's corporate headquarters in Kansas City. It suggested that the company was bringing out its "heavy artillery"' for this round of meetings. I wondered whether Gallagher was still in town. *Well*, I thought, *there's one simple way to find out.*

I found a worn telephone book, looked up the number of the Donovan Corporation, and dialed it. After several transfers, I was connected to Ms. Abigail Brimmer, one of their public relations representatives. After I identified myself and the purpose of my call, she informed me that she'd be more than happy to meet me later that same day, or the next, if that would be convenient. Or, she said, perhaps she could send me out an information package (translation: propaganda) that would outline the company's position and provide useful background information for any story I was preparing.

I politely but firmly let Ms. Brimmer know that I wasn't interested in speaking with anyone other than Michael Gallagher himself. She coolly replied that Mr. Gallagher was only in town for two more days and that he'd be tied up in meetings the entire time.

"It's highly unlikely," she went on, "that he could find time to meet with you Mr. Harrison."

Her tone was brusque and business-like. I was getting the corporate version of the bum's rush and I didn't like it. But I knew I'd get nowhere by being antagonistic. I decided to bait the hook and see if she'd bite.

"I'm afraid it's imperative that I speak with Mr. Gallagher personally. I have very sensitive information that I know he'll find important."

There was a pause while she considered this. The word *sensitive* had probably snagged her attention. "And what would be the nature of that information?" Her voice dripped with curiosity, and I knew I had her.

"I'm very sorry, Ms. Brimmer, but the story I'm working on has a few new angles that haven't been made public yet and are of such a nature that it's only fair that I hear directly from the principals on both sides of the issue – Mr. Gallagher as well as Mr. Tall Horse."

I was stretching the truth a bit, but I didn't want to tip my hand prematurely.

I needed to keep my sense of unbiased journalistic diligence clearly in view.

She said nothing, but I could feel a chill coming through the telephone line. I was put on hold for several minutes, and I became increasingly annoyed and anxious.

Without another word, I was transferred to Gallagher's office. The telephone was answered by a woman with a very pleasant voice.

"Mr. Harrison? Hello. I'm Julia Baxter. I'm handling Mr. Gallagher's appointments while he's in town. May I ask the nature of your business?"

I was encouraged to be a step closer to my goal.

"Thanks for taking my call, Ms. Baxter," I said warmly. "I'm the interim editor of *The Climax Gazette*," I said, making up my title as I went along. "I'm working on a story on the Donovan Corporation's planned development here and I have developed a few new leads that may have an impact on the negotiations. I need to speak with Mr. Gallagher as well as Mr. Tall Horse to make sure that I have the facts straight before going to press."

"May I ask what sort of information you need?"

She was polite and tactful, but I could tell that she was used to protecting her boss from unnecessary interruptions and distractions. Her job was to find out as much as she could so he could decide whether or not it was worth his time to speak with me. She was professional but persistent and I respected her for that.

I was pretty sure I had her hooked, but I still needed to reel her in. Now was the time for charm to get the job done. With as much persuasion as I could muster, I said, "I can assure you, Ms. Baxter, that Mr. Gallagher will not regret sharing just a few minutes of my time. I promise."

There was a pause while she considered my heartfelt plea. I imagined the wheels turning in her head. Then she said, her voice cordial but firm, "Surely, Mr. Harrison, you can give me some idea of the nature of this information you are seeking. I'm sure you can appreciate how busy Mr. Gallagher is at this moment. Any interruption to his schedule must be of the greatest importance."

"Very well, Ms. Baxter. Please inform Mr. Gallagher that I've uncovered information that could prove damaging to the Donovan Corporation if it's made public. Before I go that route, I owe Mr. Gallagher the opportunity to give me an explanation, if there is one."

There was another, longer pause before she said, "Can you hold just a moment, Mr. Harrison? I need to confer with Mr. Gallagher."

I felt a tingle of excitement race down my spine. Perhaps the newspaper business was in my blood after all!

In less than a minute she was back on the line. "Mr. Harrison? I'll put you through to Mr. Gallagher. Please hold a moment more."

The goal line was in sight, but now I needed to think about what I could tell Michael Gallagher that would convince him to see me. Ms. Baxter had been only the initial line of defense. Now that I was nearing the inner perimeter of corporate insularity, I had to be up to the challenge.

A few seconds later I heard a man's deep voice saying, "Mr. Harrison? This is Michael Gallagher. How may I help you?"

Gallagher sounded as if he were in his late fifties and spoke with a bit of a west Texas drawl. I knew immediately that he was all-business, so I got right to the point. "Thank you for taking my call, Mr. Gallagher. I'm aware of your busy schedule and I need just a few minutes of your time to go over some new information I've uncovered that could have a direct bearing on the negotiations you're having with the Sequoia Indian Tribal Council."

"I'm afraid, Mr. Harrison, that there's very little new information that can change the outcome of our negotiations. In fact, I'm absolutely confident that the federal authorities will come down in favor of our position very soon."

Somehow, I needed to convince Gallagher that my "new information" was of critical importance to him, but I didn't want to tell him more than I needed to.

"I can only assure you, Mr. Gallagher, that you will personally want to review the information I have and respond to it so that there will be no misunderstanding on the facts. I intend to make the same offer to Mr. Tall Horse."

I hoped I would win Gallagher over with my offer of fair play as well as his own curiosity about this "new information" I'd uncovered. Moreover, he wasn't likely to give Tall Horse an edge that might tip the scales in his favor. My strategy must have worked. After several seconds, he said, "May I ask the source of you information?"

I figured he was trying to determine if I was bluffing. *Probably a solid poker player*, I thought.

"I can only say it is from a reliable source – someone who's provided accurate information to us in the past," I replied. This was a slight exaggeration, I knew, but it was all I had. I crossed my fingers and waited.

After another long pause he said, "Can you be here this afternoon at 5:30? I can give you fifteen minutes – no more. I hope that will satisfy you."

I told him that it would be entirely satisfactory. Without another word he disconnected. I replaced the receiver and considered my next move. I needed to find some way to contact "Pete" to find out just what he knew about the conspiracy within the Donovan Corporation.

My thoughts were interrupted by Melanie, who bustled into the room in a buoyant mood.

"I've got some very good news, Clint," she said breathlessly.

"Let me guess" I said, trying to match her happy spirit. "The doctor says your father is making a speedy recovery!"

A shadow fell over her face and I knew I'd stumbled down the wrong path.

"No, I'm afraid there's still no change in his condition, but the doctor assures me that there's still every reason to hope he'll be back with us soon. His vital signs are good and there have been no new complications."

I sighed and said, "Well, that's a relief! What's your other news?"

"Well, I had a long chat with Jim Pemberton – you know, at the bank – and I explained to him how things have changed since you and Sam Dooley have agreed to work with me until Daddy's able to return. He's agreed to extend our line of credit for another thirty days!" Her eyes sparkled like blue diamonds, and she was bubbling over with enthusiasm. I couldn't help but be as excited as she was. To my surprise, she rushed over and planted a kiss on my cheek.

"That's twice in one week you've been a lifesaver, Clint, and I won't ever forget it!"

Before I could respond, she turned on her heels and was gone. Her heartfelt display of gratitude warmed me inside. Then I reluctantly forced myself back into the real world. I needed to develop a strategy for dealing with Michael Gallagher and time was running out.

I gave the situation some serious thought while I enjoyed a late lunch at the Main Street Café. Neither Mary Alice nor Mabel were working the lunch shift. On the way out, I stopped at the register where a small, wiry man was casually perusing a six-month-old copy of *Sports Illustrated*, and asked him for directions to the Donovan Corporation offices. He told me what I needed to know and returned his attention to the magazine. I stuffed some of my notes and notepad into an old briefcase I'd picked up at *The Gazette* office and headed Amos' station wagon in the direction I'd been given. It was just after five o'clock and I would be right on time. I couldn't overcome a bit of apprehension, and I wondered what kind of reception I'd get from Mr. Michael Gallagher.

CHAPTER TWENTY

The offices of the Donovan Corporation were perched on a high bluff providing a panoramic view of the valley below. The corporation was housed in a sprawling complex of modern buildings favoring a Southwestern motif with clean, angular lines, squat adobe walls, and red tile roofs. The property was protected by a ten-foot chain link fence that reminded me of the security provided to a prison or a military post. *Security must be a top priority for the Donovan Corporation*, I thought, as I approached the main gate. An alert, uniformed security guard stationed inside a small guardhouse checked my name against a roster of appointments, then checked my personal identification. The guard spoke into a microphone attached to his lapel, received the answer he needed through an earpiece, then thanked me for my patience and pushed a button on small remote-control device attached to his belt and watched as the electronic gate swung open.

"Straight ahead to the first parking lot on the left, Mr. Harrison. It's marked for 'visitor parking'. Enter through the main entrance and stop at the security desk in the front lobby. You'll be directed from there. Have a very nice day."

I thanked him and drove another quarter mile until I came to the visitor parking lot. Upon entering the main building, I found a large foyer where sunlight cascaded through large skylights arranged at irregular angles and heights. The stucco walls were covered by large murals with Southwestern themes, including stagecoaches, pony express riders, American Indians, cowboys, and the vast expanses of desert and mountains. I admired the spectacular display of art.

Another uniformed security officer sat behind a large elevated desk at the center of the room. A number of television screens allowed him to monitor key locations throughout the interior and exterior of the building. A modern communications console periodically spat out garbled voices and served as the command-and-control center for the security operation. It was an impressive display of modern technology. Could there be a more sinister reason for making security such a high priority?

The security officer checked my identification a second time, lifted a telephone receiver, and announced my arrival. He hung up and said pleasantly, "Ms. Henderson will be with you shortly."

I thanked him and seated myself in one of the leather chairs against the wall. The lobby was empty except for me and the guard, and I realized that it was after normal business hours. The only sound was the gentle whooshing of the air-conditioning system and an occasional crackling from the communications console. I glanced at a large antique clock on the wall when it struck half-past five, just as a very attractive middle-aged woman emerged from a nearby doorway and greeted me warmly. She had dark brown shoulder- length hair and wore a trim, two-piece gray suit.

"Mr. Harrison, I'm Tracy Henderson. Mr. Gallagher will see you now. Please follow me."

Without waiting, she turned and strode down the hallway, her heels clicking sharply on the tile floor, and I followed close behind.

We walked down a long hallway, passing a maze of offices, some of which were occupied, despite the time of day. She ushered me into a large, elegantly furnished conference room, then left, saying that Mr. Gallagher would be right in. The room was dominated by a long, massive oak table, ringed by a score of heavy leather armchairs. One wall was covered by ceiling to floor bookshelves filled with heavy, bound volumes. I was attracted to a large picture window that adorned the outer wall and offered a breathtaking view of the distant mountains. It was easy to understand why local people call this part of the world "God's Country". *One could get used to living in a place like this*, I thought.

"Quite a view, isn't it?"

The booming voice startled me from my reverie. I turned to see a tall, well-built man striding toward me, exuding confidence and cordiality, with his right hand extended in greeting. He gripped my hand firmly with a hand that bore signs of long years of hard work and manual labor. This was no corporate dilettante. Strength, power and self-confidence exuded from his very pores.

"I'm Mike Gallagher and I presume you're Mr. Harrison." Without waiting for an answer, he said, "Please have a seat," gesturing to one of the armchairs.

His voice and demeanor were business-like but friendly. He wasn't at all what I had expected. Although impeccably attired in a grey suit, white shirt and dark tie, he impressed me as someone who had probably come up through the ranks of the organization. His skin tone was a healthy tan, which I suspected didn't come from tanning lamps or lotion, but from spending a great deal of time outdoors. His grey hair was cut short with almost military precision, as was a neatly trimmed mustache. He wore no glasses, and his eyes were a deep cobalt blue. When he spoke, he looked directly into my eyes as if he were trying to read my thoughts. There was something magnetic about his personality, and I suspected he knew how to use it to his full advantage. I could tell he was used to being in charge.

Gallagher didn't waste any time and asked me to explain this "new information" that was so important that he's interrupted his already-crowded agenda to meet with me. "I must admit that you've piqued my curiosity, but I must ask you to be quick about it. I have only a few minutes to spare before I really must leave."

"Before I get into the information I have to share with you, Mr. Gallagher," I said, "can you first give me a rundown on the status of your negotiations with state and federal authorities regarding your proposal to mine the lands claimed by the Sequoia Indians?"

He showed just a hint of irritation, looked at his watch, and said, "Mr. Harrison, I believe our position on the negotiations for the development we've planned is on the record, and time does not permit me to go over it with you now."

I didn't want to lose him, and I needed to convince him of my neutrality. "I understand your position, but I'm starting from scratch, and I want to examine the negotiations from a fresh perspective." He signed, spread his large hands palms down on the table, shrugged his shoulders, and said, "We still maintain that we have a legal and legitimate claim to the land in question, but the tribal leaders still maintain their steadfast opposition."

"Can you run it down for me?"

"It's very simple," he said. "We have a legal claim to an area of 2,400 acres in the Blackhawk Mountains north of here. We wish to mine this land for coal. The specific area we are interested in is known as the Blackwater Canyon region. Blackwater Canyon was formed a million or so years ago by a river that has long since run dry. Our geologists have assured us that this particular area holds enough coal to keep every steel mill in this country operating for another 25 years. It's a huge natural resource simply waiting to be recovered."

"I understand the Indians have other ideas," I said.

"Yes, well, unfortunately for us, they have made a counterclaim to the federal government in which they insist that they have tribal rights to this land by virtue of an ancient treaty which no one except the Indians seems to know much about. They are relying on their own tribal records, which we claim have no legal standing and which cannot be independently validated. The tribal leaders nevertheless insist their records are as authentic as any maintained by the federal government."

"What do you see as the ultimate outcome?"

He looked me directly in the eyes and said, "We're extremely confident that we'll eventually prevail in this matter. We've invested heavily in acquiring the rights to this land, plus geologists' fees and legal expenses, and there's no good reason why our claim should be denied. Beyond that, we've made a generous offer to the tribal leaders, but they don't seem to be interested."

"May I inquire into the nature of the offer?" I asked.

"I'm sorry, Mr. Harrison, but I'm not at liberty to discuss this subject any further since we are still in negotiations."

I was about to respond when he said, "I will say, though, that I cannot understand the tribal leaders' unwillingness to even consider our offer. The fact is, the Indians could really use the financial assistance we have offered. The Sequoia tribe, as you may know, aren't a wealthy people."

He shook his head and said sadly, "This really could be a win-win situation, but they simply don't seem to see it that way."

I wondered why the tribal leaders would turn down an offer that would serve their own financial interests. If I could arrange a meeting with Mr. B. J. Tall Horse, perhaps he would be willing to share their reasons with me.

"You still haven't allowed me to state our position, which is what I thought you came here looking for, and our time is nearly up."

He was still pleasant, but his impatience was showing. I needed to get to the point before I lost him.

"Mr. Gallagher, I have in my possession a journal that Mr. Ben Griffin, the editor of the Gazette, had been keeping before the automobile accident in which he was nearly killed. Mr. Griffin's journal contains several entries in which a confidential informant, here at Donovan, alleges that members of the Donovan Corporation have engaged in what amounts to a criminal conspiracy to gain state and federal approval of its planned development."

Gallagher started to speak, but I pushed on, not wanting to lose my momentum.

"The journal also describes efforts by the Donovan Corporation to sabotage the *Climax Gazette* in retaliation for its opposition to the Donovan Corporation's plan."

The expression on Gallagher's face grew grimmer, and I wondered how he'd react to what I was telling him. He might just deny everything I'd said, since there was no real proof of any of the allegations. If that was his reaction, I didn't know what my next move would be. I felt a tight knot growing in the pit of my stomach while I waited for his response.

The self-confidence had drained from Gallagher's face and was replaced by signs of deep concern. "Frankly, Mr. Harrison, what you've just told me is so bizarre that I'm speechless. My first inclination is to call the whole thing a preposterous hoax, which is exactly what it sounds like."

The knot in my stomach grew larger and I started to respond, but he wasn't finished.

"You see, Mr. Harrison, I don't take accusations like this lightly, and I intend to get to the bottom of this whole thing. Before I can do that, though, I need as many of the details as you can give me."

It took a few seconds for the full impact of his words to register. I'd expected a blanket denial, along with counter-assertions aimed at either myself or Ben Griffin attempting to undermine the Donovan Corporation's proposal. Instead, it sounded like he was taking the offense by initiating his own investigation. Although this could merely be a clever ploy to divert suspicion and find out just how much I knew, I didn't think that was his motivation. Instead, I was convinced that, if there was any truth to the allegations, he was determined to uncover it.

I didn't know the man, but I had to admire the forthright way in which he handled the situation. I suspected that it was indicative of the way he met just about any challenge he faced. I was anxious to know what his next move would be. He didn't keep me guessing long.

CHAPTER TWENTY-ONE

P lease excuse me for a moment, Mr. Harrison." Without waiting for my reply, he picked up a telephone from a console, punched two buttons, then said, "Julia, please call Harold Ferguson and advise him that I will be late for the reception. Something has come up that I must attend to immediately. Also, get in touch with Bob Sharp and tell him I need to see him now. He should still be in his office."

He placed the telephone on the cradle and turned back to me. Fierce determination flashed in his eyes.

"Mr. Harrison, while I'm inclined to regard what you've told me as nothing more than malicious gossip, I'm not one to take anything for granted. I'd like you to repeat your story to Bob Sharp, our director of security here in Climax. He's totally reliable and I'm going to ask him to initiate an immediate investigation into these allegations. Believe me, if there's any truth at all in what you've just told me, I want to know about it."

"I'll be more than happy to assist in any way I can," I said with all sincerity. If he was serious about conducting an investigation, I could see no reason not to cooperate with him. While we waited, he filled me in on Bob Sharp.

"He's a capable and skilled investigator. We were fortunate to hire him when he retired after more than twenty years with the San Diego Police Department, where he spent several years as the head of their Criminal Investigation Division. I have total confidence in his ability." At that moment, there was a knock on the door, then a large African- American man entered the room. Robert Sharp stood an inch or two over six feet and carried about two hundred and fifty pounds on his broad frame. He was an imposing man with short, jet-black hair, neatly-trimmed, with just a shade of gray showing around his temples. A pencil-thin mustache hovered above his upper lip. I was willing to bet he'd played college football and I mentally winced as I imagined the bone-crunching tackles he must have made in his younger days.

Michael Gallagher introduced us, and I found myself looking into piercing, coal-black eyes set into a large oval face that stared impassively back at me. He extended his large hand to me, and it nearly engulfed my own.

"Mr. Harrison, good to meet you, sir!"

His deep, baritone voice resonated with authority, and he carried himself with military-like bearing. He impressed me as the kind of man you'd want on your team, regardless of what sport you're playing. As a cop, I could visualize him chasing unfortunate hoodlums down a darkened alley, while they pleaded for mercy. The very thought of this brute of a man thundering after me would have been enough to make me surrender instantly.

Michael Gallagher wasted no time in telling Sharp who I was and the gist of what I'd told him.

"As far as I'm concerned, these allegations are preposterous," Gallagher said emotionally, "but we nevertheless need to conduct an immediate internal investigation to determine their veracity, or lack thereof. After Mr. Harrison fills you in on the details, I'd like you to let me know how you plan to proceed."

Sharp nodded silently, withdrew a small notebook and pen from his inside coat pocket, and began taking notes while I repeated my story. Like any good investigator, he let me tell the story completely, without interruption, and wrote quickly. When I finished, Sharp had several questions.

"Mr. Harrison, have you talked to Mr. Griffin regarding this journal?"

I explained to him that Ben Griffin had been in a traffic accident and was still in a coma. His eyes narrowed at the news, but he said nothing.

"So, then, you have no way of knowing whether this information is authentic?"

His tone was slightly accusatory and made me uncomfortable, but I knew he was just doing his job. I'd walked in his shoes, and I knew the drill.

"No. Other than the fact that I found it in his personal papers, and I've every reason to believe that he took the information at face value."

"But, as far as you know," Sharp continued like a pit bull, "Mr. Griffin made no effort to determine the true identity of this informant?"

I could see where he was heading, but just because there was no real evidence to back up the allegations in Ben Griffin's journal didn't mean they weren't true.

"Not as far as I know. In fact, that's the reason for my interview with Mr. Gallagher. I was hoping to obtain information that would help me determine the authenticity of these allegations."

Sharp continued to eye me as he might inspect a cancer cell with a microscope.

His critical attitude did nothing to ease my discomfort. I was being grilled by a professional and I didn't like it, but I had to play along.

"Mr. Harrison, to your knowledge, have any of these allegations been reported to the El Dorado Sheriff's Department?"

I hadn't anticipated this question. I didn't want to misrepresent the facts, but I couldn't divulge my conversation with Sheriff Jenkins either.

"As far as I know, Mr. Griffin didn't report any of these incidents to the Sheriff's Department," I said, hoping that my version of the truth would satisfy him. But apparently it didn't.

"Is there some reason why you've made no effort to contact the sheriff yourself?"

His persistence was admirable, but it was pushing me further and further down a very slippery slope from which I might not recover. Once again, I had to be very careful about how I answered his question.

I shrugged my shoulders and said, "I wanted to get Mr. Gallagher's side of the story first. It seemed the only fair thing to do. If criminal offenses have been committed, I'm sure the sheriff will take whatever action is required to put the responsible parties behind bars."

I figured this was a good way to show Gallagher that I was not on a vendetta, and it appeared to work. Out of the corner of my eye I caught Michael Gallagher nodding in agreement, and the tension in my stomach eased up a bit. Then Sharp asked, "Did you bring the journal with you?"

I had expected this question and was prepared for it. "I'm not willing to turn over the actual journal for obvious reasons," I said, with a show of confidence, "but I did make a copy of the pertinent pages, which should satisfy you about its authenticity."

Sharps' eyebrows arched with interest as I reached into my briefcase, took out a manila envelope, and handed it to him. I didn't want them to begin asking questions about the identity of our confidential informant, so I had been careful not to include any pages that referenced "Pete". Sharp opened the envelope, withdrew a dozen photocopied pages, and studied them for several minutes. When he finished reading each page, he handed it to Gallagher, who read silently, his expression intent.

After he'd finished reading, Sharp collected them from Gallagher and returned them to the manila envelope. Gallagher said nothing and appeared to be deferring any decision to Sharp. Both Gallagher and I waited expectantly for Sharp to announce the next move.

Sharp looked first at Gallagher, then at me and said, "Can I speak off the record for a moment, Mr. Harrison?"

I was wary of agreeing to this, but I knew he wouldn't tell me anything useful unless I went along with him, and I was anxious to hear what he had so say. "Sure, off the record then."

He looked again at Gallagher, as if waiting for a silent signal. If there was one, I missed it. Sharp's eyes narrowed and he looked directly into mine, and I could feel his penetrating stare. "Let's just say that we know that there are certain factions in our midst who oppose our efforts to develop the disputed land in the Blackhawk Mountains. Let's also say that we are aware of certain efforts by members of these factions to disrupt and undermine our negotiations."

He paused for a moment to organize his thoughts, then went on. "If, hypothetically speaking, that were true, the accusations you've made would seem to dovetail with information we've uncovered on our own."

I was startled at his statement. Was he admitting that there was some kind of internal conspiracy working within the Donovan Corporation?

I sorted through the possibilities in my mind, then said, "Do you actually believe the persons responsible are members of your own organization?"

Sharp's face was expressionless, but the look in his eyes answered my question.

"Let's just say that we believe that the persons responsible – whether they are internal or external – are in it for themselves."

This was probably as far as he would go on that subject, but it was enough.

"What possible motive could they have?"

This time it was Gallagher who responded. "The kind of negotiations in which we are engaged, Mr. Harrison, are worth billions of dollars to the corporation, to say nothing of the millions of dollars that will be realized by the local economy. We don't know why the Sequoia Indians have mounted such fierce opposition to our proposal, but when that kind of money is at stake, greed can be a very powerful motive."

I was beginning to get the picture. This dispute was a lot larger than I'd imagined and a lot more complex as well. Then I thought of a more practical concern.

"But how can I be assured that any investigation you conduct won't be to simply protect the interests of the Donovan Corporation?"

Michael Gallagher responded, "Because, Mr. Harrison, that isn't the way this company does business, and it is certainly not the way I do business. I will give you my personal guarantee that, if any of these allegations prove to be even half true, the person or persons responsible will be discharged and any evidence our investigation uncovers will be turned over to the Sheriff's Department."

He'd spoken with conviction, and I had the impression that no better guarantee of his good faith was needed.

"Will you contact me as soon as you learn anything definitive?" I asked.

Bob Sharp nodded and said, "You will be kept informed of any significant development in the case."

He looked at Michael Gallagher, who nodded his head in agreement. This was about as much as I could expect under the circumstances. I thanked both men and left them to their deliberations. I returned to the car and drove back to town, thinking that my next move would be to arrange a visit to the Sequoia Indian Reservation, where I hoped to have a conversation with Mr. B. J. Tall Horse.

It was nearly seven o'clock by the time I returned to the inn, and I felt both exhilarated and exuberant. My meeting with the sheriff, plus the conversation I'd had with Michael Gallagher and Bob Sharp, had invigorated me like nothing else had in quite a while. Although the death of my loving wife and child was still very much in my mind, my experiences in Climax had awakened an excitement that had been dormant for some time. I was ready for a good dinner and a couple of cold beers to help me celebrate what I considered to be a rewarding day with the promise of more surprises to come.

CHAPTER TWENTY-TWO

I returned to the inn, took a long, hot shower, and changed clothes. I called the front desk and asked Amos Greer if there was any decent nightlife in Climax.

He chuckled and suggested that I try Sam's Place. It didn't sound terribly exotic, but I'd learned by now to trust Amos' judgment, so I accepted his recommendation and asked him for directions.

Sam's Place was located on a quiet residential street, just a few blocks from downtown. Its unimpressive exterior made me wonder if this was the best Climax had to offer the discerning diner. But my spirits were high, and my sense of adventure was at its peak. I was ready for just about anything.

The incomplete phrase, "Sam's Pla-e," winked at me in pink and blue neon lights from a front window and competed for space with a flashing *Miller Light* sign. The other window featured a dingy *Coors Beer* logo, along with a badly-printed, hand-printed sign announcing that "Happy Hour" was from 5:00 PM until 7:00 PM on Tuesdays and Thursdays. Regrettably, I would miss that festive event, but I decided not to let my disappointment spoil the evening. Perhaps I would just have to drown my sorrows, one cold beer at a time. A sign above the door offered "Hot Food, Sandwiches, Lunch, Dinner".

I hoped the menu would be somewhat more extensive, but it was after all, a neighborhood tavern, so what could I expect? I was reassured by the thought that Amos Greer hadn't given me bad advice yet.

The place was dimly lit inside, and it took my eyes a while to adjust as I guided myself to a seat at the bar. A jukebox in the corner crooned an old ballad by Hank Williams, who mournfully lamented his empty arms and broken heart. A sense of melancholy swept over me and my thoughts drifted back to happier days. I fought back memories of my son and lovely wife, and I wanted a beer in the worst way.

Several couples were seated in a dining area, and several more were sitting at the bar, which extended the full length of the room. At one end of the bar, a middle-aged man and woman were engaged in an animated conversation with the bartender, a tall, balding man who sported a large handlebar mustache, a prominent nose and large, dark eyes nearly hidden beneath a set of menacing jet-black eyebrows. I managed to catch his eye, and he approached me warily, the way a mouse eyes a hunk of cheese in a trap. He grunted what may have been a greeting, and I ordered a Coors Light, nodding to the draft beer handle in front of him. Without a word, he filled a frosted mug with the golden brew and placed it before me. I shoved a twenty toward him and he snapped it up, pushed a couple of keys on the register, and spread my change in front of me.

His indifferent attitude suggested to me that he was not a likely candidate to run the local welcome wagon. His duty done, Mr. Friendly retreated to the other end of the bar and resumed his conversation with the couple as they did their hardest to solve the problems of the world.

The beer was just what the doctor ordered so, like any good patient, I signaled the bartender to bring me another. When he did, I asked him for a menu. The master of solemnity handed me a worn, grease-stained sheet of paper that looked like it had been around since Territorial Days. It listed several entrees, but some of them had been crossed out or were so smudged that they were barely legible.

My hunger pangs were bouncing around in my stomach, so I settled for a steak sandwich, fries and small salad with ranch dressing. I managed to get the bartender's attention one more time and gave him my order. He nodded, said nothing, and disappeared into the kitchen. The man and woman at the other end of the bar eventually departed and were replaced by three young men who looked like they might have some serious drinking to do.

The good humor man returned and busied himself by wiping down the gleaming bar and washing some glasses in a small dishwasher that made a loud, whirring sound as it worked. After he finished his cleaning chores, he apparently had nothing better to do, so he lumbered slowly in my direction, and put two meaty hands on the bar in front of me.

"Yer that Harrison guy, ain't ya?" He squinted his eyes into narrow slits when he looked at me. His coarse voice sounded like gravel crushed in a grinder.

"I'm Clint Harrison," I admitted. "How'd you know?" But I already knew the answer – news travels fast in a small town.

"Never seen ya here fore now," he answered simply. "Don't get many strangers in here."

"I'm staying at the Summit Inn. Amos Greer recommended this place," I explained.

He nodded and said simply, "Good man." Then he allowed, "Heard 'bout what ya did fer Ben Griffin. Seems like yer some kinda hero."

What a transformation, I thought. The Silent One has morphed into Mr.

Conversation. Before I could answer, there was a loud buzzing sound from the kitchen.

"Yer order's up," he announced, and went to retrieve it.

It may not have been the best steak sandwich I'd ever eaten, but I couldn't remember one as tasty. I tried vainly not to embarrass myself at the speed with which I wolfed it down. The meat was tender and juicy and literally melted in my mouth. And the fries were golden brown, plentiful, and just salty enough to make me wish for more when they were gone. For several minutes, I was in a world all my own as my taste buds celebrated with enthusiastic appreciation. I finished my second beer and this time the bartender didn't need to be asked to bring me another.

He watched with satisfaction as I finished off the few remaining crumbs on my plate and then offered, "Best steak sandwich in town."

It was no exaggeration, and I told him so.

The bartender left to wait on another customer, and I reflected on the pleasures of a good meal that was a fitting end to the day's events. I surveyed the room and noticed someone huddling over the jukebox and methodically feeding it quarters. Now it was Willie Nelson's turn to sing soulfully about *Blue Eyes Crying in the Rain*.

Despite my earlier feeling of satisfaction about the day's accomplishments, the sad refrain once again brought back painful memories of happier days. I struggled to push back a shroud of emptiness that wrapped itself around me like a cold, wet, blanket, and I fought vainly to ignore the throbbing ache in my heart.

"Nothing like a sad song to cheer a man up, I always say."

The woman's voice startled me. She was sitting next to me and I hadn't even been aware of her. I turned to see Mary Alice, the waitress from the Main Street Café. She wore a wide smile that glowed Ike a bright candle in the darkness.

She was dressed simply in a faded red blouse and jeans. Her hair was drawn up in a ponytail held in place with a red carnation. Her lipstick matched the flower in her hair and her blouse and gave her a clean, wholesome look. A touch of eyeliner highlighted her sparkling blue eyes. She smelled of fresh flowers and pine trees, and the effect was intoxicating. Her warm smile and friendly face washed away the loneliness that had engulfed me just a few minutes earlier.

I was at a loss for words, but managed to say, "Nice to see you again."

She beamed brightly. "Nice to see you too, Mr. Harrison. I see you've discovered my favorite hangout."

This piece of news boosted my original assessment of Sam's Place. "It came highly recommended," I said with a grin.

Then my friend, the genial bartender, approached, and I said, "May I have the pleasure of buying you a drink?" She thanked me and ordered a Bloody Mary. I still had some beer left in my glass and decided to nurse it for a while. Now that I had company, I wanted to maintain some level of dignity.

"So, Mr. Harrison, do you plan on staying in town long?" "Please call me Clint," I said.

"Okay, Clint, then," she said, smiling again. "And you know my name already."

"I do indeed, Mary Alice."

The bartender brought her drink, and she winked at him and said, "Thanks, Harry. You make the best Bloody Mary!"

Something that could have been a smile appeared on Harry's face. Now that I knew his name, I was beginning to feel right at home.

"I gather you come here often," I said, wondering if Deputy Potter might be lurking nearby.

"No, not really. The truth is, I don't get out much at all, but when I do, this is one of my favorite places. I live not too far from here, so I can walk and get a little fresh air."

I raised my nearly empty glass to her in a mock salute and said, "Here's to Manhattan Beach."

She joined me in the toast and her face brightened at the mention of her former hometown.

I was curious about how she'd made the transition from Manhattan Beach to Climax. "So, how'd you end up way out here?"

She sighed, sipped her Bloody Mary, and said, "It's a long story."

"I'm in no hurry," I replied. The night was young, and I was enjoying her company.

She gazed wistfully into her own reflection in the mirror behind the bar, as if looking into her own past. "My dad died when I was just a kid – nine or ten, I think."

We had both grown up in the same area and my own father had died when I was just about the same age. I was intrigued to learn that we had a few things in common.

"Dad had no life insurance, and Mom was out of work, so we had to go live with my Aunt Roberta, who was an alcoholic and a very mean woman."

Her voice dropped an octave, and there was sadness in it as she told her story. "I tried, but I couldn't deal with my Aunt Roberta, who was my dad's sister. She had no kids and didn't want any, and she made sure to let me and my mom know that I wasn't welcome under her roof."

Family members can sometimes be very mean to one another, I thought. Thankfully, I've never had that experience, but I could understand how devastating such a situation could be for a young girl, and to her mother.

"That must've been tough on you," I offered.

She nodded her head. "It was. My mom and I talked it over and we decided to pack me off to live with my Grandpa Bob and Grandma Betty, here in Climax. It was hard to leave Mom, but it turned out to be a good thing for me. I made a lot of new friends and really liked all my new teachers, except for one – I hated science, and Mr. Baxter hated me just as much."

When she mentioned her former tormenter, she laughed and said, "He was no Mr. Rogers." I got the picture and laughed with her. She was easy to talk to, and the conversation kept my mind off of my own past troubles.

She finished her Bloody Mary, and I offered to buy her another. "Thanks, but two's my limit."

Harry acted on cue and set the drink down in front of her while I continued to nurse my beer.

"Did you and your mom ever get back together?"

She frowned and shook her head. "No, she got the cancer not long after I moved – she was a heavy smoker. I never got to see her before she died. But she went quick and didn't suffer much, and for that I'm thankful."

She got quiet then, and I couldn't think of anything else to say, so we just sat and listened to the music on the jukebox. Marty Robbins was singing about *El Paso.*

Finally, she broke the silence. "So, what brings you to our little slice of paradise? Are you just passing through or will we have the pleasure of your company for a while?"

I laughed and said, "It's hard to say. I'll be working with Sam Dooley down at the *Gazette* while Melanie's dad is in the hospital." "That's a very nice thing for you to do. I like both Ben and Melanie a lot, and I hope he pulls through this okay."

"I hope so too. Melanie's quite a gal, but she needs all the help she can get right now."

"It's nice to know we'll have you around for a while longer," she said and grinned.

Then she hopped off the bar stool and walked to the jukebox, studied the selections for a few seconds, placed several coins in the slot, and punched a few buttons. When she returned to her stool, Patsy Cline began to sing *Crazy.* Mary Alice took another sip of her drink, tugged on my arm, and said, "C'mon, Mr. Harrison, let's dance." Her request – or was it a command – caught me off guard, but I didn't know how to turn her down.

CHAPTER TWENTY-THREE

I hadn't been on a dance floor in a very long time, and I was no Gene Kelly, but she ignored my protests and maneuvered me to a spot near the juke box. I awkwardly took her in my arms and hoped I wouldn't self-destruct in an embarrassing display of clumsiness. She laughed gaily and implored me to relax, but my nervousness – and perhaps a sense of guilt – must have been obvious. She drew me to her and nestled her head on my shoulder as we moved our feet in unison to the slow, throbbing tempo of the melody. My initial awkwardness and apprehension began to fade as we eased into a comfortable rhythm, our bodies gliding about gracefully in time with the tempo of the ballad. It felt good to hold her in my arms, but I couldn't entirely escape the feeling that I was being unfaithful to my dearest Janet, who still lived in my memory. I tried to think of something to say, but couldn't, so I simply surrendered myself to the moment.

"You're a very good dancer," she whispered in my ear.

I was relieved that she had broken the silence. "It's been a long time," I said lamely. "I'm sure it shows."

She laughed softly and said, "Not at all, Clint. You're doing very well. Maybe you just need more practice."

I thought to myself, *If practice makes perfect, I'd be a willing student with her as a partner.*

She hummed the melody softly and I was captivated by the scent of her hair and the tenderness of her embrace. For the briefest moment, the pain and suffering of the recent past began to ebb, just as the last rays of the setting sun slipped into the western horizon. She pulled herself even closer to me and we danced as if we were one, moving with a single motion, our hearts beating in unison and our thoughts lost in the fantasy of our dreams. It was as if the world didn't exist beyond this time and place.

Patsy finished her soulful song, and I made a move to head back to the bar, but Mary Alice held me in place and said, "Not so fast."

She wrapped my arms around her again just in time to hear George Jones sing about *The Green, Green Grass of Home.*

This time I didn't resist, and we were once again gliding around the dance floor as if it been put there just for us.

"You picked some great songs," I said, hoping to get the conversation going again.

"You like country and western?" She sounded surprised.

"Not the modern stuff," I replied. "In fact, I don't really consider much of anything done in the last two decades *real country.* It's too loud, it makes no sense and sometimes the lyrics don't even rhyme."

She laughed and said, "Be careful, Clint, you're showing your age."

"Could be," I said, "but I like traditional values and country songs that have a message."

"A message?" life."

"Yeah, you know, love, betrayal, heartbreak – all the important things in

She nodded knowingly and smiled. She knew exactly what I meant. We spoke very little but continued to dance for as long as the music played. When the last tune ended, we returned to the bar, and I offered to buy her "one more for the road."

"I can't, really, but thanks anyway. I've got an early shift tomorrow. I need to get going."

I wasn't ready for the evening to end, so I said, "Let me walk you home."

She hesitated, then said, "That's not necessary. It's only a few blocks." "I insist," I said. "I could use the fresh air."

She put on a light jacket while I threw a few bills on the counter and waved at Harry.

The evening air was cool but invigorating. A full moon hovered over the mountains and cast its unique glow on the landscape below. It had turned out to be a perfect evening, and I felt alive and energized. She took my arm and put it around her shoulders, as if it was the most natural thing in the world.

"It's a lovely night for a walk," she said as we turned a corner and strolled down a quiet, tree-lined street. We walked together and she told me more about herself. She'd married her high school sweetheart, who'd signed up for a hitch in the Army just in time to get a free trip to Iraq. He was badly wounded during his tour and was shipped back to the States, but his recuperation led him to a terrible addiction to pain killers. After being in and out of hospitals and rehab clinics for nearly three years, he died of an overdose just days before their fifth wedding anniversary. It was a terribly sad story, but she told it calmly and dignity, and had managed to put the grief behind her. Then I realized we had something else in common.

"What about you, Clint? You haven't told me much about yourself."

I wasn't ready to share my heartache with her, but I didn't want to be evasive with her either.

"I lost my wife and child a while back. It's still hard to talk about it."

She reached out and gripped my arm tenderly to show her empathy. "I'm so sorry, Clint. We don't need to talk about that anymore."

But I wanted to talk about it. I hadn't been able to talk to anyone about that horrible experience, and I didn't want to keep it bottled up inside me any longer. But this was probably not the best time. No need to spoil a perfectly good evening. I felt very comfortable with her, and perhaps there would be another time and another place to share my grief with her.

We arrived at her place, and I struggled to find a polite way to end our conversation, but she beat me to it.

"I've had a lovely evening, Clint." She pulled my head down to hers and kissed me tenderly on my cheek.

I was caught off guard and didn't know what to say. Then she ran up the stairs, slipped in her front door, and I was left alone with my thoughts. I stood there for a while, trying to sort out my emotions. The guilt was still there, nagging at me, but I couldn't deny a desire to see Mary Alice again. I wanted to know her better, and for her to know me better. She'd kindled a deep-seated urge that yearned to be satisfied. I felt like we were kindred spirits who had much more to share.

But I had other responsibilities that couldn't be ignored. My obligation to assist Melanie at the newspaper, as well as the mission I'd accepted from Sheriff Jenkins, had to come first. I walked back to where I had parked Amos Greer's loaner and felt a spring in my step that hadn't been there before. All in all, it had been a very satisfying day, and I had an idea that tomorrow would offer even more challenges. Without even realizing it, I found myself whistling a merry tune and felt more alive at that moment than I had in a very long time.

CHAPTER TWENTY-FOUR

I drove back to the Summit thinking about the events of the day and the good time I'd had with Mary Alice. I was also anxious to see if I could set up a meeting with Mr. B. J. Tall Horse. I needed to know if he would share with me the Indians' side of the story in their dispute with the Donovan Corporation. I made a mental note to check with Amos or Martha Greer in the morning to find out if they'd heard anything yet from Estelle or William. Maybe there was something more I could do in that regard as well.

By the time I'd undressed and got into bed, I was ready for a good night's sleep, and I hoped that the demons who tormented me in my dreams would give me peace for just one night.

I awoke early, physically and mentally rejuvenated and ready to meet the challenges of the day. My first thought was to drive into town and have breakfast at the Main Street Café, just to see Mary Alice, but I decided against it. As much as I wanted to see her again, I didn't want to seem too eager, nor did I want to run the risk of another confrontation with Deputy Potter.

Instead, I went down to the dining room where I found Martha Greer busily taking orders. The place was crowded, and Estelle was nowhere in sight. When Martha approached me with a pot of steaming coffee, I asked her if she or Amos had heard from either Estelle or William, but she shook her head and frowned gravely.

"No, and I'm just worried sick about both of them. It just isn't like them to miss work and not contact us."

"I mentioned it to Sheriff Jenkins yesterday," I said, "but he says he doesn't have much of a relationship with anyone at the reservation. Seems like they stay pretty much to themselves."

"I'm afraid so, Clint, but I still don't like it – and Amos is just as worried as I am."

Martha took my order and headed into the kitchen, and I began to read a day-old *Denver Post* that someone had left on the table. I tried to concentrate on keeping up with the news of the rest of the world, but Martha's concern for the well-being of Estelle and William continued to bother me. I made up my mind that, if I did get a chance to speak with Mr. Tall Horse, I'd do my best to see what I could find out about the young Indian maiden and her cousin.

I was still mulling this over in my mind when Martha arrived with a large platter of steaming hot cakes and bacon and a refill of my coffee. I lost no time in attacking the food and it was, as usual, quite good. I didn't stop until the platter had been picked clean and I felt totally satisfied. I was enjoying my third cup of coffee when Amos Greer walked in and sat down across from me. He wore his usual pleasant smile, and he greeted me warmly.

"Yer lookin' better ever' day, Clint. Glad to see our little town is agreein' with you!" He chuckled and his round belly jiggled.

"I'm getting to feel real welcome here, Amos, that's a fact."

"So, how's the newspaper business, Clint? You get that rascal Sam Dooley tamed down yet?" He laughed again and this time I laughed with him.

"I'm not sure he's tamed down, but he's been working hard on those presses. I think it's a labor of love."

Amos chuckled and nodded his head knowingly.

"By the way, Amos, I understand there's still no word on either Estelle or William."

His smile became a frown; he shrugged his shoulders. "Nope – and I'm real worried 'bout them, Clint. Somethin's not right 'bout this whole thing. I can feel it in my bones."

I felt a chill go down my spine, like I was getting some kind of premonition about something very bad.

"I spoke with Sheriff Jenkins about talking to someone on the reservation, but he wasn't hopeful that it would be much use."

Amos sighed. "I think he's right about that. They just kinda take care of themselves out there – always have, and I guess always will."

"Well, I'm not going to let that stop me. I've got to call Mr. B. J. Tall Horse to see if he'll speak with me about their feud with the Donovan Corporation. Maybe I can learn something while I'm out there."

"Well, good luck with that," Amos said, his voice reflecting a lack of enthusiasm for my chances.

"Isn't there someone else who might be able to help me – someone who knows about what goes on at the reservation and who may be more willing to tell me something useful?"

Amos looked at me for several seconds and I could see that he was giving my question a lot of thought. He obviously knew a lot of people in town, and there was a slim chance that he could think of someone who might help me out.

Finally, he offered, "There is one person who you might want to talk to." "Who's that?"

"Lydia Raven. She works down at the Chamber of Commerce. She was raised on the reservation but left there years ago. She supposedly had some kind of run-in with Mr. Tall Horse. Bottom line, she'll know as much as anyone about what goes on out there, but she's absolutely a straight arrow – no pun intended – and will give you an honest answer."

I wrote her name on a paper napkin and thanked him again.

"Plus, she's purty as can be, and smart too." He winked at me and grinned slyly.

I asked him for directions to the Chamber office, and it sounded easy enough to find. I figured I'd stop there on my way to the *Gazette* and see what Miss Raven might be able to tell me. I added this to my "to do list" and realized it was going to be a very busy day, which was good. I needed something to occupy my mind and give new purpose to my life.

Amos got up from the table and was about to leave, then turned back to me and said, "By the way, Clint, a friend of yours was here checkin' on you last night."

I looked at him and there was an amused twinkle in his eyes. I was puzzled.

"A friend of mine? And who might that be?"

"Why, your old buddy, Deputy Potter," he said, chuckling heartily as his large belly shook with amusement.

What in the world would Potter want with me? I wondered. I asked Amos that very question.

"Didn't say. Just wanted to know if you were about. I told him I thought you went out for dinner, and he asked did I knew where. I said you don't make it a habit of informin' me of your comin' and goin,' and I'm not one to be nosey."

"What time was that?" I asked, trying to act casual.

"Oh, I'd say it had to have been somewhere 'round ten-thirty or so. I was workin' late in the office when I seen him drive up, popped on in and asked was you here. Course," he said with an impish grin on his face, "I knew where you said you were goin', but I didn't see as how it was any of his business."

I thought for a moment and realized that it must have been about the time I was dancing with Mary Alice, and the memories of our evening together made my face blush. I prayed that Amos couldn't read my thoughts.

"Did he say what he wanted?"

"Nope. He just asked if you were in, where'd I think you went, and when did I think you'd be comin' back."

The grin on his face grew wider. "Like I said, 'fraid I wasn't very helpful."

Amos turned once again to go, then looked back at me and said in a fatherly tone, "Just a word to the wise, Clint . . ."

At first, I thought he was playing with me, but then I realized he was dead serious.

"J. D. Potter ain't someone you wanna have interested in you, so be careful."

With that, he was gone, leaving me alone to wonder what the deputy had been up to. I had an idea that I'd probably find out before very long. A cold lump began to form in my stomach and I tried to put Deputy Potter out of my mind. I had better things to do than worry about the pudgy lawman.

CHAPTER TWENTY-FIVE

I stopped by the front office and asked Amos for directions to the Chamber of Commerce. It turned out to be just around the corner from the courthouse. On the way there, I stopped at the *Gazette* and told Melanie I had a few calls to make. She was furiously typing an article for the next edition, and she quickly waved me off. I went into the press room and found Sam Dooley busily attending to the presses. He was so deeply involved in his chores that I decided not to interrupt him.

I arrived at the Chamber office shortly after nine o'clock. I parked Amos' loaner car around the corner and entered to find an empty outer office. The counter was piled high with mail, books, file folders and colorful brochures, but no one was in sight. Then I heard someone moving around in a rear office. I spotted a small bell on the counter next to a sign reading: "Please ring for service", so I gave it a friendly tap.

A few seconds later, a very attractive woman emerged from the back. She had copper-colored skin, large round eyes and jet-black hair that trailed neatly over her shoulders. She had on a yellow blouse, open at the neck, and jeans that nicely accentuated the graceful lines of her hips. She wore a turquoise and silver necklace with matching earrings and bracelet.

She flashed a warm smile and said, "I'm sorry. I'm a little late getting the office open today. My assistant is home with a sick two-year-old. How may I help you?"

"Quite all right," I replied. "I'm looking for Lydia Raven." "That would be me," she acknowledged. A hint of curiosity played in her eyes. "What can I do for you?"

Her voice was as warm and friendly as her smile. Her personality seemed a good match for the job she held.

I introduced myself and said, "I'm helping Melanie Griffin run the *Gazette* while her father's laid up in the hospital and I . . ."

She cut me off and said, "Yes, Mr. Harrison, I've heard all about what you've been doing. I think it's wonderful. Let's go into my office where we can talk."

I followed her into an inner office that was tastefully decorated with traditional oak furniture, solid oak paneling and two stuffed leather chairs. She sat behind a large, neatly organized desk. She offered me a cup of coffee from a Mr. Coffee on a table behind her desk and I gratefully accepted. She filled a cup and handed it to me.

"Now then, Mr. Harrison, I will be glad to help you if I can. Just what do you want to know?"

I sipped the coffee and savored the rich aroma. Then I took out a small notebook and said, "I'm working on an update of the dispute between the Donovan Corporation and the Sequoia Indians, and I need to understand the conflict from both points of view, I was hoping you might have some useful background information about the tribe and this fellow B. J. Tall Horse."

Her reaction was obvious and immediate. At the mention of B. J. Tall Horse, the color in her cheeks darkened and her eyes narrowed. The big smile was gone too, and her lips were now a solid line. I had somehow managed to strike a raw nerve.

"I'm afraid I can't help you, Mr. Harrison."

The warmth that had been in her voice earlier was replaced by a cold and matter-of-fact tone, and I wondered why.

"Ms. Raven, I apologize if I somehow offended you, but . . ."

She shook her head. "You've not offended me, Mr. Harrison. It's just that I cannot be totally objective when it comes to Mr. B. J. Tall Horse."

I thought about this for a moment. It was obvious that she wanted to avoid any discussion about the man, but her reluctance only made me more curious. I wanted to respect her wishes, but I was pretty sure that she knew something about Mr. Tall Horse that could be important, and I needed to find a way to get her to open up.

"Ms. Raven, you're clearly reluctant to talk about Mr. Tall Horse, but I can assure you I have no interest in your personal relationship with him. I'm simply looking for background information that may help me to understand the conflict between the Donovan Corporation and the Sequoia Indians. If you can help me, I'd be very grateful."

She said nothing for several seconds, and appeared to be considering what, if anything, she was willing to tell me. I mentally crossed my fingers and hoped that she'd give me something I could run with.

Finally, she said. "What I am about to tell you is very personal and I must ask you to respect my privacy. I believe you call that 'off the record.'" I had no problem with her request. And, since I wasn't going to write an article, nothing she'd tell me would end up in the newspaper. I put away the notebook and said, "Then off the record it is."

She took a deep breath as if preparing for a difficult ordeal, then told her story. I just listened, completely captivated by what she told me.

"I wasn't born on the reservation," she began, "but I am a full-blooded Sequoia. My father was Jason Raven. My grandfather, Reuben Raven, was on the tribal council with James Tall Horse, the father of B. J. Tall Horse. Things were very different in those days. The tribal elders couldn't agree on anything and were much divided among themselves. My grandfather was bitterly opposed to the tribal council's failure to stand up to the state and federal authorities, who had done nothing to protect the rights of the American Indians for two hundred years. This led to a terrible dispute between my grandfather and James Tall Horse that was never resolved. Both have passed away and each hated the other until the bitter end.

"My mother was a niece of James Tall Horse, and she fell in love with my father when she was only sixteen and he was eighteen. They begged their parents for permission to marry, but it was hopeless because of the ongoing feud between my grandfather and James Tall Horse. Both families were against my mother and father getting married, so they did the only thing they could do, which was to leave the reservation."

She looked wistfully out the window at the far horizon while describing the events preceding her birth. Her story was getting more interesting as she talked, and I became totally captivated by the tale, but I was not prepared for what she was about to tell me.

CHAPTER TWENTY-SIX

Lydia sipped from a bottle of water and appeared to be re-living her story as she spoke. "My parents drove to Junction City, found someone to help them forge their identification papers, and were married in a civil ceremony the very next day. My father got a job as a mechanic in a large truck stop on the interstate highway and my mother worked as a waitress in the restaurant. It was a difficult life, but they were very much in love, and it was all they needed. I was born shortly after they were married, and my mother had to quit work for a while to care for me."

She paused again and said, "I hope I'm not boring you, but you need to know something of the history to understand what is happening on the reservation today."

"No," I said, "it's a fascinating story. Please go on." She took another sip of water, then continued.

"My father died just a few days before their first anniversary. He was killed when a jack that had been improperly placed beneath the rear end of a large trailer collapsed and crushed him beneath it. My mother was devastated and consumed with grief for a very long while. The people who ran the truck stop were very kind to her and saw to it that she had food, clothing and shelter, and that my father was given a decent burial. She stayed on at the truck stop for a few months after my father's death, but she finally decided she needed to be with her own people." It was a sad story, but I kept wondering what it had to do with my inquiry about B. J. Tall Horse. I figured if I was patient, she'd get around to that part, and she did.

"So, my mother returned to the reservation, and I grew up there. B. J. Tall Horse and I went to school together, and he was a spoiled brat even then. He was very big for his age, and he loved to pick on smaller boys and tease anyone who wouldn't or couldn't stand up to him."

I could hear the bitterness in her voice, and I began to understand her resentment toward this Tall Horse fellow.

"When we grew older," she continued, her voice trembling slightly, "he tried to get me to go out with him and I refused, which isn't a good thing to do because he doesn't like rejection or opposition. He was taught as a very young boy that winning is everything, regardless of the issue, and that losing is a disgrace. As a result, he made up his mind never to lose at anything, regardless of how the game is played."

She paused again, breathed deeply and looked directly at me. I saw something in her dark eyes that told me the story wouldn't have a happy ending.

"I used to like to wander through the woods in the foothills, several miles from the reservation. I'd go there to think and to dream, and it was wonderful. One day, B. J. followed me there. He'd been drinking and he attacked me. I tried to scream for help, but he pulled out a knife and threatened to kill me if I continued to resist."

I felt something cold and clammy gnawing at the insides of my stomach. I wasn't sure I wanted to hear any more, but if it made her feel better to talk about it, I wasn't going to let her down.

"I tried to fight him off, but he was very powerful, and my struggles only made him more determined. I think he actually enjoyed seeing me in fear for my very life. He tore my clothes off and held the knife to my throat while he forced himself inside me. It hurt more than anything I'd ever experienced. I almost wished he'd killed me so that I wouldn't have to endure the pain and humiliation."

She turned away, but I could see the torment she was experiencing as she explained, "I'd never been with a man before and always dreamed the first time would be something wonderful – not this."

Her voice was low and trembling as she recounted the horrible memory, but telling me about her horrific ordeal must have been therapeutic.

"When he was done, he stood over me, zipped his pants and sheathed his knife. I'll never forget that evil look in his eyes as he mocked me and told me I should be grateful that he'd been the first to have me. It was like he was proud of what he'd done to me. After he left, I snuck home the back way, hoping desperately that no one would see me and ask me what happened. I just wanted to be alone, with my own thoughts to deal the best I could with what I'd been through."

"When I got home, I took a long, hot shower, but somehow, I could still smell B.J.'s scent all over me. I hid my torn and bloody clothes so my mother wouldn't find them. But she's very intuitive, and she could tell that something was very wrong. I knew it was useless to lie to her, so I told her what had happened, and she was furious."

"I pleaded with her not to say anything about it to anyone, but she wouldn't listen and immediately called a member of the Tribal Council and demanded that B. J. Tall Horse be arrested and put on trial. I tried to talk her out of it, but she never liked B. J. and insisted that he was the one who should be ashamed, not me, and that he should be punished for what he'd done."

It had to have been a terrible ordeal, and I was surprised that she'd taken me into her confidence in such an intense personal matter. But I could see that she was a very strong woman. She wiped a single tear from her eye and continued with her story.

"My mother's pleas to the Tribal Council were brushed away like so many grains of sand in the desert. They promised to investigate, but, out of respect for James Tall Horse, they did practically nothing – a slap on the wrist. They gave my mother money – I don't know how much – and asked her to say nothing more about the incident. In return, they promised that B. J. would be sent away from the reservation and not allowed to return until he could conduct himself with honor."

It was a classic cover-up, and I'd heard others like it too many times before, but this one sounded much more sordid coming from her. I was amazed that she could remain as calm as she did while telling this heartbreaking story.

She explained that her mother was foolish enough to think that B. J. was being punished, but this wasn't the case. Instead, he went to live with relatives in Arizona until he graduated from high school. Then the Tribal Council got him enrolled at Stanford Law School and paid his tuition and all expenses while he studied law.

"To make matters worse, we found out later, through a friend of my mother, that there were other girls on the reservation who'd suffered the same fate. The Tribal Council did what they could to keep it quiet, but everyone eventually knew what he'd done. One of his victims, unfortunately, couldn't take the humiliation and hung herself. She was only 14 years old."

Tears were streaming down both cheeks now. I said nothing while she tried to regain her composure. I now understood why she bore so much bitterness toward B. J. Tall Horse. It was as if he'd been rewarded with a college education for his foul deeds! I knew things like this went on in my world, but it was hard to comprehend how it could happen on a peaceful Indian reservation. As incredible as it seemed, I had no reason to doubt her story.

She went on to say that when B. J. graduated from law school, he returned to the reservation as something of a local celebrity, and no one mentioned the dark side of his character again.

"They tried to make like it was all in the past and should be forgotten," she said bitterly.

"But I never forgot, and I know a lot of other people on the reservation who will never forget what he did to me, and to others like me."

"That's an incredible story," I said, finally able to find words to express my thoughts. "I'm amazed that he's been able to maintain his leadership role on the reservation, given what you've just told me."

She nodded sadly and said, "I told you earlier that B. J. cannot tolerate losing or even being opposed. He's also very intelligent and crafty. He will use anything he can to undermine anyone who gets in his way or disagrees with him. He doesn't always play by the rules, either. In fact, as far as he's concerned, the rules be damned if they stop him from getting what he wants!"

An idea popped into my head, and I asked her, "Do you think he's capable of playing dirty tricks or making false accusations against the Donovan Corporation to defeat their development project?"

It occurred to me that maybe all the accusations from "Pete" may have originated from someone other than a member of the Donovan Corporation. If what Lydia said was true, Mr. B. J. Tall Horse was capable of something like that.

Not surprisingly, she laughed derisively at my inquiry. "That's exactly what he'd do. He has a devious mind and he's always looking for weaknesses in the opposition. If he has a chance, he'll manufacture something to make the opposition – in this case, the Donovan Corporation – look bad."

Her description of B. J. Tall Horse as an evil, scheming person, put a whole new twist on the dispute between the Sequoia Indians and the Donovan Corporation. Was it possible that Ed Griffin had been intentionally misled about what was really going on? I realized that my investigation had suddenly taken an entirely new direction.

Several questions raced through my mind as I digested Lydia's story. Was there something more to the Indians' opposition than what I'd first surmised? What Lydia had told me was certainly enough to cause anyone to question the motives of B. J. Tall Horse. But what I didn't understand was what he might hope to accomplish by his opposition to the Donovan Company's proposal. According to Michael Gallagher, the Indians would stand to gain a lot by agreeing to the Donovan offer. Why would Tall Horse fight something that would benefit his own people? I asked Lydia that very question.

She shook her head slowly and said, "That's a very good question and I don't have the answer. I know only that he isn't speaking for the people on the reservation. While he may have the support of the Tribal Council, they will say and do anything he tells them to because they are terrified of retaliation if they oppose him."

I was amazed and said, "It sounds as if he has a very powerful hold on them."

Lydia nodded in agreement. "Indeed, he does. He must have a powerful motive to defeat the Donovan Company's proposal, but what that motive may be is a mystery to me."

"There's one other thing you might be able to tell me," I said. I told her about Estelle Pigeon and her cousin failing to report for work at the inn, and concluded, "Amos and Martha are very worried about them."

Her face darkened. "I have heard stories about people missing from the reservation, Mr. Harrison, but until now, I thought they were just the work of someone's overactive imagination. Maybe there's something to it after all." I considered what she was telling me and realized that the mystery was growing more bizarre by the moment.

"Ms. Raven, is there anyone at the reservation who could help me check on their welfare?"

She thought for a moment. "Yes, there's one person who may be able to help. But he is of the old ways and doesn't care for white men." "Who is that?"

"His name is Charles Bird. He's one of the tribal leaders. He's well respected by most of the Indian people, although he and B. J. Tall Horse don't get along at all."

She frowned, then said, "He's very reclusive and doesn't trust many people. I'm not sure he'll speak to you."

I shrugged and said, "I'm willing to make the effort to speak with anyone who might be able to help me find Estelle and William. At least it's worth a try."

She wrote his name and directions to his house on a slip of paper. On a separate slip of paper, she jotted a note, folded it and gave it to me.

"If you find him, give him this. It may convince him to help you."

I put both slips of paper in my pocket and thanked her for sharing her story with me. Before leaving, I repeated my promise to respect her privacy.

"Thanks," Lydia smiled. She continued, with less confidence in her voice, "I wish you well on your journey to the reservation, although I'm not at all certain you'll accomplish what you hope."

On my way back to the *Gazette*, I thought about her story. She had provided some very useful information about B. J. Tall Horse, but there were still many questions bouncing around in my head. Now I was more eager than ever to meet Mr. Tall Horse. Could he really be the evil character Lydia had portrayed? I was anxious to make my own assessment.

CHAPTER TWENTY-SEVEN

When I returned to the *Gazette* office, I called Sheriff Jenkins. Skipping introductions, he asked, "Whadaya have?"

His voice was coarse like gravel and it didn't sound like he was in a good mood.

"I wanted to bring you up to date on my meeting with Michael Gallagher."

"I'm listening," he said.

I summarized my conversation with Gallagher. "He flatly denied any involvement by the Donovan Corporation in any illegal activities," I concluded.

The sheriff snorted sarcastically and said, "What did you expect?"

"I'm inclined to believe him. If there are any shady dealings by his people, I don't think he knows about them."

"Well," the sheriff retorted, "just because he doesn't know anything 'bout it doesn't mean it's not going on!"

He was still skeptical and I didn't blame him.

"I'm not sure of that either. I have a feeling that there's very little that goes on out there that Michael Gallagher doesn't know about. He impresses me as someone who is on top of things that concern his organization."

"I suppose you could be right," Sheriff Jenkins admitted, but he still sounded doubtful. "So where does that leave us?"

I ignored his question and asked him one of my own. "Sheriff, do you know anything about Donovan's Security Director, a black fellow by the name of Sharp?"

"I know Bob Sharp, all right," he replied. "We worked together once on some internal thefts and employee problems at the plant. He's a straight shooter, so far as I know."

The sheriff's endorsement of Sharp reinforced my own assessment. "That was my take on him too. Gallagher brought him in as soon as he heard what I had to say. He instructed him to begin an immediate investigation. This could have been solely for my benefit, but I don't think so. I think Gallagher was being straight with me and this Sharp fellow seems reliable."

"I have to agree," Sheriff Jenkins said.

His mood seemed to improve slightly, and my confidence was on the rebound.

"I also had an interesting interview with Lydia Raven earlier today," I said. He grunted in acknowledgment, but said nothing.

"It seems that there may be a dark side to B. J. Tall Horse."

"Meaning what?" His curiosity was showing, but I'd promised Lydia not to divulge her story to anyone and I intended to keep my word.

"I can't give you the details, but I learned enough about Mr. Tall Horse that made me question his credibility. Now I need to authenticate the information I've been given."

"Sounds like you've got a mystery on your hands, Clint. How will this impact our investigation?"

"I'm not sure, Sheriff, but my gut instinct tells me all this is somehow tied together, I'm just not sure how."

"You may be right. So, what's next?"

"I've got to see B. J. Tall Horse," I replied. "I have a number of things to ask him about – including the welfare and whereabouts of Estelle and her cousin, William."

"I understand he can be a very cagy character," Sheriff Jenkins drawled.

"Don't be surprised if you get the runaround when you call out there." "I know, but I've got to give it a try."

Besides, I thought, *what good reason would he not have to see me? As far as I can tell, he hasn't been bashful with the press before. Why start now?*

I was about to disconnect when I remembered one more question.

"Sheriff, do you know a man on the reservation by the name of Charles Bird?"

He hesitated. "Well, let's just say I know of him. I've never met the man, and I don't know much about him. Why do you ask?"

166

"Lydia Raven said that he's one of the tribal elders and I might be able to get some help from him if I strike out with Mr. Tall Horse." The sheriff seemed doubtful on this point. "First off, from what I hear, he doesn't take to white men much. They say he's a strange one – some sort of medicine man. He stays pretty much to himself and doesn't even associate much with his own people."

"Lydia Raven told me pretty much the same thing but seemed to think he might have some useful information if I could just convince him to talk to me. I've made up my mind to try and see him." I signed off with, "I'll call you just as soon as I talk to B. J. Tall Horse."

He grunted once again and was gone.

I retrieved the telephone directory from Ben Griffin's desk and thumbed through the dog-eared pages until I found a listing for the Sequoia Indian Reservation. I dialed the number and wondered what kind of reception I'd receive. I was greeted by a pleasant female voice who courteously inquired about the nature of my call.

I asked to speak with B. J. Tall Horse and the female voice politely inquired, "Is he expecting your call?"

I told her no, but that I was the acting editor of the *Climax Gazette* and that I wished to speak with Mr. Tall Horse regarding a story I was preparing for the next edition.

The tone of her voice changed perceptibly as she recognized the purpose of my call. She asked if I would mind holding for a few seconds, and I was greeted by the muted sounds of light rock.

A very contemporary Indian reservation, I thought. No more than thirty seconds later a man's voice came on the line. He spoke flawless English and had an agreeable, business-like voice. "This is B.J. Tall Horse."

I was surprised at how quickly and effortlessly I had reached him. Perhaps this was going to be easier than I'd expected.

I introduced myself and he said, "Yes, I know who you are, Mr. Harrison. What can I do for you?"

He was polite, but it was obvious that he wanted me to get right to the point, so I did.

"I'm preparing a story for this week's edition on the opposition you've mounted against the Donovan Corporation's proposal to mine the hills near the reservation. I'm hoping you'll give me some insight into the situation."

"Before I answer any questions, Mr. Harrison, I'd like to say that I applaud you for standing in for Ben Griffin during his recuperation. What is the latest on his condition?"

His sincerity and interest in Ben Griffin caught me off guard. Lydia Raven had led me to expect a much less agreeable reception from Mr. Tall Horse, but I never take anything at face value, and I kept my guard up.

"The last I heard, he's still unconscious, but he's doing as well as can be expected. The doctors are hopeful that he will make a full recovery."

"That's good news," he said pleasantly. "Ben Griffin and I don't see eye to eye on everything, but he's a man of honor and trust, and I admire those qualities." *Was this the same man Lydia Raven had warned me about?*

"So, Mr. Harrison, in what way may I assist you? I'd think that, with everything that has been in the paper over the last three or four months, there's very little that hasn't been said. I'm not sure what else I can tell you."

"That's true, Mr. Tall Horse, but the article I'm preparing is primarily an update and review on what has occurred since the last article appeared. For example, I know that both you and Michael Gallagher have recently had a series of meetings with state and federal environmental experts, and I was hoping to get your view on the outcome of those meetings."

If he was as cunning as Lydia Raven said, he'd probably find some way to avoid seeing me. On the other hand, if he truly had nothing to hide, why wouldn't he want to meet with me?

"I'm afraid there's not much to talk about, Mr. Harrison. Those meetings are ongoing and I'm not at liberty to reveal the substance of our discussions at this time."

He sounded just like the lawyer he was, but I wasn't going to give up that easily.

"Yes, I understand, Mr. Tall Horse, but to be truthful, I'm trying to put a fresh perspective on the Donovan Corporation proposal, and on the Sequoia Indians' objection to it. If you can just give me a few minutes . . ." I let my voice trail off, hoping for a favorable response.

He hesitated for a moment and I waited to see how he would play his hand. "I'm afraid my schedule is very tight, Mr. Harrison. I'm leaving this afternoon for a meeting in Denver and will be gone until the weekend. But I can give you a few minutes if you could meet me here before noon."

Was he calling my bluff? There was only one way to find out. I looked at my watch. It was a few minutes before eleven. It would take me less than thirty minutes to get to the reservation.

"Would eleven–thirty be too late?" I'm a fair poker player myself.

He paused again, then said agreeably, "That will be fine. Do you need directions?"

I found a yellow pad and pencil and took down the directions and repeated them back to him. "I'll see you at eleven-thirty, then, Mr. Tall Horse. Thank you very much."

After we were disconnected, I told Ellie I'd be out for a while and headed for Amos Greer's station wagon. I couldn't suppress the feeling of excitement as I drove out of town. A dozen questions bounced around inside my head. I was determined to see for myself if this man was really the monster Lydia had described, or if he was merely the faithful and dedicated advocate of the Sequoia Indians. I couldn't wait to find out.

CHAPTER TWENTY-EIGHT

Shortly after eleven o'clock I was on the highway out of town, heading toward the Sequoia Reservation. The air was cool, and dry and the sky was an ocean of azure blue, broken by an occasional cumulus cloud drifting lazily in the upper air currents. I was struck by a sense of serene solitude as I drove into the vast emptiness. It was sparse, desolate country, marked by rolling sagebrush and ragged cactus standing silent vigil over a sea of sand populated by an occasional rattlesnake, lizard, and jack rabbit. Spotted here and there, clumps of juniper and mesquite looked as old as the ancient hills around them.

I thought of the hardships endured by the pioneer families who first drove westward through this barren country, and of the Indians who had made this land their home centuries before the white man's invasion. In our fast-paced age, it's impossible to appreciate the difficulties and challenges faced by our hardy, determined forefathers, and by the ancients who had once roamed the countryside with little but the skins of animals to clothe them, and the crudest weapons to protect them from the attacks of man and beast alike.

About fifteen miles out of town, I spotted a large wooden sign informing me I was entering the Sequoia Indian Reservation. After several more miles, I began to see signs of civilization, or what passed for it on the reservation. There were occasional mobile homes, small, one-story stucco buildings, and small, ramshackle frame houses, many of which were in various stages of disrepair. They were constructed with a combination of pale stucco, bare wood, sheet metal, or corrugated plastic. A few were painted in an odd assortment of faded pastels and most were badly weathered. The houses sprawled over both sides of the road in a crazy-quilt sort of way, with no semblance of uniformity or design.

Telephone and electric wires clung to tall poles that sprouted out of the ground at irregular intervals. The road appeared to be the main highway into the reservation, but it lacked curbs, gutters, sidewalks, streetlights or road signs of any kind. I passed a rundown gas station and one or two neglected-looking buildings that could have passed for convenience stores, which seemed to be the principal commercial outlets on the reservation. No Macy's, Targets or Sears were anywhere to be seen.

Here and there I observed small groups of men with dark brown faces, wearing jeans, denim shirts, cowboy boots, and cowboy hats, lounging on folding chairs or wooden crates. There were also clusters of young, scantily-clad children, running around the buildings, playing some game that only they knew, their bare feet sending up clouds of pale brown dust into the listless air. A wrinkled old Indian woman sat on a car seat in front of a small mobile home, watching silently as the children played. There was an occasional disabled car resting on cinder blocks, the tires long ago removed. An old, yellow school bus, badly faded after years of exposure to the sun, huddled against the side of one building. Clothes hung from a clothesline that was strung between the school bus and a nearby tree that lacked foliage of any kind. People could be seen moving about inside the school bus. I suspected that the bus might be home to some of the people who lounged nearby. *Not exactly the Sequoia Hilton*, I thought. It was a sad commentary on a once proud and independent people.

I reached the business district, and I looked for something that resembled a government building. To my left, I spotted a small adobe building that could have been a post office. Just beyond it was a two- story brick building with sparkling white trimmed windows. A large wooden sign in front told me that it was the headquarters of the Sequoia Indian Tribal Council. It was surrounded by a neatly manicured lawn. Several lofty ponderosa pines added color to the scene, which stood in stark contrast to its surroundings.

I parked in small visitor lot at the rear of the building and entered through the main entrance. I noticed the humming of air-conditioning as I entered an attractive but sparsely furnished lobby. A glass-enclosed directory listed an assortment of tribal officers and officials. The name of Byron J. Tall Horse, chairman of the Sequoia Tribal Council, was prominently displayed at the top of the directory.

I found my way to a large office at the end of the main hallway. A pretty young woman rose from a desk and greeted me warmly. Her jet-black hair cascaded naturally to her shoulders. She wore a simple dark skirt and white blouse. She had high cheek bones and a wide mouth and piercing dark eyes. She needed no makeup to accentuate her natural beauty.

"May I help you?" she said cheerily, smiling widely to show sparkling white teeth that seemed even brighter in contrast to her copper-colored skin.

I introduced myself and said that I had a meeting with Mr. B. J. Tall Horse. I glanced at my watch and noticed that it was just eleven thirty. I mentally congratulated myself for being right on time.

She returned to her desk, picked up a telephone, punched in two numbers, and waited. I heard a man's voice answer, and she announced that I had arrived. There was a muffled response, and she nodded and hung up the telephone.

"Please follow me, Mr. Harrison. Mr. Tall Horse will see you now."

She led me down a short corridor that was paneled in knotty pine and smelled faintly of pine trees. The interior of the building was simple yet clean and well-maintained, just the opposite of the decay and disrepair I had witnessed on my way through the reservation. It was an interesting dichotomy, and I wasn't sure what to make of it.

The woman ushered me into a large room that was dominated by a massive fireplace on one wall. It was so large that I could imagine roasting an entire hog on it and having room left over for three or four side dishes. A huge bison head was mounted above the fireplace. It must have stood at least eight feet tall when it was alive. Even in death, it displayed a fierce image.

The room's furnishings were tasteful and attractive, but not extravagant. There was a leather couch and three matching chairs, a spacious oak desk, a coffee table and two end tables. One wall was covered with bookcases which were nearly filled to capacity with what looked to me like legal texts. The opposing wall featured a full-length window that offered a breathtaking view of the snow-capped peaks of the Sequoia Mountains in the distance. The desk was neatly organized with several stacks of papers piled on either side of a green blotter. A laptop computer sat on one side of the desk opposite two telephones. A small table behind the desk held a printer and facsimile machine. It was the office of a busy executive.

The young woman asked me to be seated and said that Mr. Tall Horse would be in shortly. I chose one of the comfortable looking leather chairs near the coffee table and had just begun to relax in it when a side door opened and a man entered, strode toward me, and extended his right hand. He smiled warmly and grasped my hand with a solid but not overbearing grip.

"Mr. Harrison, I'm Byron Tall Horse. It's indeed a pleasure to meet you."

I started to rise, but he waved me back down, drew up another chair, and sat facing me. I was immediately impressed with his open and friendly attitude. My limited knowledge of and experience with American Indians had given me a distorted and obviously inaccurate notion of what a tribal chieftain would look like. There were no moccasins on his feet, no colorful shawls wrapped around his shoulders, and no floppy western hat on his head. Instead, what I saw before me was a very handsome, well-built and neatly attired businessman. Byron James Tall Horse stood a few inches over six feet, was lean and angular, and hadn't yet reached his fortieth year. He wore faded jeans and a western-style cotton shirt that stretched against broad shoulders that tapered off to a narrow waist that most men only wish for, and most women dream of. He was wearing cowboy boots that may have added another inch or two to his already impressive height. He wore his black hair long and tied it at the back with a turquoise-colored bandanna, allowing his long ponytail to fall to just above his shoulders. He was a physically impressive man, and I imagined that women would probably find him irresistible.

Byron Tall Horse impressed me immediately as a man who had power and who knew how to use it. If I was going to be able to deal effectively with him, I needed to gain his respect. Some successful men measure their own success by how well they can impose their will on others. They respect men who think and act like they do. I had been warned that the man standing in front of me respected only strength and power, and I wanted to convince him that I possessed these qualities in abundance. I mentally prepared to do just that.

CHAPTER TWENTY-NINE

T he tribal leader thanked me for being punctual.

"I have an extremely crowded schedule and punctuality is something I prize dearly," he said with a wide smile on his lips and a delightful twinkle in his dark eyes. His charisma was obvious, and it was easy to see how he managed to stay in a position of such power among his people.

Before I could say anything, another man entered. In stark contrast to Tall Horse, he was short, square-shouldered, and broad-chested with short dark hair over an expansive, weathered face that only a mother could love. He too wore jeans and a western-style shirt, but they fit him badly. He wore a large silver chain around his neck, on which hung a silver and turquoise medallion.

We both rose and Tall Horse introduced the second man as Lester Crow, his security chief. Crow neither spoke nor offered to shake my hand. He didn't sit down but chose to stand sentinel-like behind Tall Horse with his arms folded across his chest. He eyed me coldly, as if inspecting a dead fly, he had just swatted. I couldn't shake a sense of uneasiness in his presence. His ice-cold scowl, piercing dark eyes, and menacing body language told me he wasn't the chairman of the tribe's Welcome Wagon. His official title might be security chief, but he looked more like a surly bouncer in a strip joint. I had seen friendlier faces on mob enforcers.

Without wasting time on trivialities, Tall Horse said, "And now, how may I help you?" His tone was cordial but business-like and I wasted no time in getting to the point.

"I'm interested in anything you may be able to tell me about the current talks going on between the Sequoia Indian tribe, the Donovan Corporation, and state and federal officials. Has there been any progress that you can share with me? What do you see as the ultimate outcome?"

My question must have struck a nerve in Lester's brain, and I noticed that he uncrossed his arms and put his hands on his hips, poised for action. His attitude was definitely hostile and did nothing to allay my uneasiness.

Tall Horse didn't seem to notice, but looked thoughtfully at me, choosing his words carefully.

"While we continue to be optimistic about the ultimate outcome of this struggle, we are disappointed at the Donovan Corporation's callousness and utter disregard for the age-old rights and historic claims of the Sequoia people."

He paused to evaluate my reaction before continuing.

"Although the Donovan Corporation's high-priced attorneys have skillfully prepared a complex and confusing legal foundation for their proposal, it's only a facade intended to mask their real objective."

He spoke impeccable English, and his college education was obvious.

Tall Horse clasped his hands on the table and looked directly into my eyes. "Tribal records clearly indicate that the land in question was deeded in perpetuity by the federal government to the Sequoia Indian Nation in the Randolph-Nicholson Treaty of 1873 – three years before Colorado's statehood. Unfortunately, the precise boundaries of the land in question were never conveyed from the treaty itself into federal law, and this loophole provides the basis for the entire Donovan proposal."

I had never heard of the Randolph-Nicholson Treaty, and I didn't understand why it wouldn't be sufficient to support the Indians' claims, so I asked him to explain.

"I've forgotten, Mr. Harrison, that you're a newcomer to this area and probably don't know much about our people."

I admitted that knowledge of the area and its history was limited.

"If you know anything about the Southwestern United States during the late nineteenth century, you may appreciate the fact that relations between the United States government and the American Indians were chaotic at best. Treaties were broken – on both sides, I might add – as soon as the ink was dry on them. As a result, many Indian leaders made no attempt to abide by their terms. This, in turn, led to more and more hatred of the Indian people by the white man. They believed us to be untrustworthy, immoral and treacherous, when, in fact, there was more than enough treachery on both sides."

I hadn't planned on getting a lesson in U. S. History, but it was his show, and I was all ears. I noticed that Lester Crow hadn't moved a muscle – he was like a stone statue, and about as cold and impersonal. "As the United States government continued to push further west and move the American Indians from one disputed territory to another, the Indian tribes became more and more resigned to their fate and attempted to negotiate treaties with the

United States government with as much good faith as could be expected. Unfortunately, government representatives, including the Indian agents themselves, often didn't reciprocate in kind. Indeed, as the Indian people became weaker in strength and fewer in number, government officials took even more advantage of them."

I knew enough about the precarious relations between the white settlers and the Indians during the 19th century to know that his depiction of the treatment of the American Indian by the federal and territorial governments was a terrible reflection on the American people, and I couldn't help feel a sense of shame.

I still wasn't clear on the specific deficiencies of the Indians' claims in this case, so I said, "But what exactly was wrong with the Randolph-Nicholson Treaty?"

Tall Horse paused for a moment, looked at Lester Crow, then back to me and said patiently, as if attempting to explain a very simple topic to a child, "If you examine the treaty, you'll find that it, like many of the treaties of the day, was written in a prose that was common for the time, but which, by our standards, left much to be desired. For example, when speaking of specific boundaries, the writers referred to geographic landmarks that were commonly understood in that time, but which do not have the same meaning today. They would refer to names of topographical features of that time which today no longer exist or which have changed, through erosion, floods, earthquakes, and other natural causes. While these landmarks coincide substantially with the records maintained by our people, they do not coincide in all cases with modern usage."

I was beginning to get the picture, but I wanted to learn more, and he obliged me.

His smile turned into a tight grimace as he continued his story. "We can only presume, Mr. Harrison, that the drafters of subsequent legislation purposely misrepresented the intention of the treaty as a means of denying the Indians their rightful heritage. Bear in mind that the American politicians wrote the laws, not by the Indians, and most Indians of those days could neither read nor write English, the language in which the treaties were written. They were merely told that the spirit and intent of the treaty had been fully incorporated into the legislation that was ultimately passed by Congress. Sadly, government officials relied upon the ignorance of the Indian to commit this treachery."

It was as if the treaty had been written in invisible ink. The naivete of the Indians had been their undoing, and they had been cleverly duped by the drafters of the treaty, who knew exactly what they were doing. I was getting a much better understanding of the Indians' natural distrust of the white man.

"You see, Mr. Harrison, our tribal records clearly demonstrate, at least to our satisfaction, that the lands in question – that is the Blackwater Canyon area – were included in the Randolph-Nicholson Treaty, even though this particular area was never specifically deeded to the Sequoia Nation by Congress when the treaty was signed into law more than one hundred years ago."

"How much land area is in dispute, Mr. Tall Horse?"

He went to a large wall map and pointed to an area outlined in blue. It was rectangular in shape and ran along the base of a mountain range.

"This is the Blackwater Canyon. The boundaries of our reservation are shown in white."

He pointed to a white dotted line that covered most of the mountain range and the adjacent valley. A large part of the area within the blue rectangle was contained within the dotted white line.

"You can see that the Blackwater Canyon lies well within the western perimeter of the Sequoia Reservation. It consists of some 85 square miles and it's especially important to our people due to its religious significance."

The term "religious significance" caught my attention and I asked him what he meant by it.

His coal-black eyes stared directly into mine and I must admit that I felt just a little intimidated. He had center stage and he used his position of power expertly.

"The Blackwater Canyon has long been regarded by my people as the home of our ancestors, Mr. Harrison. I will not bore you with the religious beliefs of the Sequoia Nation, but suffice it to say we believe that the land within the canyon is sacred and represents the origin of our race. This makes the proposed invasion by the Donovan Corporation even more onerous to us." I could certainly understand his point, and I told him so. Then I asked him, "I understand that the Donovan Corporation has offered substantial financial inducements to the Sequoia people for the relinquishment of their claim on the disputed land. Would you care to comment on these offers?"

He took his seat at the table, and I could feel the tension emanating from his body. It was almost electric. A hint of anger blazed in his eyes, and he retorted quickly.

"The Donovan Corporation believes that there is a price for everything and that because my people are poor, money will persuade us to give up our sacred land. Nothing could be further from the truth!"

As if to emphasize his point, he slapped his open palm down on the table with a loud crack that startled me with its effect. He rose again and walked around the table to gaze out the window at the vast expanse before him. With his hands tucked into his hip pockets, he paced back and forth, as if deep in thought. Meanwhile, Lester Crow remained fixed in place, his expression just as menacing as ever.

"No, Mr. Harrison," Tall Horse said, shaking his head slowly, "these offers will not tempt our people. We are a proud people, and we will never accept this blood money in return for the desecration of our sacred land."

His determination was evident, but I was equally determined to pry every piece of information I could from him.

"May I ask the amount of the offer?" I fully expecting him to decline to reveal the details, and he did. "No, Mr. Harrison, I will not divulge the nature of the offer, but you may be sure that it was substantial. I know that the officials of the Donovan Corporation are desperate to acquire this land without a prolonged court battle and will go to any lengths to get what they want, but they will not succeed. The amount they've offered is irrelevant. We will refuse any offer. We only pray the state and federal authorities can appreciate the travesty that the Donovan Corporation is attempting to perpetrate at the expense of the Sequoia people."

Tall Horse looked at his watch and said, "I'm afraid I must leave now. I hope I have been helpful, Mr. Harrison, and that we can continue to count on support from your newspaper."

I'd been warned by Lydia Raven not to trust Tall Horse, but I was having a hard time reconciling the image she portrayed with my own gut reaction. Nothing he'd said or done during our meeting even hinted at the kind of duplicitous and manipulative person Lydia claimed him to be. But I couldn't completely discount the things she'd told me, though I had to admit that he came across as being much more open and honest than I'd expected.

"You've been very helpful," I replied sincerely. "I understand your position much better now and it has helped put this whole thing into perspective."

I stopped short of promising him a wholehearted endorsement, but I wanted him to think that, for the time being at least, I would say or do nothing to oppose the Indians' position.

I rose to go, and Tall Horse grasped my hand, smiled broadly and escorted me to the door. Just as I was leaving, I thought of one last question. "Oh, Mr. Tall Horse," I said as I turned back to face him, "there is one more thing. Do you happen to know anything about a place called 'Heaven's Gate?'"

His eyes narrowed and the muscles of his cheek tightened, and I knew I had struck a nerve. "No, I've never heard of the place, Mr. Harrison. Is it important?"

"I'm not sure," I replied candidly. "I found a reference to it in some of Ben Griffin's papers and I was hoping that you might know something about it."

He shook his head emphatically and walked along with me. "I'm afraid I cannot help you, Mr. Harrison, but if there is anything else I can do for you, please let me know."

I thanked him, but I was certain that he was holding something back, and I wondered why. He wasn't going to tell me, that much was certain, so I didn't bother to pursue it. He waved as I reached the lobby and stood looking after me as I left. Lester Crow was standing next to him with his arms again crossed over his chest, watching me with great interest. As I drove away, I couldn't escape a feeling of apprehension that was bounding around inside me. Had I unwittingly unleashed some sinister force that I'd soon regret?

CHAPTER THIRTY

I left the Tribal headquarters and followed the directions Lydia Raven had given me, passing more of the same squalor I'd seen on my way into the reservation. Despite the absence street signs, her directions were easy to follow, and I found Charles Bird's house without difficulty. It was a clay and adobe brick structure with faded yellow shutters and a rusty sheet metal roof. There was no driveway, so I parked on the street in front.

The yard was red clay overgrown by clumps of knee-high weeds. I could see no electricity or telephone lines running to the house, and I remembered Lydia had told me that Charles Bird had no use for modern conveniences. I had a hunch that meeting with Mr. Bird was going to be a very intriguing experience.

The front door was open when I arrived. A ragged screen door hung awkwardly on one hinge but failed to keep out a swarm of flies that hovered lazily overhead. I knocked on the door frame and called out for Charles Bird, but there was no answer. I knocked again and shouted his name twice more, with the same result. I wasn't sure if B. J. Tall Horse had been totally honest with me and I hoped Mr. Bird could provide some valuable information, but this was apparently not to be. Reluctantly, I turned to go when I sensed a presence somewhere close. I turned to see an old Indian man standing only a few feet away, staring intently at me. It was as if he'd materialized out of thin air. I was so startled that I jumped back and cried out involuntarily, "Whoa!" He was very tall and broad-shouldered, with an angular, slightly- stooped frame. I could tell that he'd been powerfully built at one time, but the years had taken their toll. He wore a tall black hat that accentuated his height but failed to cover the thick mass of grey hair that fell in tangled cords down his back, reaching nearly to his waist. His skin was the color of aged copper and looked like worn leather. He had a prominent, hooked nose and large ears, but my attention was drawn to his eyes. They were large and seemed to penetrate my very soul as he looked at me. He was dressed in faded jeans held in place by a hand-tolled leather belt with a large buckle that bore the figure of a bucking bronco. He wore a faded western-style shirt that might have once been gray. He stood erect in dirty and scuffed cowboy boots with worn down heels.

After enduring his piercing stare for several seconds, I finally managed to ask him, "Are you Charles Bird?"

The words tumbled from my lips and my nervousness was obvious.

He continued to stare at me and gave no indication that he'd heard my question. I decided to try again. "I'm looking for Charles Bird."

He acted as though he either didn't hear me or couldn't understand me, and I wondered if he spoke English. Wouldn't Lydia Raven have warned me if he didn't?

Finally, he nodded his head slightly and then said softly, in a near- whisper, "I am Charles Bird. Why do you come here?"

He spoke softly, but his English was good, and I had no problem understand-ing him.

"Mr. Bird, I am Clint Harrison, the interim editor of the Climax Gazette.

I'm filling in for Ed Griffin while he is in the hospital."

He gave no sign of recognition and continued to look at me with a penetrating stare. "I know who you are, but that does not explain why you seek me."

He spoke the words simply and without inflection. There was neither hostility nor warmth in his voice.

I handed him the note Lydia had given me, hoping it would prove more effective than my words. "Perhaps this will explain why I have come to you."

He accepted the note and studied it silently. Finally, he folded the paper and handed it back to me. He looked at me without expression and said simply, "Come with me."

He turned and walked to the house and entered through the creaking screen door. I followed him and was surprised to see that the interior of the home was neat, clean, and orderly. The house consisted of a small living room, a kitchen, and a bedroom in the rear. There was an old but comfortable looking sofa on one side of the living room and an ancient rocking chair sitting across from it. I saw no sign of electricity, but there were several oil lamps and a number of well-used candle holders situated throughout the room.

Charles Bird sat down in the rocking chair and motioned for me to sit on the couch opposite him. I obeyed without a word, wondering what to make of this strange old man. When I was seated, he asked, "Why has Lydia sent you to me?"

I briefly explained my interest in knowing more about B. J. Tall Horse and the tribe's dispute with the Donovan Corporation.

"I asked Lydia if there was anyone on the reservation who could be trusted and who might know if there is more to the tribe's claim to the disputed land than meets the eye."

He gazed impassively at me for several seconds, then said, "There are forces here on the reservation, Mr. Harrison, that cannot be controlled. They are like the wind and the clouds and the rivers. They go where they must and they do what they will, and you and others cannot stop them. The things that you speak are beyond your control. I urge you to go now and to look no further into matters that do not concern you."

His words sent a nervous tingle down my spine. It was as if he were speaking of evil spirits rather than human beings, and his response had only aroused my curiosity even more.

He offered nothing further, so I decided to try another tact. "What can you tell me about B. J. Tall Horse, Mr. Bird? Is there something beneath the surface about his dispute with the Donovan Corporation that I should know?"

He shook his head and his face twisted into a grimace. "Nothing but harm will come to you if you pursue this matter any further, Mr. Harrison. Mr. B. J. Tall Horse is not a man who will tolerate anyone who stands in his way."

His words echoed what Lydia Raven had said about Tall Horse. Clearly, there was more to this man than meets the eye. But what was it? I was determined to find out.

"Are you saying that Mr. Tall Horse has something to hide, Mr. Bird? What else can you tell me that I . . ."

"I cannot discuss Mr. Tall Horse with you any further, Mr. Harrison, and you would do well to keep clear of him."

This wasn't getting me anywhere, so I decided to change the topic. "There is something else I have to ask, Mr. Bird. Can you tell me anything about the whereabouts or the well-being of Estelle Pigeon or her cousin, William?"

I thought I saw a spark of recognition flash in his eyes, but it was gone in a second and I wondered if I had only imagined it.

He remained expressionless, and then said, "What has happened to Estelle and the others is of no concern to you, Mr. Harrison. There are many things about our way of life that are beyond your comprehension. I cannot tell you more."

The finality of his words and his utter lack of emotion angered me, but I managed to control myself. And what did he mean by "the others"?

"Then you must know what has happened to them?" This was both a statement and a question – one I hoped he would answer, but no such luck.

If he knew something about Estelle, why wouldn't he tell me? And, again, who were the others he spoke of? I had to know. I struggled to maintain my composure while he continued to look at me stoically. His silence made me even more determined to find out what he knew. "If you know something about Estelle and William's disappearance, you need to tell me," I said, then upped the ante, "Friends of hers are very worried about them. If she's in some kind of trouble, perhaps I can help her."

But he ignored my concern and said, "You must go now, Mr. Harrison."

He spat out these words as a warning: "You may be in danger if you persist.

I urge you to inquire no further into these matters!"

This time I could detect something in his voice that made me believe he knew a lot more than he was willing to share with me. But the steeliness was gone from his eyes. For the first time, he showed emotion, and I realized his concern for me was genuine, but I was determined to solve this deepening mystery.

I rose to leave, but I had one more question to ask him. "Mr. Bird, what do you know about a place called 'Heaven's Gate'?"

At first, he didn't reply. I was about to repeat the question when he said, "Mr. Harrison, I must say again that you are intruding into matters of which you should not be concerned."

The tone of his voice was cold and carried a clear warning. I felt a lump of something cold and clammy form in my stomach, and I flashed back to my days in patrol when, while searching a dark building for an intruder, I was fearful of being ambushed. I was clearly getting into an area where danger lurked, but I felt compelled to press on.

"I have reason to believe that this Heaven's Gate may have something to do with the accident in which Mr. Griffin was nearly killed." There was a long, awkward silence. Finally, he seemed to resign himself to the situation, as if sensing that I wouldn't cease until he gave me something I could use. His eyes dimmed with sadness, and he turned once again to stare directly at me.

"I fear you do not have long to live, Mr. Harrison. If it becomes known that you are seeking information about this forbidden place, your fate has already been sealed."

He spoke these words in a harsh whisper and seemed to be prophesying my death. For the very first time, I began to doubt the wisdom of my coming here in the first place. I felt a sudden impulse to flee, but I was froze in place, either by fear, or uncertainty, or both.

I eventually mustered up enough courage to say, "I respect your judgment, Mr. Bird, but I must ask you to tell me what you know about Heaven's Gate."

There was another long pause, and I think he may have been waiting to see if I would obey my better instincts and leave, but when I didn't, he seemed to accept the inevitable and proceeded to tell me about a Sequoia Indian lore.

"The place of which you speak," he said somberly, "is a passage within the Blackwater River Canyon that guards the entrance to a series of caverns that travel deep into the ground and which are believed to be the birthplace of our ancestors."

I remembered that B. J. Tall Horse had made a reference to the birthplace of their civilization somewhere in that area, but he denied any knowledge of Heaven's Gate, and I wondered why.

"For centuries, no man has entered that sacred area, although there are many stories of those who have tried and have been lost forever. It is believed that there are evil spirits guarding this place and who stand vigil over its secrets. We have many legends that bear witness to the evils that lurk beyond Heaven's Gate, and we respect the solitude that the spirits demand."

As he spoke, he seemed to be visualizing the mysteries of the place he described, and I wondered what Ed Griffin had discovered about this place. *Had Ed Griffin been on his way to Heaven's Gate when he was nearly killed? Were Estelle and William's disappearance connected with these other events?* These questions made me even more determined to get to the bottom of this eerie mystery.

"Mr. Bird, earlier today I asked B. J. Tall Horse if he knew anything about Heaven's Gate and he said the term meant nothing to him. Can you think of some reason he would lie about this?"

He stared out the window and seemed to be recalling things from long ago. Finally, he said, "Mr. Tall Horse also has many secrets. As I said before, you would do well not to intrude into his affairs."

Once again, his words reinforced what Lydia Raven had told me about Byron Tall Horse, and I was convinced that the tribal leader wasn't someone I should underestimate.

"Mr. Bird, is it possible that someone made an attempt on Griffin's life because of what he knew, or what he may have been trying to learn about Heaven's Gate?"

"There are those among us who, I fear, have very dark, deep secrets and who will go to any length to keep others from knowing what those secrets are."

Unfortunately, the only person who could tell me what I needed to know was Ed Griffin, but he was in no condition to reveal anything. I was convinced that I'd have to go to Heaven's Gate myself. Perhaps there I would find something to explain this entire series of strange events. But I still needed to know where it was.

Charles Bird must have read my thoughts.

"I can see that my efforts to convince you to abandon your investigation into this matter have been like throwing sand in the wind. I can only urge you to be very careful, and to be aware that your venture will not be welcomed by the spirits who guard that place."

His words were a clear warning to me, but I pretended not to care. "Mr. Bird, can you help me find Heaven's Gate?"

He nodded slowly in silent resignation and took a small tablet and pencil from a table and drew a crude map showing me the route to take from Climax.

He told me that it was several miles off the main highway and through rough terrain, but his directions looked simple enough and I didn't think I would have any trouble following them.

He rose from the rocking chair and walked to the door, signaling the end of our conversation. I followed him into the bright sunshine, where a slight breeze rustled the branches of a tall ponderosa pine tree and drove small. clouds of dust skittering across the dirt roadway.

I thanked him for his time, and he responded by saying, "You have nothing to thank me for, Mr. Harrison, for what I have told you is likely to cost you your life."

"That may be, Mr. Bird, but I've cheated death more than once, and I will do it again if I have to. I'm determined to get to the bottom of these events, and I believe that Heaven's Gate is where I must start. Thank you for sharing this information with me."

Charles Bird looked deep into my eyes – maybe trying to see what was making me ignore his advice – then removed a leather string from around his neck and handed it to me. On it was a small leather amulet bearing the figure of an eagle in flight.

"Keep this with you on your trip to Heaven's Gate, Mr. Harrison. I pray the gods will look after you."

Before I could protest, Charles Bird turned from me and walked back into his house. I stood there for several seconds, examining the odd gift, wondering how it could help me. But he was gone, and I was left alone to ponder his earlier warnings.

On my way back to town, I thought carefully about everything Charles Bird had told me. I don't believe in the supernatural, but the old man's warnings continued to worry me. I was also intrigued by what he told me about Byron J. Tall Horse. If there was something going on beyond this place called Heaven's Gate that Mr. Tall Horse didn't want me to know about, there was no doubt in my mind that he'd do everything in his power to keep me away from there.

But I'd dealt with powerful opposition in the past, and I was in no mood to back down now. I couldn't renege on my commitment to Sheriff Jenkins, and the disappearance of Estelle and William introduced a new element that increased the stakes. In any event, I figured I had passed the point of no return. I was irrevocably being drawn into a precarious situation, but I would have no peace of mind until I completely unraveled this mystery. I intended to keep going, regardless of the consequences.

CHAPTER THIRTY-ONE

On my way out of the reservation, I wondered what if anything, I'd accomplished. Other than obtaining directions to Heaven's Gate, what had I gained? I was several miles from the reservation when I noticed a cloud of dust behind me. I studied the image in my rear-view mirror and realized that the dust cloud was trailing a dark-colored pickup truck that was keeping pace behind me. There was no other traffic on the highway, and I couldn't escape the uneasy feeling that I was being followed. Charles Bird's warning played through my mind, and I instinctively gripped the steering wheel a little tighter and tried to estimate how much farther it was to town.

I eased my foot down on the accelerator and watched as the needle rose gradually until the front end of the old car began to vibrate in protest. The truck accelerated just enough to keep pace with me, neither closing the gap between us nor widening it. I eased off the accelerator until the front-end shimmy faded. Once again, the truck's speed adjusted to keep pace with mine. There was no longer any doubt that I was being followed, and my pursuer was making no secret of it. Maybe that was the whole point. My pulse raced and my palms grew moist as I considered my options.

If the driver of the pickup truck was planning to ambush me, he'd had a good opportunity several miles back. The area was remote and uninhabited – a perfect place for another "accident" or something even worse. But that didn't seem to be the plan. Instead, the driver of the pickup truck was apparently content to keep me in sight, perhaps as a warning, or perhaps to follow me to my destination. In either case, my initial fear gradually gave way to irritation. I was tempted to turn around and confront my pursuer, but my better sense prevailed.

I decided to call Sheriff Jenkins to report my unwelcome follower. With any luck, he might be able to intercept the driver of the pickup truck by the time we reached town. I pulled the cellular phone from my pocket and punched in his speed dial number. He answered the second ring and I explained my situation.

"Where are you now?" He sounded glad to hear from me, but I detected a note of concern in his voice.

I gave him my best estimate of my location, and he asked, "What's the truck look like?"

"Looks to be dark blue or black, but I can't say for sure at this distance, and I

don't particularly want him to get any closer."

"Just continue to drive normally," he said calmly, trying to reassure me.

"After you turn off the highway, drive toward the center of town."

I heard him say something to someone, then he returned to me. "We'll be waiting for your friend somewhere along Main Street. We'll find an excuse to stop the truck and check him out. I'll let you know what we find out."

We arrived in Climax less than 15 minutes later, and I followed Jenkins' instructions and turned onto Main Street. Traffic was light and I soon spotted the sheriff's car pulled in behind the pickup truck. At the town square, the pickup turned left while I continued to the newspaper office. The sheriff's car continued to follow the pickup truck but made no attempt to stop it.

When I reached the office, I waved to Sam Dooley, who was in the back room having a rather colorful argument with one of the large presses. He paid me no attention, and I entered my office just as my cell phone rang. It was Sheriff Jenkins.

"We didn't need to stop the driver of the truck," he said, his voice low and even.

"Why not?" My annoyance was obvious. "Couldn't you at least find out what

he was up to?"

"Because it wasn't necessary, for one thing, and because it might have complicated matters for another."

"What do you mean?" I said, trying to control my frustration.

"The man driving the pickup truck is well known to us," the sheriff continued patiently. "His name is Lester Crow. He's the sidekick of . . ."

"Of B. J. Tall Horse," I interrupted, more agitated than ever. "I met him earlier today." I suppressed an involuntary shudder when I recalled the piercing black eyes that had stared coldly at me. "He doesn't impress me as a very friendly person."

The sheriff snorted derisively. "You're right about that. Tall Horse refers to him as his security chief, but in reality, he's a muscle man who's capable of being quite violent."

"It sounds like you've had personal experience with him." The sheriff snorted again. "He's killed at least one man we know of, and probably others we don't know about."

"You mean he's done serious prison time?" I said, visualizing Lester Crow working on a chain gang.

"Not for murder," the sheriff said with disappointment. "He was never charged. They had a half-dozen witnesses who testified that it was self-defense. We figured they were either bribed or threatened, but we couldn't prove it, and he got off."

"He sounds like a real sinister character," I said. A nagging uneasiness rumbled deep inside me.

"He did jail time for drug use and possession several years ago, but that was before he got hooked up with Tall Horse, and he claims to have been straight ever since. We have no evidence to say otherwise."

"He's definitely someone I want to stay clear of."

"That would be a good idea," Jenkins said with finality.

"But I'd still like to know why he followed me all the way from the reservation."

"Your guess is as good as mine – but even if we'd stopped and questioned him, he would have denied following you. There's only one road between here and the reservation and he has as much right to be there as you or anyone else."

Despite my irritation, I knew he was right. "Besides, we don't want to do anything to suggest that we may be investigating him or Tall Horse. The less they think we're interested in him, the better off we are. Now that we know he's interested in you, we can keep an eye on him. If he does anything stupid, which I think is unlikely, we'll be there to nail him."

His reassurance comforted me, and I decided that it was all I could expect under the circumstances.

Changing the subject, I gave the sheriff a rundown on my meeting with Tall Horse and he grunted without commenting.

When I finished, he was silent for a moment, then said, "Well, I can't say that your meeting was particularly helpful. He didn't tell you anything we didn't already know."

I thought I'd let him down, but he didn't see it that way.

"On the other hand, something must have been said that spurred his interest

in you. Any idea what that was?"

I thought about it for a minute. "Not really, Sheriff. Our meeting was amicable and I left on a positive note." Then I thought again and remembered the Indian leader had denied knowing anything about Heaven's Gate. I told the sheriff about Tall Horse's reaction when I'd asked him about it.

The reference to Heaven's Gate registered quickly with the sheriff. "That's the place that was on the note we found in Ben Griffin's pocket!"

"That's right," I said emphatically. "I'm sure Tall Horse was lying to me – I could read it in his eyes. He knows where it is – or perhaps what it is – and

didn't want to tell me about it. There has to be a reason for his evasiveness."
"You're probably right about that."

Then I told the sheriff about my talk with Charles Bird. "This Bird fellow seems like quite a character."

"He is indeed. But what he told me reinforces what Lydia Raven said about B. J. Tall Horse. I'm more convinced than ever that he has some ulterior motive in this legal battle with the Donovan Corporation. And I think it may have something to do with this Heaven's Gate."

The sheriff sighed. "So what's your next move?"

"I've got to get a look at this Heaven's Gate. The Indians won't go near there because they think it's guarded by evil spirits. Something in my gut tells me that's where I need to start looking for some answers."

Sheriff Jenkins was silent for a moment, then said, "You may be right, Clint,

but I think we need to handle this from here on out."

I was stunned. Was he taking the case away from me?

"I don't understand," I said, doing my best to conceal my disappointment. "I thought the whole reason you wanted me on this investigation was because you needed someone who would not be suspected!"

"You bet I did!" he retorted, a slight edge to his voice. "But if you've managed to arouse their suspicions, your usefulness to me has been com-promised. We've lost whatever advantage we may have had!"

I started to object, but he cut me off. "Besides, I don't need non-authorized personnel being unnecessarily exposed to danger."

"That wasn't what you said when you asked me to give you a hand." I was having a hard time keeping my composure, but I didn't want to get into an argument with him because he had the final say, but I wasn't about to bow out gracefully. I meant to finish what I started.

"I signed on for the long haul, Sheriff, and I have no intention of backing out now, just as it gets interesting!" I was on a roll, and I meant to say my piece.

He started to object, but I pressed on. "Besides, you've got no one else you can trust. You told me so yourself! Why, I . . ."

"Enough!" His voice roared so loud that I was sure I could hear him without using the cell phone. I'd probably gone too far, but my emotions had taken over and I meant every word I said.

"Damn it all, Harrison, you're a real pistol when you get riled up, aren't

you?"

I thought I'd detected a note of humor in his voice.

"If you know anything about me, Sheriff," I said, "you know that I'm no

quitter. You gave me a job to do, and I intend to finish it!"

There was an audible sigh on the other end of the line. "Yep, I know all about you, Harrison. I checked you out pretty thoroughly before I offered you this assignment. I just wanted to give you a graceful way out if you wanted one. I guess I just got my answer."

He sounded almost relieved, and I was too. He chuckled and said, "All right, Harrison, what's your plan?" "I'm going to Heaven's Gate and do a little nosing around."

"How do you plan on finding the place? It's not on any map I know of and I've never heard of it before we found that note in Ben's pocket!"

I told him I was given directions from Charles Bird, and I didn't think I'd have any trouble finding it. He offered to send someone with me.

"That won't be necessary," I said. "I only plan to have a look around and see what's there. Once I check this place out, we may have a better idea of what we're dealing with. Then I can get back to you, and we can decide how to proceed."

He still didn't like the idea of my going out in that desolate country alone, but I insisted and he grudgingly gave in.

"Well, all right then," he said finally, realizing I had my mind made up. "But you are to take no unnecessary chances and make sure to keep me informed of every step you take!"

I assured him that I'd be in touch with him by cell phone and we disconnected. I looked at my watch and saw that it was nearly four o'clock – time
to get moving. I had many things to do.

I left a brief note for Melanie, telling her that I was out on a story, feeling
a bit guilty about my deception. Then I made a mental list of things I needed
to do before setting off to find Heaven's Gate.

CHAPTER THIRTY-TWO

S utter's Merchandise Mart was not much to look at from the outside, but inside I discovered a veritable treasure trove of clothing, equipment, and accessories for nearly every outdoor purpose, from skiing to mountain climbing. I'd been warned by Charles Bird that I'd be going through some rugged territory on my way to Heaven's Gate, and I wanted to be prepared. In 45 minutes, I'd collected an impressive assortment of gear and I figured I was ready for just about any eventuality.

The clerk at the register, a very large man with a barrel chest, broad shoulders, a huge handlebar mustache, and a tangled mane of fire-red hair that hung in snarled braids below his shoulders, eyed me skeptically. I didn't fit the profile of the typical outdoors man, but he said nothing, and I returned the silent treatment, prompting his imagination to work overtime.

I arrived back at the inn and stopped by the office to see Amos Greer. He was whispering profanities while poring over a pile of receipts and laboriously making entries on a computer keyboard. The glazed look in his eyes and the frustration in his voice told me that he'd not yet mastered the wonderful world of computers. His countenance brightened when he looked up through his rimless glasses to see me standing at the counter.

"Have you heard anything from Estelle or William?" I asked, hoping they might have contacted him.

"Nope, not a thing," he said, rising from his desk. He put his hands on his hips and said, "Martha and I are really worried that something has happened to them." The concern in his voice was clear. I knew that both he and Martha considered Estelle and William to be like members of their family.

"I've made some inquiries of my own," I said. His eyes widened, hoping for good news. "I don't really have anything solid, but I'm working on a few leads." This was a bit of a stretch, but I wanted to give him something to bolster his spirits. "When I get back, I hope to have better news about them."

Amos started to say something, and I could see the curiosity in his eyes. Before he could ask me for the details, I said, "I can't really go into it right now, Amos, but I promise that I'll do everything I can to check on their welfare. You and Martha will be the first to know if I find something out."

I felt guilty leaving Amos in the dark, but I couldn't let anyone other than Sheriff Jenkins know about my mission. Amos reluctantly returned to staring at the screen of his computer, just as confused as before.

I hauled the large bundle of equipment I'd purchased to my room and spread it out in a heap on the bed. It had been many years since I'd spent much time outdoors, but I had fond memories of my days as a Boy Scout. I'd made it as far as First Class, but my dream of becoming an Eagle Scout had eluded me. Later, after our marriage, Janet and I spent many marvelous evenings in the mountains near Big Bear, embraced under the stars, snuggling together in the warmth of our Polar Bear double sleeping bag, while the last red embers of our campfire glowed in the darkness.

A wave of nostalgia washed over me, and I realized that some of the items before me were remarkably similar to the things I'd hastily packed into boxes and hauled off to a Salvation Army secondhand store not too long ago. I tried to put those memories out of my mind and concentrate on the task at hand. Had I forgotten anything? I ran over my mental checklist: wooden matches in a waterproof container; a small first aid kit with gauze, bandages, tape and protective ointment; gloves; a waterproof compass; extra heavy-duty socks; hiking boots; flashlight; flares; nylon rope; a package of high-protein nuts and dried fruit; a canteen with belt carrier. It looked like enough gear to sustain me through a long trek, and I didn't expect to be gone for more than a day, but my combat experience in the Marine Corps had taught me to be prepared for anything. I was going to be out in a rather desolate area by myself, many miles from civilization, and every bit of the gear I'd bought could come in handy. *Better to have it and not need it than to need it and not have it*, I reassured myself.

Satisfied that I had everything I needed, I packed my gear into a large backpack. What seemed like an insurmountable task took me less than thirty minutes. When I was finished, I surveyed my handiwork with pride. Some things you just never forget.

It was after eight o'clock when I finished my preparations and I toyed with the idea of heading out to the Main Street Café for a late dinner, but then I realized that my motive had more to do with wanting to see Mary Alice again than satisfying my hunger. I was excited about what the next day might hold, and I wanted to get an early start, so I settled on going to the dining room, where Martha Green was kind enough to fix me a delicious club sandwich and salad, which I washed down with two bottles of Coors beer. I returned to my room and was suddenly very tired. I stripped off my clothes and fell eagerly into the cool sheets of my bed. Somewhere in the trees outside my window, an owl made mournful sounds, and I fell asleep wondering how many things could go wrong in the life of an owl.

I was awakened by a sound, but I didn't know what it was. I listened intently and wondered if my imagination was playing tricks on me. Then I heard it again – a faint scraping of metal on metal. The second time it was louder and more distinct, and I was instantly on the alert. I sat bolt upright, ready to spring into action, but I didn't move. The digital readout on the bedside clock said 2:35AM. I tried to control my breathing and the silence felt suffocating. Then I heard it a third time, and I was sure that it was coming from just outside my door. My body tensed. Adrenalin raced through my nervous system as I realized that someone was trying to get into my room. The door lock was ancient but solid and would offer resistance to even an experienced lock picker.

I held my breath and gently pulled myself out of the bed, trying my best to avoid making any sound. I was grateful for the firm mattress and bedsprings and solid wooden floors, which allowed me to crawl soundlessly from the bed and creep to a spot behind the door where I waited anxiously to spring on the intruder. I searched frantically for something to use as a weapon but found nothing.

I froze when I heard a faint click as the tumbler fell into place and the door slowly opened. A dark form silently crept into the room and moved toward the bed. The intruder appeared to be a man, but it was difficult to tell with certainty in the faint moonlight that streamed through the window. He held an object that could have been a knife or a gun in his left hand. Without a weapon of my own, my only advantage was surprise, which can be a great equalizer.

I allowed the intruder to clear the door before I sprang into action. I locked my fingers together to form a human hammer, raised my arms over my head, and swung them down with as much force as I could muster, striking the intruder on the left forearm. He grunted in pain and the object in his hand clattered to the floor and skidded somewhere out of sight. Before he had time to recover, I hammered him again, this time aiming for his head. He dodged and my blow fell on his collarbone with a crunching thud. He bellowed in anger, and I knew I'd done some damage. I seized the advantage and struck him one more time with all the force I could summon, and he staggered and dropped to his knees. Just as I thought he was going to go down for the count, he sprang back to his feet, crouching low and snarling savagely.

He swung a powerful right hook at my midsection, but I managed to step back, and his blow glanced off my side. Even so, it felt like I'd been punched with a sledgehammer. He charged at me again and I could smell his body odor. He threw another punch, this time with his left and it caught me on the side of my head. I saw fireworks and pain shot through the side of my face. I could taste my own blood and my vision was blurred. I swayed crazily but managed to stay on my feet. I somehow found the strength to land a solid haymaker to his head. It stunned him just long enough for me to hit him with a series of short jabbing punches to his chest and stomach. He was hurt, but he refused to go down.

He lunged for me, and we both went down, with me on the bottom. The impact knocked my head against the fireplace and daggers of white-hot pain knifed through my head and warm blood filled my eyes. His hot breath was on my neck, and I struggled to free myself. His two large hands were around my throat, and I frantically sucked in air. He was powerfully built, and I knew that it would only be a matter of seconds before he broke my neck or I suffocated. I struggled to escape his grasp, but it was useless.

I flung my free arm out wildly, searching desperately for something to use as a weapon when I knocked the fireplace poker to the floor. I was beginning to black out as the pressure on my windpipe increased. Using what little strength I had left, I seized the poker, and with one last effort, I swung it wildly at his head. I missed the first time, but I connected the second and was rewarded as warm blood sprayed my face. This time it was his, not mine. The blow did some damage, because he released his hold on my throat just enough for me to twist free. Then I gripped the poker in both hands and swung it high over my head and struck him as hard as I could on the side of his head. I heard the reassuring sound of breaking bone and soft tissue being torn as my attacker roared in pain and fury.

He released me and grasped his head with both hands, and I knew that he'd been seriously hurt. He staggered to his feet and kicked me savagely in the groin. For a brief moment, I thought my life was over. I lay helplessly on the floor as he charged into the hallway. By the time I could get to my feet, he was out of sight, and I was in no shape to chase him down. I half fell; half stumbled into the hallway to find Amos Greer in pajamas charging toward me in frightened amazement. "What in tarnation's all this ruckus?" Then he took one look at me and said, "You look like you been in one hellava fight!"

"No time to explain," I gasped, ignoring the pain that shot through every nerve in my body. "Call 911. He's getting away!" I wanted desperately to pursue my attacker, but the best I could do was to struggle to my knees.

Amos gently pushed me down aid said, "You stay right there."

He lumbered down the hallway, and I collapsed where I was. I couldn't remember a time when I'd felt as beat up and sore as I did at that moment.

Moments later, Amos reappeared and bent over me with his hands on his knees, gasping to catch his breath. Wheezing terribly, he finally managed to say, "Sorry Clint. I got to the parking lot just in time to see a dark colored pickup truck roar away and speed down the driveway without lights."

When he finally caught his breath, he helped me get to my feet and led me back to my room. I was dizzy and weak, and I swayed like a drunken Marine, but he managed to steady me and helped me into a recliner.

"How bad are you hurt, son?"

Before I could answer, Martha Greer appeared in her bathrobe and slippers. She took one look at me and left, returning minutes later with gauze,

206

bandages, and iodine, and began patching me up. She made mewing sounds as she prodded, wiped, and bandaged. When she finished, she drew back to examine her handiwork and assured me that I'd live to see another day. "Yer gonna have a real shiner for a few days, Clint," she warned. I winced in pain as she patted my cheek. "But I expect you'll heal just fine." She handed me a glass of water and three tablets. "Take these," she said authoritatively. "They'll kill the pain and help you sleep."

My head felt like it was in the jaws of a vice, so I accepted the pills from her gratefully, swallowed them, and washed them down with water, hoping for quick relief, but it didn't come.

Heavy footsteps in the hallway signaled the arrival of Deputy Potter. He entered my room without knocking, casually surveyed the surroundings, then looked at me with cold, lifeless eyes. He showed no emotion, but his mouth twisted into a sneer. He stood with his thumbs locked into the gun belt that sagged around his fat belly, and he continued to stare at me, as if waiting for an explanation.

Amos Greer finally spoke up. "Clint's been hurt, J. D." he said, his voice urgent. "Fella jumped him in his room, and he barely escaped with his life."

Potter ignored Amos, said nothing, and looked bored. He sauntered slowly around the room, as if conducting a mental inventory of its contents.

Showing a total lack of concern, Potter finally got around to asking me, "You wanna tell me what happened here?" He spoke in a monotone and showed as much compassion as someone who'd just stepped on a small bug.

Amos angrily answered for me. "Fella shot outta here in a pickup truck just a minute or two before you pulled in, J. D. You didn't see anything on your way up here?"

Potter looked briefly at Amos, ignored the implication, and swung his fish-eye gaze back at me. His animosity toward me was so thick you could cut it with a knife, but I was hurting too much to care.

"He beat up bad as you?" Potter's voice showed either jealousy or disbelief – I wasn't sure which, and I didn't much care.

I shrugged my shoulders, causing searing hot pain to shoot down my side. "I got a couple of good whacks at him, and he lost some blood," I said and Potter's gaze fell to the bloody poker lying on the floor.

"I reckon so," he said, looking at the red stains on my shirt and hands. "That your blood or his?"

"Probably some of both," I said. By this time, the pills were beginning to take effect and the pain was being replaced by a dull throbbing and a powerful desire to sleep.

Potter took a small notebook out of his shirt pocket and began writing. "Get a look at him?"

"Not really," I replied. "It was dark. I was in bed when I heard someone breaking in."

Potter bent over and examined the poker. It had splotches of blood and strands of dark hair clinging to one side.

"This what he hit you with?" Potter asked, using his pen to move the shaft closer to the light. "No, that's what I used on him."

Potter's eyes met mine and for the first time, he showed something like interest.

"He had something in his hand when he came into the room," I said. "It fell to the floor when I jumped him. I think it went under the bed."

Potter threw his flashlight beam under the bed and Amos dropped to his knees to look.

"There's somethin' right there, I think," Amos said, pointing.

Potter knelt and taking a handkerchief from his rear pocket, reached under the bed and retrieved a bone-handled hunting knife by its six- inch blade. He held it up to the light and admired it.

"Now that's some kinda pigsticker," he proclaimed enviously. I didn't share his enthusiasm, and neither Amos nor Martha appeared to either.

"Now Martha," Potter said, "I'm gonna need a coupla large paper bags, if you got 'em, or plastic will do."

He looked at me with a sly grin and said, "You know, I gotta protect the evidence of the crime, don't I?" He said it sarcastically, but I was in no condition to care.

Martha slipped out and returned moments later with two large, brown paper bags and wordlessly handed them to Potter, who made a show of putting the knife into the first bag and the poker into the second one.

"There," he said with a satisfied grin, "that should do it." In his mind, I suppose he'd done all that was needed.

Since there was little left for them to do, Amos and Martha bid me goodnight, but Martha warned me to stay in bed as long as possible so my wounds would heal. I didn't bother telling her that I had a full day ahead of me and I needed to get an early start in the morning. I also had no intention of letting Potter know about my plans to find Heaven's Gate. The fewer people who knew my secret, the safer I'd be.

After Amos and Martha left, Potter asked me a few more questions and made some entries in his notebook. The medication Martha gave me was seriously kicking in, so I asked Potter, "Do you have all you need for now?"

He looked at me coldly. "Anything else you can tell me 'bout this fella you say attacked you? Not much fer us ta go on."

I shook my head and tried to stay focused on him, but I was ready to collapse. "Not really, except that he seemed powerfully built. I'd say he was shorter than me – maybe five nine or five ten – but very solid."

"Color of hair or eyes?"

I shook my head. "Couldn't say – lights were out." I struggled to keep my eyes open.

"Did he say anything? Would you recognize his voice if you heard it again?"

"I . . . ah . . . don't know. He didn't say anything." I said. I wasn't giving him much to go on, but it was all I could do to stay awake. "How 'bout the truck? Color, model, year, anything?"

I shook my head again. "Amos said it was dark-colored, but he didn't really get a good look."

"Well, that's it then." He flipped his notebook closed and stuffed it into his shift pocket. "We'll see what we can do."

His words were not encouraging, but they weren't meant to be.

Before he left, he said he'd turn his report into the sheriff the first thing in the morning. I thanked him and closed the door behind him. I nursed my wounds while my mind churned with flashbacks of the attack, and I worked to chase away dark fears about what other dangers might lie ahead.

CHAPTER THIRTY-THREE

I woke from a deep sleep just as the blazing red ball of the sun began its journey over the eastern mountain peaks. The side of my face was still tender to the touch, but I felt much better than I had any right to expect. The human body has a powerful rejuvenating capacity, and Martha's capable nursing probably had something to do with it as well.

I stepped into the shower and let the pulsating stream of water massage my aching muscles and wash away the pain and soreness. I toweled myself dry and dressed in the clothes I'd purchased the day before. I chose faded jeans and a lightweight shirt, as it promised to be a beautiful day with lots of sunshine. I pulled on the hiking boots and found that they fit snugly and gave good support to my arches. They were comfortable and extended well above my ankles to provide an extra measure of protection while hiking in rugged terrain. I tucked a pair of workman's gloves into the pocket of my backpack, along with a small bottle of water, the compass I'd purchased the day before, and a county road map.

It was just after six o'clock when I stopped by the dining room to get a large cup of coffee to go. Martha Greer looked at me quizzically when I told her I was not having breakfast. "You should still be in bed, Clint Harrison," she said, in the voice of a mother scolding her naughty child. I knew she was right, but I was on a mission, and I couldn't explain myself to her. She told me to wait while she went back into the kitchen. When she returned, she had a thermos full of steaming hot coffee and handed it to me. "You won't listen to me, but you'd better take this with you. I'm betting' you'll be glad you had it before this day's over."

I'd no idea then how right she'd turn out to be. I thanked her and she walked away, shaking her head and muttering under her breath. I left wishing I could be honest with her about my plans, but it wasn't possible.

A few minutes later, I was on the road, wondering just where this day would take me. I felt a sense of excitement and anticipation that I'd not experienced in some time. It was a pleasant feeling, and I let it wash over me while I sipped the coffee and mentally thanked Martha for her thoughtfulness. I felt the caffeine's jolt as I turned north toward the Sequoia Mountains, which loomed dark and foreboding several miles distant.

In less than thirty minutes I found myself traveling down that same mountain road that Ben Griffin had traveled on the fateful day of our accident. An eerie feeling of dread came over me as I passed the very point where our vehicles had collided and I flashed back to the terror of that moment. I pushed the memory of that incident from my mind and focused on what lay ahead. Then my mind drifted back to the events of last evening, and I found myself reliving the attack in slow motion. I was convinced that my attacker was Lester Crow, but I couldn't prove it. Perhaps when I returned from my journey, Sheriff Jenkins might have some solid leads. For the time being, though, all I had was a lot of suspicion, and that would get me nowhere.

A couple miles further, I came to a fork in the road. On that fateful day, I'd driven the right fork, coming the other way. Today I chose the left fork, leading me to Heaven's Gate. As I drove, I couldn't escape the uneasy feeling that, once again I was being watched, and I began to check the rear-view mirror for any sign of a dark pickup. There were few vehicles on the road, and my apprehension ebbed as I got closer to my destination.

At the bottom of the grade, I turned right and headed toward another range of mountain peaks that etched the northern horizon. The sun had been bright in the eastern sky when I left Climax, but low clouds drifted in from the west and before I knew it the sky grew dark, and small pellets of rain were skittering across the windshield. The rain increased in intensity, and before I knew it, I was in the middle of a cloudburst, complete with thunder and lightning. It occurred to me that I'd not seen rain since arriving in Climax. Any other time, I would've welcomed the rainfall, but it's sudden arrival complicated my plans, and I wondered if the spirits Charles Bird had spoken of were warning me to stay away from their sacred ground.

Very quickly, the rain increased in intensity, and the visibility became so poor that I was forced to pull to the shoulder of the road to wait until conditions improved enough for me to continue on. After 15 minutes or so, the storm broke almost as suddenly as it had come, but the clouds remained and the rain continued intermittently. My spirits sagged with the low gray clouds and showers casting a somber pall over the landscape. What had started out to be a wonderful day was now dark, cold and uninviting, but I was determined to press on.

The directions Charles Bird had given me took me past the Indian reservation in a northwesterly direction and into the foothills that eventually led to Blackwater Canyon. About thirty miles past the reservation, I turned onto a small country road that Charles Bird had told me to look for. It was paved but unmarked and quite narrow, and appeared used much.

I followed the road through low foothills and rugged arroyos, as the elevation gradually increased and the surrounding landscape became more barren, desolate, and forbidding. After a few miles, the road eventually deteriorated, and I was forced to maneuver around one large pothole and rut after another, and I hoped Amos Greer's loaner would hold up under the beating it was taking.

I continued up the rut-choked road and thought about the ancient Indian tribes that had roamed this land centuries ago. I marveled at their ability to survive in such a desolate and unforgiving environment. My reverie was interrupted by a loud, incessant ringing noise coming from the cell phone in my jacket pocket. I stopped driving to retrieve the phone and pushed the "answer" button. I was greeted by the booming voice of Sheriff Jenkins.

"What in thunder is this I hear 'bout you bein' attacked in yer room last night?" He was very angry, and I realized that I should've called him earlier to tell him about the attack, rather than letting him get the news from J. D. Potter. Before I could say anything, he asked, "Where in the hell are you now, Harrison? I called the Summit and Amos Greer told me you left at first light."

"I'm fine, Sheriff," I said. "A little sore is all. Any leads on my attacker?" I hoped to deflect his anger, but it didn't work.

"Well, hellfire and damnation," he said, colorfully displaying his exasperation. "If you were where you're supposed to be, which is in yer room and restin', you'd already know that we don't have much more now than we did last night."

"But I am where I'm supposed to be, Sheriff," I replied defensively, feeling like a schoolboy being sent to detention for something I almost didn't do.

"Goddamn it, Harrison," he bellowed, "that trip coulda waited till yer in better shape. Those mountains are no place to be if yer not physically fit."

"Take it easy, Sheriff," I replied casually. "I figure I'm about five miles from Heaven's Gate now, and I should . . ."

But he wanted none of my excuses and cut me off in mid-sentence. "Look here, Harrison! Accordin' to what I been told, yer in no shape ta be any place but in yer bed. Ya must be crazy ta be out there climbin' 'round in those mountains after gettin' the tar whipped outta ya last night!" He was mad as hell, but I appreciated his concern about my well-being.

"I'm okay, Sheriff," I replied confidently. "I really am. I have some soreness, no broken bones, and a couple of bruises that will heal just fine. In the meantime, you gave me a job to do, and I intend to get it done."

There was silence for a moment, and I could imagine the conflicting thoughts going through his head, knowing full well that nothing he could say would get me to turn around and wait another day to begin my quest.

When he spoke again, his voice was softer and the anger was gone. "Well . . . okay then, but don't go takin' no chances. When you reckon you'll be back?" "I'm not really sure, "I said, "but I'll be in touch with you no later than tomorrow. You can count on it."

He started to say something when static filled my ear. The sheriff's voice was badly garbled. Then the connection was broken, and all I could hear was static on the line. I tried to call him back, but the indicator told me that there was no signal. I was apparently in an area where the reception was being blocked by the mountains, and I realized that I'd just lost my only link with the one person who could help me if I got into trouble. I suddenly felt very much alone, and once again I wondered what I'd gotten myself into.

I gazed up at the sheer cliffs and jagged peaks jutting high into the sky on all sides, and a sense of dread overcame me. Charles Bird's ominous warnings flashed through my mind, and I wondered if the spirits guarding Heaven's Gate were eyeing me as I drew closer to their sacred ground. I had a premonition that I was about to be tested as I'd never been tested before, and I could only hope that I'd be up to the challenge.

I reluctantly put the cell phone back in my pocket, hoping that I'd find a stronger signal later on. It was my one hope for survival if things got rough, but I had no way of knowing just how rough they were about to get.

CHAPTER THIRTY-FOUR

The sun eventually emerged from the clouds, but the rain had turned what was left of the road into a muddy trench. When it was no longer possible to drive, I found a level spot beneath the overhang of a large cliff, parked the car and gathered up my backpack and jacket and headed up a path made more difficult to navigate by heavy undergrowth. I began to realize just how out of shape I was for this kind of activity, but it was too late to turn back now.

A huge spire of rock resembling a tapered church steeple loomed in the distance. This was the place Charles Bird had called Eagle Point. I was now less than a mile away from my destination, and an electric current of anticipation ran through me, spurring me on with a sense of excitement.

The narrow path became much steeper, and in less than thirty minutes, fatigue was wearing on me, but I forced myself to press on, pushing higher up the slope, thankful that the skies were finally clear. The trail faded away, and I reached a small clearing. Just ahead, a large rock formation rose several hundred feet in the air. It resembled a medieval castle, complete with turrets, archways, and balustrades. Its multi-hued granite face sparkled in the brilliant sunlight – it was a magnificent geological formation, and I stood there looking at it, fascinated by its majestic character.

The lower portion of the fortress formed a huge arch that rose above an entrance into the side of the mountain. This, according to Charles Bird, was my destination – Heaven's Gate! The arch was at least one hundred feet above ground, and I saw no easy way to reach it from below. But reach it I must if I was going to discover the secrets that lay beyond it. I stood beneath the massive rock formation and studied the cliff surface. It was irregular and stratified, the effect of millions of years of weather and erosion. Then I spotted a narrow ledge that traversed the face of the cliff. From where I stood, I couldn't be certain, but it extended all the way to the peak of the arch. If the ledge was wide enough, I might be able to follow it to a point where I could jump to the floor of the arch. With a full backpack, it would be risky, but it was the only chance I had to gain access to Heaven's Gate.

I checked my gear to make sure everything was in place, whispered a brief prayer for divine guidance, and began climbing. I soon discovered that the ledge was narrower than it appeared at first. My progress was slow and laborious. The angle of the ledge increased sharply as I neared the halfway point. I avoided looking down, but the adrenalin was pumping through my veins, and I was unable to control my nervousness. The climb was taking its toll on me as I struggled up the precipitous ledge.

The outcrop became narrower the higher I climbed, and I was forced to press my body against the sheer cliff wall. My progress was measured in inches rather than feet. Just ahead, what appeared to be a tree branch lay across the ledge. I'd need to be careful stepping over it not to lose my balance. My heart skipped a beat when the dead branch moved, and I realized it was actually a very large and very much alive rattlesnake! It was less than six feet in front of me and had me squarely in its sights. The snake was pale grey with dark stripes running horizontally along its body. I knew it was a rattler because I could see the segmented sections of rattles on its tail, which was held erect but motionless.

My mind raced as I tried to think of some way out of my predicament. I wanted to retreat, but I was frozen in place. Cold beads of sweat dripped from my forehead. I watched as the snake slowly slithered its way toward me, moving its head from side to side. I knew one false move on my part – the slightest twitch – might provoke the rattler to strike.

My heart was beating wildly as the snake inched ever closer to me. It would soon be within striking distance. I had nothing to use to defend myself and I felt entirely helpless while I stood there like a statue. I tried to prepare myself for the inevitable and imagined the pain of the rattler's fangs sinking deep into my flesh, its deadly venom flowing into my bloodstream. My nervous system would soon be paralyzed, and my body would be wracked by fatal convulsions.

The swift attack was over before I knew what had happened. I heard a shrill, piercing shriek, and, from out of nowhere, something dark and powerful flashed before my eyes and pounced on the snake so suddenly that it had no time to react. In an instant, the snake had vanished, and I heard the sound of powerful wings beating the air above me. I looked up and saw the snake dangling helplessly in the powerful talons of a large eagle with a six-foot wingspan. The eagle soared high above the mountain peaks, carrying the snake in its powerful talons. My heartbeat resumed its normal cadence as I watched the eagle climb until it disappeared behind the mountain peak.

It may have been dumb luck that sent the eagle swooping down at that precise moment, but I thanked God, nonetheless. It was several minutes before I recovered my composure enough to move on. My progress came to an abrupt halt when the ledge ended several feet from my intended destination. I needed to reach a spot directly above the peak of the arch, from which I hoped to be able to jump and land on the level floor of the arch. I was fully aware that a slight miscalculation could send me down the face of the mountain to the jagged rocks below. I needed to climb another two or three feet higher to have the best chance of making the jump.

The surface of the cliff was covered with a series of crevices and rock outcroppings which might provide footholds and handholds to allow me to advance to a position where I could make the jump safely. I'd done some rock climbing in my youth, but nothing to match the challenge I now faced. Morbid images of my body splattering over the rocks below flashed through my mind, but I forced myself to remain focused on the task before me.

I pressed myself against the face of the cliff and found a crevice just above my head to use as a handhold while I searched for somewhere to place my foot. I found one about two feet away and moved my right foot tentatively to it. When I was sure it would hold my weight, I shifted my body along the cliff face, moved my left hand to the crevice above me, and carefully edged along the cliff face, inch by inch, until I was able to place my left foot alongside its partner.

Slowly, moving at the speed of a caterpillar, I traversed the face of the cliff using the irregular surface to gain purchase. My breathing labored and beads of perspiration streamed down my forehead. Once again, I questioned my own sanity and wondered what had made me take on such a task, but it was too late to worry about it then.

It took thirty minutes for me to reach a point directly above the peak of the arch. I'd have to jump down about 15 feet to land on the floor of the arch that protruded slightly from the face of the cliff. And, I'd need to gauge my jump and angle of fall carefully, or I would miss the slight protrusion and plunge to the rocks below.

But, even if I could make the jump safely, how would I be able to get back up once I'd completed my mission?

I withdrew a twenty-five-foot coil of rope from my backpack and looked for some way to anchor it. Just a few inches above my head, I spotted a large, tube-shaped rock jutting out from the surface of the cliff. Putting the skills

I'd learned as a Boy Scout to good use, I fashioned a loop from one end of the rope and drew it tight around the rock. I gave several good pulls to make sure that it was secure.

I decided my chances of success would be better if I shed my pack, so I carefully maneuvered myself out of it. I took one of the shoulder straps and held it against the face of the cliff and let it drop to the floor below. It landed with a soft thud, but my aim had been slightly off and it came to rest only inches from the edge of the cliff.

I gave one more tug on the rope, and when I was satisfied it would hold me, I took a deep breath, gripped the rope tightly with both hands, and dropped over the ledge. I used my feel to rappel down the cliff face, one foot at a time, while my arms ached from muscles I'd not used in a very long time. I was no more than halfway down when I felt something give. I looked up to see that the rope was beginning to slip off the rock, and I knew only seconds separated me from the jagged rocks below.

I scrambled to reach the floor below me before the rope gave way, but I didn't quite make it. I was still several feet above the floor when I began to fall. With the rope still in my hand, I half-fell, half-jumped, another six or seven feet, kicking my legs wildly in a frantic effort to control my fall. In a split second, I knew I'd miscalculated. I missed the ledge but landed hard on a large rock protruding from beneath the archway floor. My momentum carried me to the edge of the rock, and I frantically reached for something to keep me from falling into the gorge. The breath was sucked from my body and sharp pain knifed through my side. I frantically clung to the rope as my body swayed back and forth in the gentle breeze, and I tried not to think about what waited for me below. I tried desperately to maintain my balance and managed to find a large crack in the cliff wall above me. I dug both hands into it, used all the strength I had, and finally managed to pull myself up and over the edge.

I lay there hurt and exhausted for several minutes, recovering my strength.

I was bleeding from a cut on my arm, and every muscle in my body cried out for relief.

So much for my escape route, I thought. All I could do then was hope to find another way out of the cave. I tried to push all the negative possibilities out of my mind as I struggled to my feet and surveyed my surroundings. It was an impressive sight.

CHAPTER THIRTY-FIVE

T he arch towered high above me and was perfectly symmetrical. It resembled the entrance to a medieval castle, and I imagined armored knights carrying lances and brightly colored heralds marching on their way to defend the kingdom from the murderous invaders. But I was the only warrior present, and I felt more like a wayward tourist than a soldier on horseback.

The archway opened onto a large grotto that appeared to lead deep into the mountain. I retrieved my flashlight from the backpack and was comforted by the strong beam of light that it emitted when I directed it into the depths of the cavern. I took a long sip from my canteen and forged ahead. A strange feeling came over me, as if a mysterious force was drawing me into in bowels of the mountain. I could almost feel the presence of the Indian spirits Charles Bird had spoken of.

I'd spent one summer of my youth in southwest Illinois, in an area that was known for its intricate network of caves, much like those that had been explored by Huck Finn and Tom Sawyer a century before. I had enough experience to know what to expect. The inky darkness and the eerie sounds of my footsteps echoing off the walls of the cavern sent chills down my spine as I forged into the deep recesses of the mountain, and I tried to imagine how Huck and Tom had felt as they ventured forth on their own mysterious explorations.

In a very few minutes, the cavern narrowed sharply, and the ground began to angle slightly downward. Too late, I realized I should have called Sheriff Jenkins to give him a progress report, but by now it would be impossible to get a signal that far into the cave. My spirits ebbed when I realized that I was now cut off from help if I needed it. Total darkness closed in around me and I was left with only the beam of my flashlight to guide me. Belatedly, I cursed myself for not thinking about bringing spare batteries. Hopefully, I would not need them.

The floor of the cave was worn smooth as if it had been traversed many times over, and I wondered if the Sequoia Indian ancestors, had once used this cave for shelter. The air was more humid as I descended lower into the depths, and I became aware of the odor of damp earth, reminding me of a freshly turned grave. The walls glistened with moisture, and somewhere in the distance I could hear the faint sound of running water. I guessed it might be an underground river. Before long, the cave's ceiling was no more than five feet above my head. I was startled by hundreds – maybe thousands – of pale brown long-legged crickets that skittered away as the beam of my flashlight flashed over them, and I wondered what other living creatures I might encounter as I continued to descend into the bowels of the earth.

It was not long before the space between the walls narrowed to just a few feet, and I felt a bit claustrophobic. The air was heavy and dank and my breathing became labored, even though I was not physically exerting myself. Then the cave floor descended even more steeply, and I had to slow my pace to keep from stumbling. The wavering glow from the flashlight illuminated a small movement ahead and I saw a six-inch red-hued salamander creeping silently from a crack in the wall. It stopped, frozen in its tracks, blinked at the beam of light, then darted into another crevice and was gone. I tried not to think about how easy it would be to become hopelessly lost, hundreds of feet deep inside the mountain. Then I remembered Charles Bird telling me about people who had gone to Heaven's Gate, never to be heard from again, and a cold, dark feeling of dread washed over me. I considered turning back but decided against it. I'd come this far, and I was going to stay the course, regardless of the consequences.

I eventually came to a point where the cave was so narrow that I had to press my body between the moist walls and hold the flashlight to one side as I edged slowly and painstakingly forward. The cave's ceiling had dropped significantly as well, and I was forced to bend my knees and hunch my shoulders to get through. In the distance, the sound of churning water grew louder, confirming my earlier suspicion that an underground river was somewhere ahead.

I looked at the luminescent dial of my watch and was surprised to see that I had been in the cave for nearly thirty minutes. I came to a place where my forward progress was blocked as the space between the walls became even narrower. This forced me to shed my backpack and pull it along behind me. Forward progress became much more difficult, and I was barely able to squeeze through the narrow opening. I reached a point where I thought I could go no further, but I was determined to continue, as if some irresistible force was pulling me deeper into the mountain. I gave one final shove and found myself in a large chamber with a ceiling that extended twenty-five feet overhead. My flashlight beam gave off an eerie glow as it reflected from the limestone walls that luminesced with shades of green, amber and orange. Huge dagger-like rock formations extended from the ceiling. Similar rock formations, in a riot of shapes and hues, erupted from the floor. I'd arrived in a chamber filled with a veritable forest of brightly colored stalagmites and stalactites.

I marveled at the surreal scene before me, then felt a cool breeze coming from the far end of the chamber. I was suddenly chilled, and I wished I had a heavier jacket than the one I wore. The cool breeze was coming from an opening in the chamber that looked as if it led into another cave. I entered it and discovered that it continued, once again at a downward angle. The sense of dread that I'd felt earlier was replaced with a feeling of excitement as my curiosity about what lay ahead of me continued to build.

The sound of running water grew louder. I continued my descent, and I appeared to be heading directly toward it. Then I heard another sound – low, powerful rumbling – like that of a locomotive. I could also feel a slight vibration beneath my feet, as if made by some kind of volcanic activity. The trembling increased in intensity as I followed the cave downward. I soon became convinced that the rumbling of the ground and the dull, roaring sound were in unison, and I couldn't imagine what was causing them.

The passageway eventually narrowed, and the opening became so small that I was forced to drop to my knees and crawl, a few inches at a time, while trying to hold the flashlight steady in one hand and drag my pack with the other. After a few minutes, my fingers grew numb from the cold, and I stopped to put on my gloves. The temperature continued to drop, and I began worrying about hypothermia. After several minutes of crawling on my hands and knees and becoming more chilled, the cave eventually widened enough for me to stand up, but as I did so, I was dismayed to discover that my journey had just come to a sudden end. No more than fifteen feet ahead of me, the path ended abruptly, and I learned the source of the rushing water I'd been hearing. There, perhaps thirty feet below me, was an underground river, with churning water coursing rapidly along, hundreds of feet beneath the surface of the earth.

The trail resumed on the opposite side of the river, but it was a good ten feet away. I'd been on the track team in college, but broad jumping was not my event. A ten foot jump would be a real feat for me under the best of conditions, and these were anything but. However, the alternative was failure, and I'd already rejected that as an option.

I carefully considered my situation and eventually accepted the fact that the only way to get across to the other side was to jump, no matter how risky that might be. I took a few minutes to build up my courage and hoped for the mental toughness and physical ability to make the jump. I tossed my backpack to the other side – if I survived the jump, I'd need it later on. I gripped my flashlight securely in my right hand to help me get a good look at my target and, when I was finally ready to make the attempt, I backed up twenty feet or so to get a good running start. When I was ready, I ran as fast as I could, used my legs to push myself off, extended my body to its full length, and tried to get as high as possible so my momentum would carry me safely to the other side.

I nearly made it. I managed to land with my arms fully extended over the edge of the shaft, but the floor was moist and slippery and I couldn't get a good grip. Instead, I slipped over the edge, falling into the dark, rapidly moving water below. The shock of the chilly water caused me to black out for a few seconds. When I came to, I was fighting to keep from being bashed to bits against the rocks beneath the surface of the river. I was thrown about with ferocious intensity, and I struggled desperately to keep my head above water. The current was strong, and I was fighting a losing battle. My body was savagely tumbled about, and I was pulled along by the rushing current. It was all I could do to push myself to the surface long enough to take a few heaving gasps of air before I was pulled beneath the surface again. I was no match for the powerful river, and I knew that my next breath could be my last.

My lungs felt as if they were about to burst, and I was beginning to lose consciousness. Then my head struck something hard and sharp. Savage pain shot through my body and brilliant streaks of red, white, and yellow light flashed through my brain. I was overcome by bone-chilling darkness, and I knew I was about to die. When I could fight no more, I surrendered to the cold, relentless hand of death.

CHAPTER THIRTY-SIX

The numbing cold wrapped its icy fingers around me, shooting sharp barbs of pain into every part of my body. I desperately struggled to escape from its paralyzing grip. I hadn't expected death to be like this, but then I realized I was still alive, but just barely. I began retching violently. Torrents of ice-cold water, bile and body waste erupted from inside me. When the convulsions were over, I was unable to move, and I lay with my face in the disgusting mess. I couldn't remember ever feeling more helpless or alone.

I was in total darkness, and I was laying half in and half out of a shallow pool of water. From somewhere inside me, I summoned the strength to pull myself out of the water. The bitter cold was gone, but I shook uncontrollably from the cold. I tried to push myself erect, but I had no strength left, and collapsed on the cold, hard ground and once again lost consciousness.

When I came to again, I forced myself to sit up, and I began to take a personal inventory. Remarkably, all major body parts seemed intact and there appeared to be no broken bones. My legs and arms were sore and badly bruised and I had an ugly laceration on one knee, but it had nearly stopped bleeding. I winced as I touched my forehead and found a large lump over my left eye. I could imagine what it would look like in 24 hours, but that was the least of my worries. Other than feeling like I'd been through a meat tenderizer, I was in better shape than I deserved.

My biggest problem was the supplies and equipment I had lost. My backpack and flashlight were gone, but my canteen still hung from my belt. I still had on my jacket, but it was soaked and hung from my shoulders like a cold, wet beach towel. I was colder than I had ever been and had no idea where I was or what my next move should be. My situation was not hopeless, but I didn't like my odds of getting out of this alive. Had I survived the raging waters only to be lost forever inside this underground tomb? Depression beckoned, but feeling sorry for myself wouldn't accomplish anything, so I struggled to push the negative thoughts out of my mind.

Then my hand was drawn to a small lump in my pants pocket. I reached in and withdrew the amulet Charles Bird gave me, and I was transfixed, thinking about what Charles Bird had told me. *Had the gods been watching over me? Was it just blind luck that I was saved from a rattler's bite by a passing eagle? How else could I have been saved from the rushing current of the underground river?* I gazed at the amulet and the depression I'd experienced only moments earlier melted away, replaced by a new sense of hope and optimism. I hadn't come this far to fail, and with the help of Charles Bird's gods, I was going to complete my mission.

I continued my inventory and was relieved to find a waterproof container of stick matches in my jacket pocket. My spirits jumped with the realization that I had a source of heat and light, if I could just find something to burn. In another pocket, I found two of the high-energy granola bars I'd brought. And I still had the cell phone. I remembered Sheriff Jenkins telling me he'd gotten it from the military – developed for use by the Navy Seals, and that it had a special waterproof case, but it was useless to me deep in the bowels of the mountain. I decided to keep it with me anyway, just in case. My spirits began to lift as I realized that my situation was not as hopeless as I first thought.

I made an assessment of my situation, I needed light. With trembling fingers, I unscrewed the metal top of the container and carefully withdrew one of the matches, replaced the lid and struck the match against the rough surface on the base of the tube. The match flared and died momentarily and then burst into flame. Holding the match high above my head, I could see that I was in a large underground grotto, fifty feet in diameter. The river was to my left, flowing as fast and relentlessly as before.

The match flickered out, and I lit a second one, trying not to think about how few were left in the container.

I used the feeble flame to explore my surroundings and, just ahead, spotted an old mine shaft. A set of rusty narrow railroad tracks led into the darkness ahead. The tracks ended just short of the river, and I saw the rotted remains of what may have been a loading dock. Perhaps at one time, the loading dock had been used to offload ore onto small barges and carried to the outside by the river. I felt somewhat relieved to know that I was in an area that had once been inhabited by human beings! That must mean somewhere ahead there was an opening that would lead me to safety. All I had to do was find it.

I could barely make out the narrow-gauge railroad tracks and wooden cross beams that led into the darkness of the old mine. The flame on the second match burned my fingers and I reluctantly tossed it to the ground. I lit a third match and looked desperately for something I could burn to help light my way. A few feet inside the shaft I discovered a crude torch inserted into a depression in the rock wall. It was made from a large piece of scrub oak wrapped in several layers of coarse cloth and then soaked in creosote, which ignites easily and burns well. There was no way of telling how long it had been used, but there was still enough of it left to burn for some time, if I could get it to light.

I picked up the old torch and held the dwindling flame of my match to it, but the flame flickered out. I lit another match and held it to the torch. At first it only gave off smelly, sooty smoke, but eventually the aged creosote ignited, and in a few seconds the torch was burning brightly. I now had both heat and light, but I wasn't ready to start celebrating just yet.

It was time for me to move on. I held my torch aloft and made my way down the mine shaft which curved at irregular angles. It had obviously been blasted out of solid rock. I envisioned exhausted miners struggling to pick and shovel their way through tons of rock and earth and I wondered what kind of mine it had been. I knew gold and silver had been mined in this area a hundred or more years ago, but how had such a mine been operated in an area that was claimed by the Sequoia Indians as sacred ground? And could the Donovan Corporation be aware of such a mine? These questions only added to the mystery, and I hoped I would soon find the answers to them.

Just ahead, I spotted an old wooden cart that had been used to carry ore. Its four iron wheels were as rusted as the iron rails carried it through the tunnel. But the body of the cart was still intact, and it looked to be in relatively good shape, despite a century or more of neglect. Clearly, this old tunnel was part of what had once been a mine of some kind, but those days were buried in the past.

I'd walked a short distance when I became aware of a rumbling beneath my feet and the thumping sound of some kind of heavy machinery somewhere ahead of me. I couldn't be sure, but it made the same rhythmic sound I'd heard before falling into the river. I continued on, and the sound became more distinct. I was sure the mine shaft was leading directly to its source. My pulse raced and I instinctively quickened my pace. The aches and pain and bitter cold I'd suffered earlier were replaced by a sense of anticipation. With any luck, my journey might be coming to a quick end, and the secrets of Heaven's Gate might soon be revealed.

The mine shaft was leading deeper into the mountain, and with each step, the rumbling sound grew slightly louder. It had a regular, pulsing rhythm, an almost staccato beat. *Whomp, whomp, whomp de-whomp*, pause. *Whomp, whomp, whomp de-whomp*, pause. The pattern repeated itself every fifteen seconds or so, and the ground beneath my feet trembled in time with the sound. My curiosity grew by the second. *What kind of machine, person or thing could be making such a commotion in the very heart of a mountain?*

My journey ended abruptly as I rounded a curve in the tunnel and found it completely blocked by fallen rock. I could go no farther unless I found a way to remove the tons of rock that blocked my way. But I knew that whatever I was looking for had to be on the other side of the rock pile, and I needed to find a way to get there.

I looked for something that I could use to remove the rock, but saw nothing. Then I spotted the end of what looked like a long wooden handle that was partly buried in the ground. I pulled on it several times before I was able to free it and was gratified to discover that it was attached to an old miner's pick – left behind decades ago and appearing before me so conveniently! I instinctively felt the lump of Charles Bird's talisman in my pocket and knew the gods were still watching over me. The pick was covered with dirt and rust, and the handle was broken, but it was something I could use to attack the rock pile.

I mounted the torch on a rock outcropping where it would burn freely and illuminate my progress. Then I began to pick away, working on the smallest rocks, trying to dislodge them and bring some of the larger ones down as well. It was slow and tiring work, and I was soon sweating profusely. I paused to remove my jacket and shirt and took a few sips of water from my canteen. I couldn't remember how long it had been since I'd last eaten, and I was starving. I retrieved the soggy remains of the granola bar from my jacket pocket and devoured it quickly, thankful for anything to ease the hunger pangs.

I was only able to work a few minutes at a time before stopping to rest, but I made good progress. In less than an hour, I'd managed to remove one layer of rocks, but there was no way of knowing how much more lay between me and the other side. Meanwhile, the thunderous sound continued to shake the ground beneath my feet. *Whomp, whomp, whomp de-whomp*, pause. *Whomp, whomp, whomp de-whomp*, pause.

I continued to pick away at the boulders, and each one that came tumbling to the ground was a small victory. My progress was measured in inches, but I knew somehow, I must find the source of the strange sound that seemed to grow louder with each passing moment.

After two more hours, I noticed that the flame on my torch was beginning to flicker. I feared it was about to go out, and I'd be left in total darkness, so I redoubled my efforts, working desperately to finish. Then I noticed that the flame was not going out, but was shimmering in a faint breeze, and I noticed a gentle current of air coming from the other side of the rock pile. The discovery energized me, and I worked furiously to dislodge more rocks and find the source of the breeze.

Eventually I could see a small glimmer of light peeking through the rocks, and I knew I'd broken through. I worked to enlarge the small hole and was eventually able to remove enough rock to have a clear view of the other side. The rumbling sound was louder, and I knew that it was coming from somewhere just ahead.

I continued pulling out chunks of rock until I was able to clear a hole large enough to squeeze through. I no longer needed the torch, so I doused the flame and left it lying on the other side of the rock pile. It might come in handy if I had to make a quick exit. I crept carefully along the tunnel, keeping in the shadows to avoid detection. As I rounded a curve, I was amazed to see that I was in a massive underground chamber that extended hundreds of yards in every direction. The ceiling was at least a hundred feet high and I wondered what force of nature had left this huge arena deep in the bowels of the mountain.

I was marveling at the spectacle before me when a loud whistle shrieked and the rumbling sound stopped. I paused breathlessly. Had I tripped an alarm? My instincts were on high alert, ready to bolt at the first sign of danger. Then, from somewhere in the distance, I heard footsteps approaching, accompanied by the sound of voices, and I feared the worst.

I looked for a place to conceal myself, and I spotted a large storage area containing huge wooden crates stacked twenty feet high along with large drums of what appeared to be diesel fuel. I squeezed through an opening between the crates, and my heart skipped a beat when I saw what was stenciled in large letters on the side of each crate: "The Heaven's Gate Corporation." I'd reached my destination!

The entry in Ben Griffin's journal flashed through my mind. Whatever was going on in this place was important enough for someone to try to kill Ben Griffin to keep it secret, and the attack on me no doubt had the same purpose. The voices were only a few feet away, and I pressed myself against the crate and listened, hoping my heavy breathing wouldn't give me away. Two men were talking, and one of them was not happy.

"Goddamn it, Frank, don't give me excuses! This shipment has to be in Denver by the day after tomorrow and that's all there is to it! The boss won't put up with any more delays!"

The man named Frank replied, "I'm tryin' ta tell ya that we're pushin' them Injuns as hard as we can, but we're usin' old men, women and kids to do man's work and they're just not up to it. Can't we get a few more bodies down in that hole?"

The first man's voice was cold and hard. "For Chrisake, no! We're pushing our luck as it is. We're starting to get too many questions about people missing from the reservation. You'll just have to make it with what you got." Frank said, "Like I say, we're doin' the best we can. How much longer do ya think we got?"

"The boss says it's just a matter a time before someone gets onto us, so we need ta shut the operation down soon – this may be the last shipment . . . I dunno."

"And then what'll we do with them Injuns? We can't just let 'em go!"

The other man paused for a moment, then said, his voice dripping with sarcasm, "We'll just have to arrange for them to have an . . . uh . . . unfortunate accident – to make sure they're never heard from again. Comprende?"

Frank sighed deeply, then said in a near whisper, "Yep. Guess there ain't no other way."

Their voices trailed off as they walked away from where I was hiding. My heart was racing even faster as it dawned on me that I'd just heard two men plan a mass murder of innocent people. The horrible meaning of the conversation jolted me, and it was at that very moment that I recognized the voice of one of the two men. A cold lump of something very unpleasant grew in my stomach when I realized that the man giving the orders was none other than Lester Crow!

CHAPTER THIRTY-SEVEN

The footsteps retreated into the distance, and my pulse returned to normal. My first impression of Lester Crow hadn't been a good one, and now I had even more reason to dislike him. I'd just overheard him sentence a group of innocent people – perhaps Estelle and little William among them – to death!

I sat there in the shadows and a dozen questions bounced around in my head. *How was this underground operation – whatever it was – connected to the land dispute with the Donovan Corporation, or with the missing Indians? And what connection did B. J. Tall Horse have with the Heaven's Gate Corporation? Could Tall Horse be the "boss" Crow had mentioned? What was going on in this place buried deep in the bowels of the mountain? What did all this have to do with the attack on Ben Griffin?* I felt like I was working a huge jigsaw puzzle and none of the pieces fit together. Somehow, I needed to get to the bottom of this bizarre mystery, but it looked like dangerous territory ahead.

When I was sure no one else was around, I crept up to get a better view of the action in the large chamber. In the distance, I saw a tall wooden derrick–like structure with a long conveyor belt leading to a large platform at its top. One end of the conveyor belt extended into the opening of what appeared to be another mine shaft at the far end of the chamber. Piles of rock were being carried by the conveyor belt into a large machine that made loud, pounding sounds that roared above the clattering and chattering of other machinery. A large wooden chute was attached to one side of the building. Crushed rock spilled from the chute into large dump trucks parked alongside the structure. The noxious odor of diesel fumes and fuel oil hung thick in the air. I realized I had stumbled onto some kind of mining operation deep inside the mountain.

A loud whistle shrieked and almost immediately the sounds of machinery clanking, grinding and chugging stopped. I heard shouts coming from the mine shaft, and seconds later, a small group of men and women trudged slowly from the mine. Their backs were bent, and their shoulders were stooped, and they moved as if they were on a chain gang. Their clothes were dirty and ragged, and I was reminded of scenes of prisoners of war in Nazi prison camps during World War II. Two men with rifles followed them and one shouted orders in a language I couldn't understand.

The men and women walked single file and came to a halt in response to a sharp command from one of the two armed guards. The small group – I counted six in all, including a small boy of eight or nine years who walked with a limp – stood facing the guard, waiting for further orders. They looked completely helpless and defeated – apparently worn out from heavy labor. One old man was having difficulty standing and leaned on another man for support. One of the women turned to help him and my pulse raced when I recognized Estelle. The mystery of Estelle's disappearance had finally been solved, but I was in no mood to celebrate. Instead, I was filled with dread as I realized the dangerous situation she was in. My stomach churned as I wondered how I'd be able to free these unfortunate people from the terrible fate that awaited them.

I looked at my watch and was surprised to see that it was eight o'clock in the evening. I'd lost all sense of time since my journey began more than 12 hours earlier. It was the end of the workday for the captive Indians. One of the guards shouted at them, and they moved in unison to an old picnic table nearby. As if on cue, an elderly Indian woman, accompanied by a small boy, appeared carrying a cardboard box. She gave each of the workers sandwiches wrapped in paper and a paper cup which the young boy filled with a liquid from a large jug. The old woman handed out apples and oranges, which they eagerly accepted. The workers ate the modest meal slowly, while the two guards watched in silence.

After the workers finished eating, one of the guards – a particularly evil-looking fellow – ordered them to line up, and they obeyed silently. He barked at them and waited for a response. When none came, he walked to the old man and asked him a question in a manner that reminded me of my D.I. in Marine Corps boot camp. The old man either didn't understand the question or was unwilling to give an answer. The guard asked the question again, putting his face nose-to-nose with the old man, who shrank away in fear and nearly stumbled to the ground. The guard turned away in anger and said something to the second guard, who watched with an amused look on his face. The evil-eyed guard suddenly turned back to the old man and swiftly struck him with the butt of his rifle. The old man fell to the ground, crying out in pain. Estelle rushed to him and cradled his head in her arms, while the other workers looked on in fearful silence. I watched the vicious attack and silently cursed my own inability to intercede.

Then a man I hadn't seen before appeared, walked quickly to the two guards, and shouted for them to "Knock it off!" I recognized the voice as the man named Frank I'd heard earlier having a discussion with Lester Crow.

Frank got into an animated argument with the two guards, who didn't seem to appreciate his intervention. Frank pointed to the old man lying on the ground, obviously angry at the beating the guard had administered. He turned to the workers and said something to them. Without replying, they turned and walked slowly toward two nearby tents. Estelle and the other man helped the old man to his feet and half-led, half-carried him to one of the two tents. Then Estelle, the old woman and the young boy went into the other tent. Meanwhile, Frank and the two guards walked over to a building that looked like it could be a combination office and bunkhouse. Frank and the heavy-handed guard were still engaged in a heated conversation.

The camp became eerily quiet, and I was left alone with my thoughts. I tried to come up with a possible escape plan, but getting out of the camp without being seen wouldn't be easy. First, I needed to get a better understanding of the physical layout of the camp, and what escape routes might be available. There had to be a method of accessing this place from the outside – other than the dangerous route I'd taken – and I had to find it.

I also needed to know how many guards there were, where they were posted, and how often they made their rounds. In addition to Frank, there were at least two guards, and possibly more. I figured they'd need at least three plus the one in charge to cover three eight-hour shifts (if that's what they were working), which meant there were two more guards unaccounted for – perhaps still in the bunkhouse. And what about Lester Crow? Was he still on the scene, in the office or bunkhouse? I figured there would be one guard on duty at a time, and two or three others who could be summoned quickly if the need arises. As I considered the odds, which were not great, I wondered what weapons might be available if we had to use force to overcome the guards. I quickly rejected this as an option because I couldn't expect much help from the Indians, and the risks associated with an armed confrontation were too great. All in all, the deck was stacked against us. I tried to keep a positive attitude, but it was impossible to deny the danger we faced.

Before doing anything, I had to make contact with the Indians and gain their confidence and cooperation. I hoped Estelle would help me accomplish that objective. But I had to find a way to get to them without being discovered. To do that, I had to find out how often the guard checked the prisoners. Due to the confined area of the camp, I suspected the guard followed a regular routine. Once I knew what that routine was, I could use it to my advantage. I didn't have to wait long to find out.

It was a few minutes after 9:00 PM when I heard footsteps approaching from the far side of the camp. Moments later, a guard whom I hadn't seen before approached the Indians' tents. I saw him shine his flashlight into each of the tents and conduct a visual inspection. Satisfied that all of the workers were accounted for, he was soon out of sight. I was anxious to make contact with Estelle, but I needed to determine the guard's routine before making a move. Until then, all I could do was wait.

I was bone tired and, despite my best efforts to stay awake, I lost the battle and eventually nodded off. It seemed like only minutes later when I heard the guard's footsteps approaching again. I panicked, thinking I'd been discovered. I was relieved to see the guard check the two tents again, then retreat from sight. I looked at my watch. It was 11:15 – a little over two hours since his last check. But had I missed a round? I'd slept so soundly, I couldn't be sure. I decided to err on the side of safety and assume that the guard made his rounds every hour. This should give me time to get to the Indians' tents, find Estelle, and encourage the other Indians to trust me to help them escape from this underground prison.

CHAPTER THIRTY-EIGHT

I t looked to be about thirty yards from my hiding place to the tents where the Indians slept. The only illumination came from two security lights that hung high overhead, but they did little to cut through the dense shroud of darkness that enveloped the cave. This would work to my advantage, since I'd be able to move about in the shadows with little chance of being seen.

I'd have the cover of relative darkness to protect me as I made my way there. I removed my boots and carried them while I crept slowly out, pausing to listen for any sound of danger. Half-crawling and half-running, I kept a low profile, just in case the guard appeared unexpectedly. I felt totally exposed as I crossed the open space, knowing full well that any small sound might mean discovery.

The two tents were large enough to provide sleeping quarters for four or five people. I reached the first tent and heard the sounds of labored breathing and men snoring. I crawled to the second tent and heard a woman sobbing softly. I was about to pull back the tent flap when I heard footsteps approaching. I froze, and my heart leaped into my throat. I had to do something or I'd be discovered in a matter of seconds. My only choice was to quickly yank on the tent flap and dive inside, hoping the occupants wouldn't cry out in alarm.

I hit the ground and fell next to a sleeping body and waited, holding my breath, while the footsteps passed by. A flashlight beam played over the tent and I froze, thinking I'd been discovered, but this time the guard didn't bother to look inside the tent, and the footsteps retreated as quickly as they'd come. I waited for my heartbeat to return to something like normal and thought, *So much for routine.*

Three sleeping forms were covered by heavy, rough blankets. I moved quietly over to the one who'd been sobbing moments earlier. I was sure it was Estelle, but I knew she wouldn't recognize me in the almost total darkness. I withdrew me cell phone from my pocket and opened it up to illuminate my face as I gently placed my hand over her mouth to keep her from sounding an alarm.

"Estelle," I whispered. "It's me. Clint Harrison from the inn. Do you remember me?"

She instinctively pulled back, then flinched as if she'd been jolted by an electric shock, and her eyes grew wide with fear, but she didn't cry out. I whispered again, hoping to avoid waking up the other two sleeping forms. "Estelle, it's Clint Harrison. Remember me – OJ?"

The one sleeping next to her groaned, turned over, then was quiet. Estelle finally recognized me and reacted as if she was seeing a ghost. Her mouth moved, but no words came out. She was still in a state of shock. I motioned to her to remain silent, reached my arm out and placed it on her hand to reassure her, and whispered, "Estelle, I've come to get you out of here." I hoped I sounded more confident than I felt, knowing the odds of us making a safe escape were slim.

She slowly nodded her head, and tears streamed down her cheeks. I whispered, I'll get you out of here, but I need your help." She nodded again, remaining silent.

There was movement from one of the other two sleeping bodies, and an old woman emerged from beneath the blanket and stared at me suspiciously. She said something to Estelle, and the two of them conversed in hushed tones.

Then Estelle turned to me and whispered, "This is Mona Dove," gesturing to the old woman. "She and I were brought here together, along with my cousin, William. She wants to know how you came to be here."

"That's not important," I whispered. "Right now, I need to know if you'll be willing to help me. I can't get you out of here without your cooperation."

Estelle turned back to Mona Dove, and they talked quietly for several minutes, while I nervously listened for footsteps outside. Mona Dove eyed me warily as she conversed with Estelle. Then Estelle said, "We are grateful for what you are trying to do, but unless you have brought more men with you, our situation is hopeless. There are three guards with rifles, and we are helpless against them."

"Let me worry about the details," I said, trying to reassure her. "I'm working on a plan, but I seriously need your assistance to pull it off."

My plan was sketchy, but I needed to convince her it would work. But I needed to know more about the situation we were in. "How many guards are there?"

Estelle said, "Three guards, plus Frank, who is in charge."

"That's all?" I was displaying more confidence than I felt. I assumed all the guards were armed and we had no weapons to defend ourselves, but I made up my mind not to become discouraged.

Something in Estelle's eyes told me she trusted me. She turned to Mona

Dove and they talked again in hushed whispers. Mona Dove continued to look at me, nodding knowingly, but I couldn't tell if that meant her approval or simply her understanding of what Estelle was saying. Then Estelle turned to me and said, "Our situation is hopeless, Mr. Harrison, and I fear you have risked your life for nothing, but we will help you in whatever way we can."

I looked at my watch and figured I had another 30 minutes before the guard returned, so I asked Estelle to explain how they'd come to be in this terrible situation in the first place.

Estelle paused for a moment, then said, "There are many people on the reservation who do not like or trust B. J. Tall Horse and his associates, Mr. Harrison, but they say nothing and do nothing to provoke his wrath. Those few who openly oppose him often come to unfortunate ends. That is why we are here."

Her words made my stomach turn, and raised more questions, but they would have to wait. It was enough to know she and the others had been taken to serve as slave laborers. The whole idea was unbelievable, yet Estelle was the living proof. The sinister plot only reinforced what Lydia Raven had told me about B. J. Tall Horse, and I didn't need anything to convince me Lester Crow was just as evil as I'd originally suspected.

Estelle went on to tell me the mine was originally discovered by an old prospector who'd made many claims of "striking it rich" before, and all of them had turned out to be bogus. Then one day, the old miner turned up with a leather pouch full of very rich gold ore, claiming he'd finally "hit the big one." When B. J. Tall Horse heard about this, he sent Lester Crow to check out the old man's claim. Shortly after that, the old prospector was found with a broken neck at the bottom of a deep gorge. Officially, it was reported that he got drunk and fell off his horse. The investigation into his death, which occurred on the reservation, was conducted by the Tribal Police, who are controlled by B. J. Tall Horse. To no one's surprise, the old man's death was ruled an accident.

I was beginning to get the picture. "But why all the secrecy? Surely, any discovery of gold on Indian land would have been enough to benefit the entire tribe!"

Estelle smiled sadly and shook her head. "You underestimate the evil of this man, Mr. Harrison. He cares nothing for the Sequoia people and will do anything to serve his own interests. The only reason he remains in power is because of the fear others have of him, and the respect some of the elders have for his father."

Estelle continued, her voice trembling, "The real reason for keeping this mine a secret, Mr. Harrison, is that it isn't on Indian land at all."

"What do you mean?" I said incredulously.

"This mine is on land owned by the United States government. This has been common knowledge on the reservation for years. But when B. J. Tall Horse learned of the Donovan Corporation's plans to develop the land, he realized that he needed to do something to stop them. "What did he do?"

Estelle took a deep breath and said, "He was able to obtain a false set of documents which vaguely alluded to an old treaty between the Sequoia Indian Tribe and the federal government which altered the actual boundary of the reservation."

I shook my head in disbelief.

"The papers he obtained are obviously worthless, but they've given him all he needs to block the Donovan Corporation's plans, at least for the time being." "But surely he'll eventually be found out," I said.

Estelle nodded. "Yes, but by then, he will have made millions from the sale of the gold and will have enough to live like a king anywhere in the world."

"If this is common knowledge among your people, why hasn't someone on the reservation gone to the authorities?"

Estelle shook her head sadly and looked at Mona Dove, her eyes reflecting deep-seated resentment. "The white man has victimized my people for centuries, and they trust no one in authority. Our people trust only themselves and they would rather die than reveal their shameful secret to the outside world."

Time was running short, and I still needed to know more about our situation, so I asked her about other entrances to the mine. The only one she knew of was the way they'd come when Lester Crow's men had brought them there. But it was heavily patrolled by Lester Crow's guards and wouldn't offer a safe route of escape.

"Is that the only entrance?"

"No," she said. "There are other caves leading off from the main chamber, but they have all been blocked off to prevent anyone from entering or leaving."

It was pure luck that I'd been able to pick my way through the rock and into the secret chamber. *Or was it another sign Charles Bird's gods were still standing vigil?*

"I saw six of you earlier. Are there more?"

"No," she replied softly. "Besides Mona Dove, little William and myself, there are three men – Luther, Jacob and Isaac. Isaac is very old and not well."

I asked her if they'd be willing to attempt an escape if I could show them the way. She turned to Mona Dove, and they conversed quietly for several minutes before Estelle turned back to me. "We know Lester Crow will not allow us to leave this place alive, Mr. Harrison. If you are willing to risk your life for us, we will follow you."

That was good to know. I did my best to assure her I'd see to it they all got out of this place alive, but I had no idea how I was going to make that happen.

"I need food and rest and a better place to hide. Is there some place I can stay and be safe and get something to eat?" Estelle turned to Mona Dove and the two of them spoke in hushed voices. Then Mona Dove nodded and said something to Estelle.

"In the kitchen where Mona Dove works, there's a storeroom in the cellar. Perishable provisions are kept there. It's small, not much larger than a closet, but it would be safe for you, at least for a while – the guards do not come into the kitchen. There's a trap door in the floor that leads to a set of stars. It will not be comfortable, but it will be the safest place for you."

It sounded like the perfect spot for me to rest and spend time planning our escape. Estelle told me how to reach the kitchen. I figured I still had an hour or two before the camp came alive, so the best thing for me to do was to get to the kitchen and find the storeroom while no one was about.

I told Estelle that I'd check back with her in 24 hours, by which time I hoped to have the details of my escape plan worked out. The sooner I could get them out of that living hell, the better I'd like it. She said something to Mona Dove, who continued to eye me with something between suspicion and disbelief. I opened the tent flap, listened for footsteps, then crept cautiously out. I scanned the area for any sign of the guard. When I was convinced, it was safe, I sped quickly across the open space, headed for the kitchen.

The kitchen was in a small Quonset hut on the other side of the bunkhouse. I reached it safely and entered through a rear door Estelle told me would not be locked. There were no lights on inside, but I used the illumination from my cell phone to find the trap door exactly where Estelle told me it would be. I raised it and inched myself slowly down, carefully closing the door after I cleared the opening. I made it to the floor, retrieved the small tin of matches from my jacket pocket, and lit one. The cellar was crowded with an assortment of food in burlap bags, tins and boxes. I found a kerosene lantern hanging from an overhead beam. Touching my flickering match to the wick, I watched anxiously as it sputtered once, then once more, and went out. I adjusted the fuel knob and struck another match. This time it lit instantly. I adjusted the flickering flame and was comforted by a warm glow that threw dancing shadows on the wall.

I moved a couple of boxes out of the way and found an old tarp to protect me from the cold, damp ground as I slept. It was dirty and smelly, but it would do for the time being. I turned the lantern flame down low, laid down on my crude bed, and was asleep instantly. When I woke up, I heard people moving around overhead. And I realized I had nowhere to go if one of the guards were to look in. After a few minutes, I forced myself to relax, deciding the sounds were the old woman and the young boy preparing a meal. That realization created hunger pangs in my stomach, but I had no choice but to remain where I was until it was safe to come out. In the meantime, I thought about what I'd learned from Estelle. It all made sense now. The whole ugly picture was coming into focus, and all the pieces were beginning to fit together. I was more determined than ever to see B. J. Tall Horse, Lester Crow, and their henchmen exposed for the vicious felons they were. But first, I needed a workable escape plan, and that was going to take some serious thinking, so I wasted no time in getting started.

CHAPTER THIRTY-NINE

I was deep in thought when I heard the trap door opening, and light from the kitchen filled the small cellar. I panicked, looking for a place to hide, or for something to use as a weapon, but there was nothing. Then I saw the form of Mona Dove slowly making her way down the ladder, and I started to breathe easier. She'd lit the kerosene lantern and the cellar glowed warmly in its light. For the first time, I got a good look at her. I guessed she was in her sixties or perhaps older, but her copper-colored skin was smooth and unblemished by winkles or splotches. Her dark eyes shone brightly and radiated an inner strength. I was willing to bet she'd been a very beautiful woman in the days of her youth.

When she saw that I was awake, she said, "You sleep good. Now you eat good too." It was the first time I'd heard her speak English, and I was startled. I'd just assumed she spoke only in her native tongue. I was relieved to know that we'd be able to communicate without Estelle serving as an interpreter.

She handed me a plate of hot food and a steaming mug of coffee, which I put on a large crate. She moved another crate next to it for me to sit on. The plate was heaped with fried eggs, bacon, and hash brown potatoes. It was a magnificent feast, and I wasted no time showing her my appreciation. She watched approvingly as I ate. I couldn't remember food ever tasting better.

When I could eat no more, she grunted agreeably and said, "You eat good. I bring more later." I looked at my watch and was surprised to see it was nearly noon. I'd only had a few hours sleep, but the rest was just what my body needed.

Mona Dove took my plate and said, "Men eat soon. You stay." She retreated up the ladder, closed the trap door, and was gone, leaving behind a large metal pitcher filled with hot coffee. I eagerly poured myself another cup.

I savored the meal I'd just eaten and the warmth and pleasant aroma of the coffee. Afterward, I resumed my consideration of our options. From what Estelle told me, the only viable way out of that place was the way I'd come, but that route took us right back to the raging underwater river, and I couldn't think of any way we could navigate it to safety. Then I remembered the hole I'd made in the rock pile, and I hoped a roaming guard wouldn't spot it. If that happened, our one possible escape route would be gone, and the guards would be warned of a possible intruder. That meant we needed to move quickly.

Counting myself, there were seven of us, and we were only as strong as our weakest link. Because of her age, Mona Dove couldn't move fast, nor could little William who, Estelle told me, walked with a limp due to a severely deformed foot. The old man – Isaac – was ill and would need help moving quickly. I planned on asking Jacob and Luther, the two younger men, to take on this task. I'd look after Mona Dove, while Estelle would have to help little William. Our escape would require a great deal of physical exertion, and teamwork would be essential if we had any chance of getting out of there alive.

We couldn't overpower the guards – there were too many of them and they were too well armed, and we had no weapons. The only thing we had going for us was stealth and the element of surprise. I figured we'd need a good head start – at least an hour – before the night guard knew the Indians were missing. Our best chance was to be on the move an hour or two after the camp was asleep. I planned to tell Estelle to have the others wrap all their belongings inside their blankets so a guard making casual inspection would see what appeared to be six sleeping bodies. We'd have to travel lightly, so it would be best to leave behind anything they didn't absolutely need. With any luck, we'd be well on our way before the guards realized what had happened. I subconsciously reached into my pants pocket, rubbed Charles Bird's amulet, and hoped the gods were still watching over me.

I had barely managed to squeeze through the small opening in the rock blocking the mine shaft, and the physical limitations of Isaac, Mona Dove and little William would require us to remove more of the rock before we could all manage to get through. That would take precious time we couldn't spare, but it was something I'd need to factor into my timetable. It would also take tools we didn't have, but I hoped I could find something when I reconnoitered the area later that evening.

Once on the other side, we'd need something to block the guards from following us. I hoped to find some dynamite and primer cord in the storage area where I'd hidden the day before. I added those items to my mental wish list, and went on to consider some of the other obstacles facing us.

The underground river seemed to be our only real way out of the mountain, but there was no way of knowing where the river might take us. It was entirely conceivable that we might end up going deeper into the mountain and never reach the outside world, but I was betting it flowed into another river somewhere on the outside. The river had nearly cost me my life, and even the strongest swimmer would be no match for the raging current. We would need a sturdy raft or something like it to carry us down the river, and who knew what other perils the river might hold for us? Finding such a vessel in the heart of an underground mine might be unlikely, but I had an idea that might just work.

I wanted to go over the basics of my plan with Estelle and Mona Dove so they could convince the others to go along. I didn't think it would be a problem, since they already knew what fate awaited them at the hands of Lester Crow and his men. In the meantime, I needed to think about a few things. I was still going over the details in my mind when fatigue once again overtook me, and I fell into a deep sleep.

I felt a dull pain in my ribs and woke with a start to see Mona Dove poking me with her forefinger. She handed me another platter of steaming, hot food and sat a fresh container of coffee on the crate next to me. "Men go now," she said. "In two hour, we sleep. You come then."

I told her I'd be there as soon as it was safe. Before I did that, I needed to do some looking around. I waited until after 10:00 PM, then climbed the ladder to the kitchen. It was dark outside, and quiet. The camp had settled in for the evening, but I knew at least one guard would be making his rounds, and I had to be careful to avoid being seen.

When I was sure I could make it to safely, I headed for the storage area. I kept a low profile, stayed in the darkness of the shadows, and reached my destination safely. I caught a glimpse of the guard on the far side of the camp, so I ducked behind a stack of oil drums until he was no longer in sight.

I roamed quietly in and around a collection of packing crates, fifty gallon fuel drums, and empty packing boxes. At first glance, I saw nothing we could use in our escape, and I felt the onset of defeat growing in my stomach. But my spirits rose when I stumbled across a crate of dynamite and primer cord – exactly what I needed. I found an old burlap bag and placed six sticks of dynamite and fifty feet of primer cord into it and took it with me while I completed my search. In a small tool shed I found a miner's pick axe and a couple of shovels which we might be able to use to remove more rock blocking the mine shaft.

I was thinking about where to secure the tools and dynamite when I was startled by voices and the sound of footsteps approaching. Taking the bag with me, I crawled inside an open packing crate and prayed that I wouldn't be discovered. I held my breath and tried to keep my heart from beating like a jungle drum.

A man's voice said angrily, "What's so goddamn important, Peters? It's almost midnight. Can't this wait until morning?" I recognized Lester Crow's caustic voice immediately.

"Take it easy, Lester," Peters said. "I have to be careful when I come out here – I'm not sure, but they may be following me."

Lester Crow snorted decisively. "Keep it quiet– I don't want the others to hear us."

Peters went on, his voice an octave lower. "I'm telling you, Lester, it's only a matter of time before the law finds out what you an' B. J. are up to. There's some kinda investigation goin' on at the plant, and I need ta get out 'fore they come lookin' for me."

The response was cold and dagger sharp. "It don't make no difference what you think, Peters. Your job is to keep the Donovan people off balance and ours is to run the mine. When the boss says it's time to shut down, that's when we shut down – not before!"

But Peters didn't back down – he didn't seem to be intimidated by Lester Crow. "You know damn well you'd have had a hellava tough time with Donovan if I hadn't been working on the inside. The phoney treaty and doctored plot surveys cost them at least six months."

"The boss is well aware of your contribution," Crow said with annoyance. "And you've been paid well for your services – don't forget that."

But Peters didn't agree. "Now that you mention it, Lester, I'm not sure my pay is equal to my involvement – I think I deserve more than I'm gettin'."

"I'll give the boss your message," Lester Crow replied mechanically. "In the meantime, you need to get back to Donovan and find out what you can about this investigation. We can find a way to sidetrack it."

"I'll see what I can do," Peters said, sighing deeply, "but I'm not optimistic.

Security has really tightened up in the last couple-a days, and they're bein' very quiet about it. I think they know something's goin' on, but they haven't figured out what. It may not be long 'fore they do." Lester Crow said, "This so-called investigation may be just a bluff because they're afraid they may lose their appeal. If that happens, we may not need to close down this operation as soon as we thought. The longer we keep the negotiations going, the more gold we take out of this mine, and the richer we'll all be."

I heard them laugh and slap each other's palms, then their footsteps gradually faded into the darkness of the night. When they were gone, I thought about what I'd just heard. Tall Horse must have had the man named Peters working inside the Donovan Corporation to sabotage the company's efforts to win claim to the disputed land. Then it dawned on me that this man Peters must be the mysterious "Pete" mentioned in Ben Griffin's diary. If so, he'd been working for B. J. Tall Horse all along, and paid very well for his services. But, if that were the case, why would he leak the story to Ben Griffin? Was he a double agent? Whose side was Peters on? Did Peters know that he could wind up an accessory to murder? There were still questions that remained unanswered, but they'd have to wait.

When I was sure it was safe to move about, I returned the tools to the tool shed, along with the bag of dynamite and primer cord, hoping they'd still be there in 24 hours. Then I headed back to the Indians' tents to talk to Estelle and Mona Dove. I knew time was running out, but I needed Estelle to explain my plan to the others, so they'd be ready to go the next night.

CHAPTER FORTY

The camp was deep in sleep, and the guard was nowhere to be seen when I made my way back to the Indians' tents. I carefully slipped inside, and went to Estelle, who woke quickly.

"I need to talk to you and Mona Dove," I said. She nodded and reached over to rouse the older woman. This time the boy who slept next to her rose as well but remained quiet. Mona Dove eyed me expectantly.

"I have a plan," I said, keeping my voice low. "It's risky and it will be difficult, but it's the only way I can think of to get us out of here alive."

The two women exchanged glances and Estelle spoke. "You are in much danger here, Mr. Harrison. We know you are willing to risk your life for us, and we are grateful."

She paused a moment, then said, "We believe the chances for our survival are not good. When Lester Crow and B. J. Tall Horse close this mine, we will be killed so no one will know what they did here."

She looked me directly in the eyes and said, "We have decided that we must go with you, Mr. Harrison, if we are to survive. We are prepared to place our lives in your hands."

I was relieved they'd decided to put their trust in me. It would improve our chances if everyone agreed with the plan, and it was time to give them the details. "We need the men in on this too. Can we get you all together?"

Mona Dove shook her head and Estelle explained, "No, that is not possible. The men – Luther, Isaac, and Jacob – know we are meeting. They have agreed as well, but we risk discovery to have them here. We will . . ."

As if to make her point, we were alerted by the sound of approaching footsteps. We all dropped to the ground and huddled together breathlessly. I pressed myself behind Estelle as she pulled the heavy blanket over us.

The footsteps drew closer, and the beam of a flashlight played on the canvas of the tent. The guard stopped a few feet away. I was gripped by panic, and I tried to remember if I'd closed the tent flap firmly behind me.

I heard water rushing, then realized the guard was urinating in the shadows just a few feet away. The torrent eventually slowed to a trickle, then stopped. Meanwhile we waited, afraid to move or to breathe. Moments later, the footsteps retreated, and we all sighed with relief.

Estelle was right. It could be dangerous if all of us met at the same time.

"If you explain your plan to us, we will go over it with the men. They will do exactly as you say. They can be trusted completely."

Mona Dove said nothing, but nodded, her expressionless eyes locked on mine.

The boy was listening intently to our conversation, but hadn't said a word. Finally, he spoke up. "I understand what you have said, Mr. Harrison." His voice was calm and suggested a maturity beyond his years. As if reading my thoughts, he said, "You do not need to worry about me."

Estelle introduced me to her cousin, William. "He is a good boy," she said proudly. "He will not be a problem." I spent the next several minutes outlining my plan to them. They asked a few questions to make sure they understood but did not question my judgment. When I finished, I was confident they all knew what had to be done. Estelle agreed to fill the men in the next day during their meal break. I told them I'd come for them the following night, shortly after midnight, and lead them to the storage area. From there, we'd gather up the few tools and supplies I'd collected and make our way into the tunnel. I hoped we'd be able to enlarge the opening enough for all of us to get through without alerting the guards. Fortunately, I hadn't spotted them making a regular check of the storage area during the night.

When I finished explaining my plan, I looked into their eyes and saw no fear or apprehension, but only determined resolve, and I began to feel good about our chances.

Then Estelle asked, "What about food?"

It was so simple I hadn't even considered it.

"Good thought," I said. "Can you save some of your food from the evening meal to bring with you? We'll be traveling as fast as possible.

Mona Dove said, "I bring food."

I didn't bother to pursue it. I sensed she knew exactly what to bring, and I was glad to have her make the offer.

It was time for me to go, so I told them goodbye and carefully opened the tent flap a crack to make sure the guard was nowhere in sight. When I was sure it was safe, I crept back to the kitchen and made my way into the cellar. Once again, alone with my thoughts, I felt both elation and apprehension. It was one thing to place your own life at risk, but it was something very different to put innocent people in harm's way, even though the alternative meant almost certain death for all of them. Good plan or not, it was the only one that afforded us any chance for survival, and it was up to me to make it work.

Fatigue quickly overcame me, and I slept peacefully, confident that the gods would watch over us the following night. I awoke to the sounds of voices overhead. It was 7:00 AM, and Mona Dove was no doubt preparing breakfast for the guards and workers. I kept myself occupied by going over my mental checklist of everything that needed to be done before and during our escape. My stomach was in knots and my nerves were approaching overload.

As she had done the day before, Mona Dove made periodic trips down to the cellar to keep me supplied with hot food, water and coffee. Later, I tried to rest, but nervous energy kept me awake and on edge. As evening approached, I was unable to contain the sense of excitement that overcame me, and I remembered how I'd felt before running onto the football field just before the big game with our high school rival. But this was no game, and the consequences of this evening's contest were much more serious than anything I'd ever faced before.

Despite my anxiety about the chance of failure, and the adrenalin rushing through my veins, I managed to get a few hours sleep. It was midnight when I awoke, and it was time to put my plan into effect. I was aware that the lives of six innocent people were at stake, but I tried not to let that fact deter me. I quietly climbed out of the cellar, exited the kitchen, and paused for a minute, listening for any sound that might indicate the approach of a guard. When I was satisfied it was safe to proceed, I crept back to the Indians' tents and crawled inside to find Estelle, Mona Dove, and little William waiting expectantly, their eyes shining with excitement.

"We are ready, Mr. Harrison," Estelle whispered. "The men are ready also."

She nodded in the direction of the other tent.

"We'll wait until after the guard makes his next round, then we'll go," I said with as much confidence as I could muster.

Both Estelle and Mona nodded their understanding, and we all huddled together in the warmth of their blankets, doing our best to suppress our apprehension as we waited for the guard's approach.

In less than thirty minutes, we heard the familiar footsteps approaching, and we reclined together on the ground, covering ourselves with the blankets, hoping the guard would pass quickly by. The flashlight beam played around on the tents, and we waited breathlessly. When the guard satisfied himself that all was as it should be, he left as quickly as he'd come, and we all breathed a collective sigh of relief.

We waited another ten minutes, then I motioned for Estelle, Mona Dove and little William to follow me out. Estelle signaled for Jacob, Luther and Isaac to follow. I motioned for them to keep as low as possible and to stay in the shadows as we made our way toward the storage area. We had less than eighty yards to our destination, but progress was painfully slow, owing to the inability of the little band to move with any speed at all. I prayed that we wouldn't be spotted as my escape plan began to unfold. I was alert for the slightest sign of approaching danger, while my heartbeat inside my chest with the force and tempo of a jungle drum. The more distance we could place between ourselves and the guards, the safer we'd be.

When we reached the storage area, I noticed Mona Dove carrying a leather bag with a shoulder strap, and guessed it was the food she'd promised to bring. I didn't bother wondering what was in it and hoped we'd reach safety soon enough without needing any food, but it was good to have, just in case.

I pointed to the bag and suggested to Estelle that she carry it, but Mona Dove pulled the strap tightly to her shoulder and said, "No, I carry."

I motioned for Estelle to have the group wait out of sight behind some oil drums while I retrieved the burlap bag containing the dynamite and fuse cord and the tools I'd hidden on my last visit. Then we proceeded to the place in the tunnel where I'd entered two days before. I was relieved to find it just as I'd left it.

I pointed to the small hole through which I'd come and whispered to them, "We must make this large enough for all of us to get through safely." Estelle and Mona Dove nodded silently, then looked to the men and repeated my instructions. They too nodded and appeared undaunted by the task before us.

I decided not to risk the noise that a pick-axe might make on rock, and I instructed Jacob and Luther to work with me by moving one rock at a time from the opening. It would take longer, but it was necessary to ensure that we were not discovered. Meanwhile, Estelle and little William helped by moving the smaller rocks out of our way. Mona Dove tended to Isaac, who sat on a large boulder and watched our progress with intense interest. The need to work quietly made our progress slower than I'd hoped, but in less than an hour, I felt we'd removed enough rock from around the opening. I motioned for Estelle to enter, followed by Mona Dove. If the two of them made it through, the rest should have no problem.

Estelle made it through easily, but Mona Dove's age and girth made her progress much more difficult, and for a moment I was sure we'd need to remove more rock. But then, with Estelle pulling from her side and Luther pushing from our side, she made it, and we all breathed a bit easier. I sent William next, who zipped through easily. Then I motioned for Luther to assist Isaac. Luther managed to get to the other side, then gently pulled the old man through after him, while I pushed from the rear. Meanwhile, precious minutes had slipped away. Then I motioned for Jacob to go on through, and I followed closely behind him. Once on the other side, I stopped only long enough to allow my racing heart to resume something close to its normal rhythm, while I mentally celebrated our first, small victory, and hoped for many more.

I found the old creosote torch where I'd abandoned it and used one of my few remaining matches to ignite it, hoping it would burn long enough for us to reach the river. When it eventually glowed warmly in the eerie darkness, I whispered to Estelle to have Luther use it to lead them down the tunnel as quickly as possible. She obeyed without a word and they were on their way.

I retrieved the burlap bag from the other side, withdrew the five sticks of dynamite, wrapped the primer cord firmly around them, and placed the bundle in a small opening in the rocks where the blast should effectively seal the tunnel. By the time the guards were able to figure out what had happened and dig their way through the blasted rock, I hoped we'd be well on our way to freedom.

I'd never worked with dynamite before, but I'd attended an anti- terrorism training course as a cop and they covered the use of dynamite well enough for me to know how to attach the basting cap and primer cord, but I wasn't at all sure how long it would take the fifty foot fuse to ignite the dynamite, nor did I know how old the fuse and dynamite were, nor how their age might affect the timing of the blast. I prayed the primer cord was long enough to give us at least a ten-minute head start. By that time, I figured we'd be more than halfway to the river, even traveling as slow as we must. I decided to wait a few minutes before lighting the fuse to give the Indians just a little more time, but my plan evaporated in a flash when I heard men shouting, and I knew the Indians' escape had been discovered. I was gripped by cold fear, frozen in place, unable to think. Stark images of disaster flashed through my mind as I feared with crushing despair that my plan to save the Indians was doomed.

CHAPTER FORTY-ONE

There was no time to lose. Using my pocketknife, I cut off all but five feet of the fuse cord and quickly lit it. I watched it long enough to see that it was burning, then raced to catch up with Estelle and the others, knowing full well that our time frame had been severely altered by the premature discovery of their escape. Just as I reached them, the thunderous roar of the blast echoed off the walls of the mine shaft and rumbled beneath our feet. Estelle and Mona Dove cried out in fright.

"We've no time to waste," I said. "We must move quickly."

It was a command I didn't need to give. The sound of the blast jolted them into action, and they quickened their pace in recognition of the danger they now faced.

The air grew cold, and damp and the creosote torch Jacob carried flickered as shadows danced crazily on the tunnel walls. Then I heard the faint sound of rushing water, and I knew we were getting close to the river. The Indians were moving as fast as they could, and the exhaustion was showing on their faces. I knew they were nearing the limits of their physical endurance, and I prayed it would be enough.

We approached a bend in the tunnel, and I spotted the ore cart I'd seen when I first entered the tunnel, and I knew the river was a short way ahead. Just then, we heard two additional blasts in close succession, and I knew instantly what it meant. The guards were blasting an opening in the tunnel and would be on the way after us in a matter of minutes. Time was quickly running out. I looked into the eyes of Estelle and the others, and it was clear that they fully grasped the danger we faced.

The next few minutes would mean the difference between life and death for all of us. I ran to the ore cart and shouted for the others to follow. I directed Jacob to help Isaac climb inside while I lifted little Michael in behind him. Sensing my plan, Luther helped Mona Dove up and over the railing and Estelle climbed in after her. I motioned for Luther, who looked to be the strongest, to stay with me.

The ore cart was equipped with a wooden brake lever that held the cart in place. I pushed hard against it to get it to release, but it wouldn't budge. Luther grabbed the lever and pulled while I pushed and eventually, we were rewarded by a loud creaking sound as the lever slowly moved and the brake was released. I motioned Luther to follow me, and we put our shoulders to the cart and attempted to push it down the tracks toward the river, some forty feet ahead. There was no telling how long the cart had sat here, frozen in time, and it moved very little as we pushed against it with every ounce of our strength. I was beginning to think it was going to be impossible to move when the ancient metal wheels shrieked in protest, then slowly began to turn. In my imagination, I could see the faces of Lester Crow's men in hot pursuit, and I pushed even harder against the rear of the cart.

I slipped and fell, and Luther helped me to my feet. We continued pushing the cart, and it began to offer less resistance. In another few seconds, the cart was rolling freely down the track, and we ran to catch up. I motioned for Luther to get aboard, and he pulled me up after him. We both fell into The waiting arms of Estelle and Mona Dove as the car continued to increase its speed. In another fifteen seconds, I could see the churning water of the river just ahead and I motioned for everyone to hold on to something and keep their heads down low, just as the cart reached the end of the track and splashed into the raging river.

We were jolted by the impact, and the Indians cried out involuntarily as the ore cart was thrown about by the fast-moving current. It bobbed and spun like a cork, but remained upright, and I breathed a sigh of relief. We were all drenched by the splashing, churning water, but I saw a look of hope in the Indians' eyes as they realized we were one step closer to freedom.

The torch was lost when we hit the water, and we were in total darkness. There was no way to know how wide the river was at this point, nor where it would take us, but we were putting distance between us and the guards, who'd be hard pressed to find a way to follow us once they realized the river was our path of escape.

To our relief, after its initial plunge into the strong current, the sturdy cart held steady, from time to time bumping into unseen objects, and throwing us about, but maintaining its buoyancy and continuing us along to our unknown destination. As we bobbed about, like a bottle in an angry sea, I clung tightly to the side of the cart with one hand and to Estelle with the other, and wondered where the river would take us, and what dangers might lay ahead. Luck, or perhaps something more powerful, had been with us so far, but somehow, I knew our ordeal was far from over. We soon entered an area where the water was very choppy, and the cart rocked and swayed violently, and I feared we'd be thrown into the raging waters. We desperately clung to the sides of the cart and to each other as we were jerked and bucked savagely by the turbulent, unrelenting waters. Something warned me that disaster lurked just ahead.

Then I heard a roaring sound, but at first, I didn't recognize what it was. As it grew louder, I realized we were approaching rapids, and my premonition was quickly becoming a reality. Estelle's grip on my arm tightened, and I could feel the tension coursing through her veins. The roaring sound grew louder by the second. I knew the rapids were directly ahead, and I shouted for everyone to hold on tight and keep down to maintain a low center of gravity. Blanketed in total darkness, we had no way to navigate through the treacherous shoals and were at the mercy of the raging river. Our chances of surviving this new danger were not good, and I whispered a quiet prayer for God's intervention.

The impact came with savage fury as our small ship was thrown against unseen obstacles. We gasped for breath as chilly water rushed over us. The roar of the crash was deafening and was accompanied by the unmistakable sound of splintering wood. Our vessel tipped wildly to one side and then another, then righted itself, and I prayed we hadn't lost anyone. But the river wasn't done with us, and we were thrown savagely against yet another object. The second impact was even greater than the first, and the sound of the cart being torn apart was terrifying. Boards were being ripped loose from the bottom of the cart, and it quickly filled with water. One more impact would surely rip the small craft into pieces, and our rush to freedom would come to a sudden, violent end.

There was a brief lull and no one spoke. Suddenly we were jerked forward by a huge torrent of icy water and I feared the worst. The third collision was worse than the first two. It came without warning and sounded like a clap of thunder. There was no time to react. I lost my grip and was thrown overboard, and I felt myself pulled down into the very depths of the raging river. I struggled to hold my breath and fought my way back to the surface, only to be pushed violently back down again. I struggled back to the surface and gasped desperately for air before I engulfed for the third time.

With one last burst of energy, l managed to reach the surface again, sucking in air with heaving, gasping sobs. The current was still strong, but I'd managed to survive the rapids, and I was able to stay afloat. I was struck violently by something solid and heavy, and I reached for it, grabbing onto a wooden beam that may have been ripped from the ore cart when it had been dashed against the rocks and ripped into a dozen pieces. I thought about the others, and I was overcome with grief, fearing they couldn't have survived in the raging waters. My mind was filled with horrifying images of them fighting for their lives, then being swept under to their death. I knew I'd always feel responsible for the tragic loss of these innocent people.

I was physically and emotionally exhausted, but I held on to the beam with all the strength I had left. The current was still strong, and I was barely able to keep my head above the water. Then I noticed something different about the darkness around me. I looked up and was amazed to see a star twinkling in the deep blue sky. I'd emerged from the mountain and was gazing at a sky I thought I might never see again. From the light of a quarter moon, I could see that the river was about thirty feet across. I struggled to maneuver myself toward the nearest shore, but it was filled with heavy boulders, and there were rocky shoals just ahead.

I didn't like my chances of making it through them alive, so I looked for some way to reach shore before being thrown into them. I spotted a large oak tree on the riverbank that thrust its bony branches out over the river. As I passed under it, I reached as high as I could and grabbed the branch and clung to it with all the strength I had left. I watched as the wood beam hurtled toward the rocky shoals and hit them with an explosive crash, and I shuddered involuntarily at the sound.

I was swaying just inches above the water, holding fast to the tree branch, hoping it would support me, and praying for a miracle. Inch by inch, hand over hand, I began to move toward the shore, summoning up every ounce of strength I could muster. My arms ached and daggers of pain shot through every muscle of my body. I was just a few feet from the shoreline, but it seemed much farther. Directly below was a pile of jagged rocks. Another twelve inches and I would be close enough to drop safely to the ground. But just as safety seemed within reach, I heard a loud crack that sounded like a gunshot. As the rotted limb gave way, I fell toward the rocks below, bracing myself for the pain that was sure to come.

The tree limb partially cushioned my fall, but a sharp pain seared through my leg. I reached down and felt blood beginning to ooze from an gash on my thigh. It was soft tissue damage, and no bones or muscles appeared to have been injured, but I needed to stop the bleeding. I struggled to tear off a piece of lining from my jacket and placed it over the wound, using another strip to tie it in place. The wound throbbed painfully, but the makeshift bandage stopped the bleeding, and I was thankful that my injuries hadn't been more severe. I rested for a while, then pulled myself up a steep embankment to a grassy knoll overlooking the river. I lay there under a star-studded sky. The scene was peaceful, but my thoughts were filled with horrible images of Estelle, Mona Dove, and the others who'd died because of me, and I began to cry.

CHAPTER FORTY-TWO

I awoke from a fitful sleep as a freezing wind rushed through the canyon and gripped me in its icy fingers, making me shiver in my wet clothes. Somewhere in the distance I heard voices and wondered if the sprits were coming for me.

Then I heard a woman's voice, and I knew it was Estelle. I struggled to my feet, ignoring the pain that wracked my body. I desperately wanted to find her – to make sure she was alright – but I dared not make a sound, fearful that, by now, Lester Crow's men might be anywhere.

A pale mist shrouded the eastern horizon, and dawn would come soon, and with daylight there'd be increased danger. Then more voices were carried on the wind, and I walked slowly along the river, keeping a low as possible, using a large rock outcropping and scrub oak for concealment. The voices were closer, but where were they? Was I dreaming? Perhaps my mind was playing tricks on me, and I was actually hearing the voices of Lester Crow's men.

Then someone said, "Mr. Harrison!"

It was unmistakably Estelle, but I saw nothing. "Mr. Harrison! Here! It's me, Estelle!"

I trained my eyes on the area where the voice was coming from and then, in the dim light of the predawn, I saw a slight movement just ahead, coming from a pile of rocks. At first, I was not sure what I was seeing. Was it a mirage? Was I in some sort of trance? Then a small hand emerged from the rocks and waved to me. I drew closer and watched in disbelief as little William emerged from behind the pile of rocks, smiling from ear to ear. I'll never forget that smile and how I felt at that moment. I was overcome by relief, joy and wonderment, and I ran to him and gathered him in my arms, thankful to find him alive.

The rock pile concealed a shallow cave that extended back into the shoreline. A small opening was just large enough for someone to squeeze through. Little William motioned for me to follow him. Once inside, I was amazed to find them all there, even Isaac. I couldn't hold back the tears that streamed down my dirt-caked cheeks. My prayers had been answered.

"We thought you had drowned, Mr. Harrison," Estelle said. She had tears in her eyes too, but they were tears of happiness.

"And I thought the same about all of you," I said, my voice quivering with emotion. "I was sure you'd been crushed on the rocks or drowned in the river."

Estelle noticed blood coming from the cut on my leg and tore a strip of cloth from her jacket to use as a fresh bandage. While she worked, she explained that the impact that had thrown me clear had ripped the cart into two pieces. One of the pieces was large enough to form a makeshift raft that carried them down the river until it emerged from the mountain and finally struck a sand bar near our present location. They'd all survived the ordeal with only a few minor cuts and bruises. It was, I knew, a miracle. Had Charles Bird's amulet been responsible? I didn't know, but I mumbled another prayer of thanks. "We found this cave and decided it would be best to remain here during the day and to travel only at night," Estelle said.

"Good idea," I agreed. Through the rocks I could see the first golden rays of the new day begin to pour over the valley. "I'll bet Lester Crow's men will be out searching the area and this is as good a place as any for us to hide."

I surveyed our surroundings and assessed our situation. All in all, we'd been extremely fortunate. We'd made our escape, and the explosion delayed the guards' pursuit long enough for us to reach the river. The trip down river had been rough, but we'd made it out alive and with no serious injuries. We'd survived much better than I had any right to expect, but our situation was still precarious. Somehow, we needed to find our way to safety without being detected by Lester Crow's men, and that wouldn't be easy.

Once the guards figured out how we'd escaped, they'd concentrate their search efforts along the river. The more distance we could put between us and our present location, the better off we'd be. But we still had to travel during darkness and find a place to hide during daylight. To make matters worse, I had no idea where we were or how far we'd have to go before reaching safety, and traveling with Mona Dove, Isaac and little William would be a slow and arduous process.

I figured we were safe for the time being because the cave entrance was well concealed. Luther had placed several large bushes across the entrance, and it was unlikely that the casual observer would spot our hiding place. I was confident that we were as secure as we could be under the circumstances. "What about food?" I asked. I hadn't eaten in several hours, and we needed our energy if we were to survive. Estelle handed me the shoulder bag Mona Dove had carried earlier and said, "We have a few things." I was amazed that it was still intact and wondered what it contained. I looked in the bag and was pleasantly surprised to find three cans of peaches, several granola bars, a box of vanilla wafers, a small candle, a large container of beef jerky and one canteen of water. It wasn't much, but it would do for now.

I used a utility knife from the bag to open one of the cans of peaches and passed it around, telling Estelle to have everyone help themselves. When the can came back to me, there was plenty left, so I took some and passed the can around again. We ate with our fingers, but no one complained. The peaches were delicious, and we savored every mouthful.

Next, I passed around the box of vanilla wafers and told everyone to take a few. We ate slowly, relishing each small morsel, fully aware that it might be some time before we ate again. Finally, I passed the canteen around. The water was cold, pure, and tasted better than anything I could remember. We'd need to refill the canteen before we left the riverbank, as water would be essential to our survival.

It wasn't much of a meal, but it helped quell the hunger pangs that had been rampaging through my stomach. After food, rest was the next order of business. I figured we had a good twelve hours before it would be safe to move about. We agreed we'd each sleep a few hours, with at least two people always remaining awake to be on alert for any signs of Lester Crow's men. After some discussion, it was decided that the watches be divided between I, Jacob, Luther and Estelle, but Mona Dove insisted that she and William would take their turn. Only Isaac, who looked even more feeble than he had before, was exempted. Estelle insisted that I sleep first, and I didn't argue. I was exhausted, and I knew I couldn't go any farther without rest. After we worked out a schedule giving everyone a turn at keeping watch, I retreated to the rear of the cave, stretched out on the cold, damp earth, and feel into a deep sleep.

I woke with a start as someone grabbed my arm. I nearly cried out, but Estelle clamped her hand over my mouth, then lowered her face to mine and placed the tip of her finger over her lips. Her eyes were wide with fright, and I was immediately on alert. I looked around and saw that the others were frozen in place. In another instant I knew why. The sound of men's voices and the snorting of horses and the clatter of their hooves were unmistakable. They were near enough to hear fragments of their conversation.

I couldn't tell how many there were, but they were moving fast. I unconsciously held my breath, even though the cave was well concealed, and it was unlikely that anyone on horseback traveling fast would see anything to raise their suspicion. But if they took the time to search the area on foot, we'd be in serious jeopardy.

Fortunately for us, they had a lot of area to cover. Within five minutes the voices drifted off, and the clatter of the horses' hooves faded away. We all exchanged glances, sighed deeply and smiled nervously.

I waited another thirty minutes, then moved the bushes and looked outside – the shadows were growing long. It would be dark soon, but we needed to wait a few more hours until it would be safe to move. If Lester Crow's men pitched camp nearby, they'd probably post a guard, and we'd have to travel quietly and be continually on the alert.

I asked Estelle to light the candle; then I asked Mona Dove if she had any idea where we were. She nodded and, with a sharp stick, traced a crude map in the dirt.

"We here," she said, pointing to a large X. "This is river." She scratched a crooked line. "Reservation here." She drew a large box and then traced a line from the X to the box.

"But is it safe to return to the reservation?" I asked. "Won't Lester Crow's men be looking for us there?"

Estelle spoke up. "We will go to Charles Bird. He will help us." "Yes," I replied, "but if B. J. Tall Horse finds out . . ."

Estelle shook her head. "Many people fear B. J. Tall Horse, Mr. Harrison, but Charles Bird is not one of them. He will see that we are not harmed."

I reflected back on my meeting with the mysterious Charles Bird and decided that what Estelle said made sense. Charles Bird was probably the best person on the reservation to help us out, if we could only get to him safely.

"How far is it to the reservation?" I asked Mona Dove, pointing to the line she'd drawn.

"Ten mile, maybe fifteen," she said impassively. "That doesn't seem too bad," I said. "If we make good time, we should be able to cover that in five hours, six at the most. We might make the reservation by dawn."

"Not so easy," Mona Dove said, shaking her head. "This very bad country.

Many hills and canyons. Going be very hard and very slow."

This was something I hadn't counted on. Between Isaac and Mona Dove, we wouldn't be able to make good time, even on level terrain. Traveling up and down hills and canyons and across a rocky countryside would make it even more difficult. We'd be lucky to cover five miles in a single evening. It could take us two or even three nights to make the reservation, assuming we could find adequate cover and a place to rest. I tried not to show my disappointment, but the others could read my thoughts. Nevertheless, we'd come too far to get discouraged now. I looked each of them in the eye and knew they were as determined as I was to finish what we'd started.

I turned to Estelle. "Maybe it would be faster if I went on alone and brought back help."

She immediately shook her head, rejecting my idea. "We will all go. We will make good time, and we will find another cave to rest in by tomorrow. There are many caves in these hills – too many for them to search. We will be safe."

I thought about it for a minute, then decided she was right – it was best that we stay together. If something were to happen to me, what then – and how would they know? Just as I'd originally planned, we'd succeed or fail as a team.

When it was time to eat again, we finished off the first can of peaches and had a few more of the vanilla wafers. I passed around the beef jerky followed by the canteen. It was enough to sustain us for the time being. Finally, we each had a bite of one of the granola bars. It was sweet tasting and would give us added energy for what lay ahead.

I took my turn at watch and Jacob and Luther kept me company while Mona Dove, Estelle, Isaac, and little William slept. A sense of comradery that transcended our language barrier and cultural differences was now binding us together. We sat silently, each with our own thoughts, each praying that the gods would continue to watch over us until we reached the end of our journey.

CHAPTER FORTY-THREE

The night was overcast, and we had a strong breeze at our backs. A hazy moon was barely visible through a thick layer of clouds. The lack of illumination worked in our favor, and I silently gave thanks for this small blessing. Our little procession moved slowly across an endless series of hills and valleys that rippled the terrain like a huge washboard. The ground was rocky and covered with thick underbrush, making it painfully slow. Mona Dove was a strong woman, but her age limited her mobility. Little William quietly hobbled along, managing to keep up better than I'd expected, and I admired his courage.

We walked without speaking. Silence, like darkness, was our ally. Our safety depended on being able to move without being seen or heard. I didn't know where Lester Crow's guards were, but I was certain they were not far away. He couldn't afford to have us escape, and he wouldn't rest until we were found.

The hills were dotted with clusters of pine and aspen, and we used the trees for cover wherever possible. Following Mona Dove's directions, Estelle led the way, and I followed her, with William and Mona Dove following me. Luther and Jacob helping Isaac, brought up the rear. Mona Dove seemed to know the area well, and she had good instincts. Her courage and determination were an inspiration to me.

We'd been walking for a little more than three hours when I called for a rest break. We had arrived at a thick stand of cottonwood trees, several of which had fallen to form a natural shelter, offering both protection from the elements and concealment. I passed around more peaches, beef jerky, and vanilla wafers. We all ate silently, thankful for what little we had. Then I passed the canteen around and we drank sparingly, not knowing when we'd find water again. When we finished, we conversed in hushed tones.

"We're making good progress," I whispered, hoping to buoy the confidence. Mona Dove nodded but said nothing. The exertion of our journey was tiring to her, but she didn't complain, and I marveled at her physical and emotional endurance.

Mona Dove pointed ahead and whispered something to Estelle, who said, "Mona Dove says Elkhorn Peak lies between us and the reservation. There is an old trail that was used long ago by our ancestors, and later by the fur traders. It winds around the base of the mountain. Once we are on this trail, we should reach the reservation in another four hours."

It seemed so near, yet so far. Estelle continued, "She says there are many caves below Elkhorn Peak where we can rest during the day."

"We can probably go another three hours before dawn," I said. "Is that enough time to reach the trail?"

We all looked at Mona Dove for an answer, then she said, "Maybe – will be hard, but we try."

I wasn't overwhelmed by her confidence, but I knew she was being realistic. We might have to push on harder than we'd been doing, but I didn't want to think about the alternative. We only had enough food for another 24 hours.

With a little extra effort, we just might make the reservation by then – if Lester Crow's men didn't find us first.

We couldn't afford to linger any longer, so we resumed our journey. I did what I could to pick up the pace. Pain knifed through my leg with each step, but I forced myself to concentrate on placing one foot in front of the other. Despite the injury to my leg, I was in as good a shape as any of the others, and I had to set an example for them if I expected them to follow my lead. We had to make Elkhorn Peak before first light.

A pale quarter moon was partially obscured by broken clouds, providing just enough light for us to find our way along the difficult terrain. The cool, crisp night air was invigorating and helped quicken our pace. Before long, we were climbing a rocky slope cut into the side of a towering mountain. This had to be Elkhorn Peak. The trail was narrow and overgrown with underbrush and cluttered with fallen rock and dead tree limbs, making our progress even slower than before. We were forced to stop frequently – more than I wanted – for rest. I watched Mona Dove and I knew she had to be exhausted, but she showed no sign of it.

Against the eastern horizon, a faint pink line marked the beginning of a new day. We'd need to find refuge soon. Just ahead was a broad clearing. Beyond that, a sheer granite cliff stretched high into the sky. A series of dark crevices pockmarked the face of the cliff. This was our destination, but we were running out of time. The pink edge of the eastern horizon was brighter now, and dawn would be upon us all too soon. We were physically exhausted and needed to stop and rest, but we dared not. Our very lives depended on moving as quickly as possible. Once again, I forced myself to quicken the pace and hoped the others would be able to do the same. They seemed to share my sense of urgency and somehow managed to move along faster than before.

Just as we reached the clearing, the pristine silence exploded violently with a loud crack of a rifle. I instinctively ducked and turned my head in time to see Luther topple forward, a dark stain spreading over his right arm. Another loud crack echoed from the canyon walls and kicked up dirt a few feet from where I stood. No one moved except Estelle, who ran to Luther and knelt beside him, examining his wound. There was no time to run and no place to seek cover. In an instant, I knew our plan had failed. We were going to die – perhaps right where we stood.

There were three of them. They approached on horseback from behind us, the horses' hooves thudding dully on the rocky ground. They were in no hurry. The rifle shots were meant as a warning. We were as good as dead, but they weren't ready to kill us just yet. That thought gave me no comfort. As they drew near, I recognized the lead horseman as the evil-looking guard who'd struck Isaac with his rifle butt two days earlier. He had the look of the devil in his eyes, and I knew he must find delight in making others suffer. I tried not to think about what was going to happen to us.

None of the Indians spoke except Estelle, who held Luther in her arms and whispered softly to him. Luther was clearly in great pain. His wound didn't appear to be life-threatening, but the only thing she could do for him was to stop the bleeding.

Evil-eye dismounted and pointed his rifle in our direction. "Drop right there or the next shot will do a lot more damage!" His voice was menacing. I think he was hoping that one of us would try to make a run for it, but no one did. Slowly, we all dropped to the ground. All except Estelle, who continued to minister to Luther. The guard cranked off another round in her general direction. She ducked in terror, but didn't leave Luther's side.

Evil-eye glared at her and shouted, "You got bad hearin' little lady, or are ya just plain dumb like most-a yer kind?"

Estelle regained her composure and calmly replied, "He is hurt and needs medical attention." She showed no fear, and I admired her courage. Then she ripped off a part of Luther's shirt and used it to fashion a crude tourniquet. He moaned in pain as she placed it on his upper arm.

Evil-eye roared wickedly and said, "Where yer goin', little squaw girl, none-a ya is gonna need no doctor!" He laughed insanely and looked for approval to the other two men, still on horseback. They only stared at us without emotion.

Apparently convinced that Estelle was no immediate threat, Evil-eye turned his attention to me.

"Well, now," he said, savagely spitting the words out. "This one here don't look like no injun!" He kicked my side with a powerful thrust of his boot and white-hot pain shot through my ribs. He chuckled gleefully as I writhed in agony.

He knelt beside me, grabbed my hair, jerked my head back roughly, and thrust his face close to mine. I could smell his foul breath and strong body odor as I looked into the dull blue of his eyes and saw nothing but hate. *What kind of monster is he?*

"Well, lookee here," he said in mock delight, "I do believe this is Mr. Harrison! The same fella who's been snoopin' 'round over at the reservation and askin' a bunch-a nosey questions!"

He slammed my head down on the ground and I nearly blacked out. Blood started oozing from my nose. He broke into merciless laughter as he reveled in my suffering. I made up my mind that if I was going to die in this man's hands, it wouldn't be without a fight. I didn't know how, but I intended to make him pay for his heartless treatment of us.

Evil-eye turned to the men on horseback and said, "Harry, you an' Joe git on down here 'n tie their hands an' feet. We want 'em all neat an' purty when the boss gits here."

I could only guess that "the boss" was Lester Crow. He'd no doubt want to be around when it came time to dispose of us.

"Check 'em fer weapons, too!" Evil-eye ordered.

Harry and Joe dismounted and began roughly searching us. They didn't bother to be gentle with the women, or even little William. Joe approached me and ran his hands across my chest and down my sides and back.

"Hey, what do we got here?" Joe said, pulling my utility knife from my jacket pocket. He tossed it to Harry, who casually examined it, then put it in his own pocket. Any chance I had of making a fight out of it had just been derailed. The only weapon that could have helped us even the odds was now in their hands.

Joe continued searching me with renewed interest. He felt a lump in my shirt pocket, stuck his hand inside and came out holding the small cellular telephone the sheriff gave me. I'd just thrown craps twice in a row. Had Charles Bird's gods finally abandoned us? I tried vainly to remember who the patron saint of lost souls was.

"What the hell's this?" Joe said, turning the small telephone over in his hand. Then, realizing what it was, he answered his own question. "The sunuvabitch has a queer-looking cell phone!" he exclaimed, acting as if he'd just found a bomb. Evil-eye came over and examined the cell phone. He found the power switch and flipped it on to see if it worked. Nothing happened. The battery was probably too weak or it had been damaged in the river.

I noticed that the nearly imperceptible green light on the bottom of the phone was now on, but I wasn't sure what this meant, and Evil-eye didn't seem to notice. He decided that that the odd-looking cell phone might be worth saving and put it in his shirt pocket. Meanwhile, Joe began looping rope around my arms and legs. The ropes were tight and cut into my wrists, making movement nearly impossible. He made Jacob and me sit back to back, then tied us together. He did the same thing with little William and Mona Dove. Finally, when Estelle had finished bandaging Luther, the two of them were tied together in the same way, ignoring Estelle's pleas and Luther's cries of pain. They tied Isaac securely to the trunk of a nearby tree.

Evil-eye walked back to me and grinned at me with an ugly sneer, "So you're the hot shot what helped these Injuns escape! I figured they was too dumb ta do it on their own."

He bellowed a loud, braying laugh that sounded more animal than human and glared manically at me.

"You'll pay for this," I said, trying to project more confidence than I felt. "The sheriff will be all over you like . . ."

Whack! He'd whirled and kicked me savagely in the ribs a second time and pain shot through me like hot bolts of fire. I couldn't control my own cries as I gasped for breath. I heard Estelle sobbing quietly.

"If I was you, Mister Troublemaker, I'd think twice 'bout smartin' off again. Lester gave me strict orders ta keep ya from gettin' away, but he didn't say nothin' 'bout keepin' ya in one piece." He kicked me again, but this time it was a glancing blow, and I was already too numb to feel the pain.

Evil-eye told Harry to go find some wood for a fire. He returned a few minutes later with his arms full of dead tree branches, and Joe and Harry busied themselves building a campfire. By then, the sun was an orange ball just peeking over the eastern horizon, but there was still a chill in the air, and the ground was damp and cold. The heat from the fire felt good.

We all watched silently as Joe boiled water in a tin pot, then poured it into a small pan containing a pouch of coffee grounds, making what we used to call "hobo coffee". It wasn't made for a king, but the pungent aroma reminded me how hungry I was. Evil-eye, Joe and Harry sat around the fire, sipping their coffee and joking amongst themselves, ignoring the cruel fate that awaited us. The pain in my side was nothing compared to the anguish I felt about my failure to help the Indians reach home safely. Nothing the guards could do to me would equal the shame and sense of inadequacy I felt about how I'd led the Indians right into the hands of their foes. They might not hold me responsible, but I couldn't forgive myself for the harm I'd caused them.

CHAPTER FORTY-FOUR

The sun was a bright red ball climbing steadily over the mountain peaks as its warm rays replaced the early morning chill. The guards drank coffee and munched on beef jerky, oblivious to our hunger or discomfort. My leg still throbbed, and I was nauseated and weak from exhaustion and loss of blood. I looked at Luther. His face was pale and his eyes were narrow slits. Mona Dove, Estelle, Jacob and little William were conscious, but the grim look on their faces reflected the desperation of our situation. Isaac said nothing, his face an emotionless mask. All we could do was wait, but how long and for what?

The guards talked quietly in hushed whispers while we were left with our own thoughts about what would happen next. Then I heard the soft chirp of a cell phone, and Evil-eye separated himself from the others. He withdrew his cell phone from his jacket pocket, listened briefly, then spoke into it. He closed the phone, put it back in his pocket, and said to the others, "Lester's on his way." He looked at us, grinned meanly, and said, "Won't be long now."

I was consumed with hatred at the thought of Lester Crow. I prayed for a miracle, but knew the odds were stacked against us. My arms and legs were numb from the lack of circulation, and I felt dizzy and light-headed.

At one point, I dozed off into a troubled sleep. I awoke to the sound of an approaching vehicle, growing louder as a cloud of dust rose in the distance. The guards stood up in anticipation, and a minute later a dark blue pickup truck came into view, approaching at a high rate of speed. It looked a lot like the truck that had followed me from the reservation and may have been the same one Amos had seen speeding away from the inn following the attack on me.

The truck braked sharply and halted a short distance from us. The driver's door opened, and the sinister countenance of Lester Crow emerged, an invisible shroud of negative energy emanating from him. He approached us with haughty air and placed his hands on his hips, surveying the situation. No one spoke, and the tension in the air crackled like electricity. He eyed each of us slowly, then walked toward me, and I felt my muscles tense involuntarily. My mouth and throat were as dry as the desert floor and I was faint from lack of food and water. He stood over me and stared like a vulture eyeing its prey. A dark bruise above his left eye confirmed that he was the intruder I'd struck with the poker during the attack on me. Finally he spoke and there was venom in his voice.

"We meet again, Mr. Harrison." He paused for a response, but I didn't answer. "You have caused us much trouble, but you will trouble us no more." He hissed these last words, then said with finality, "We shall take great pleasure in putting an end to your meddling."

I knew he meant what he said, and I didn't doubt that he'd enjoy keeping his promise.

Evil-eye laughed derisively at me.

Crow turned and walked to Evil-eye and they spoke in hushed tones. Evil-eye nodded several times and said something I couldn't understand.

Lester Crow walked back and looked down at me for a long moment. It is said that the eyes are the windows to the soul, but I could see only vindictiveness as he looked at me.

"Well, Mr. Harrison," he said with mock sincerity, "I have a special treat for you. You have managed to rouse the interest of my employer, who has requested that I keep you in reasonably good condition until he arrives so that he can deal with you himself."

He seemed disappointed that he would not have the pleasure of killing me.

I twisted my body to face him and paid the price as hot barbs of pain tore into my rib cage.

"That would be Mr. B. J. Tall Hose, I presume," I said, gritting my teeth to overcome the numbing pain.

Crow grinned crookedly and said, "You should be pleased that Mr. Tall Horse has taken such an interest in you, Mr. Harrison. He's a very busy man and allows himself to become personally involved only in matters of great importance."

Evil-eye chortled again, enjoying Lester Crow's brand of humor.

"You see, Mr. Harrison, you have forced us to alter our schedule substantially. Your interference has cost us a great deal in time and money, but the price you'll pay will be much higher." His tone was cold and impersonal, and I was sickened at his total disregard for what was to become of us.

I was surprised to learn that B. J. Tall Horse planned to make an appearance. The big bosses don't usually dirty their hands by doing the killing when they have people like Lester Crow and his underlings to conduct their orders. But when Tall Horse found out that I was responsible for uncovering his mining operation and leading the Indians in their escape, he must have been so infuriated that he decided to unleash his anger on me himself. Nonetheless, I would die with the satisfaction of knowing that I'd disrupted his plans, even if I hadn't been able to stop him altogether.

The sun blazed overhead in a clear, cloudless sky, and the temperature was climbing into the 80s. My throat was dry and I desperately wanted something to drink, but I knew it would do no good to ask, and I wouldn't give them the satisfaction of begging. The others were still silent, but the desperation of their situation as well as the fatigue and hunger they felt was evident in their faces. Luther had lost a lot of blood, but he was still breathing. I wondered how much longer he could hold on. But what difference did it make? One way or another, we were all going to die – probably before the end of the day. The great getaway plan had almost worked – but almost wasn't good enough.

I tried to move my fingers so I could loosen the knots that bound me, but I couldn't reach them. Jacob must have sensed what I was doing and reached his fingers out to touch mine. He began working his hands slowly over the knots that held my hands together and I prayed he wouldn't be discovered. I shifted my body slightly to allow him more room to work – hoping he could loosen the knots enough to free my hands. *If I can get my hands on one of the guard's rifles, I can at least do some serious damage before one of them shoots and kills me. My primary target, if I get the chance, will be Lester Crow followed by Evil-eye.*

I heard another vehicle. The men heard it too and stood erect, like soldiers on the front line awaiting the arrival of the commander in chief. But this was one general who ruled by force and intimidation rather than legitimate authority. Except for Lester Crow, it was fear, not respect, that drove these men. If B. J. Tall Horse was the commanding general, Lester Crow was his chief of staff, but they were both cut from the same cloth. There was no doubt that Tall Horse was the brains of the outfit – the idea man, the organizer

– while Lester Crow, with cunning and guile, attended to the details of the operation. It was a perfect combination, and it had worked flawlessly . . . until I inserted myself into the picture.

Trailing a thick cloud of dust, another pickup truck approached, this one larger and gleaming red in color. White lettering on the door of the truck, along with a colorful seal, identified it as an official vehicle of the Sequoia Indian Nation.

The red truck braked to a halt and B. J. Tall Horse emerged from behind the wheel. He was wearing tapered jeans, a long-sleeved western-cut shirt, and a white cowboy hat. He wore designer cowboy boots that had probably set him back a week's pay, and on his belt, he wore a large silver buckle with lots of turquoise and sparkling gems. He was just as impressive as he'd been the first day I met him but, now I could see something in his eyes that wasn't there before.

Tall Horse only nodded to Lester Crow, and ignored the other men, who stood silently, in reverent obedience – not wishing to become the target of his wrath. He walked to where we sat and glanced with disinterest at the Indians. Then he glared at me with the expression of a prizefighter who'd just scored a knockout. I locked my eyes on his and tried to ignore the futility of our situation.

"So we meet again, Mr. Harrison. I regret that it is under such unfortunate circumstances." His voice was low, but the threat it carried was obvious.

I continued to stare at him and said, "If you're as smart as I think you are, Mr. Tall Horse, you'll release us now, before there's any more blood on your hands. You must know that the authorities are closing in on you at this very moment – it's only a matter of time before you're discovered."

From somewhere behind me I heard a loud, chackling laugh. It sounded like a hyena, but it was actually Evil-eye.

Tall Horse said nothing, but continued to look at me while a thin smile played on his lips. "I am touched by your concern for my welfare, Mr. Harrison, but you are needlessly alarmed. You see, we have taken great pains to maintain tight security over our operations, and we have been quite successful in plugging any . . . ah . . . leaks, shall we say."

Evil-eye chortled again, enjoying the moment.

Tall Horse let his eyes wander over the pitiful group of Indians, showing no emotion whatsoever, while I wondered what kind of man could have such a callous disregard for the plight of his own people. He was so confident, so utterly sure of himself; and I wanted so much to see him pay for his crimes. Sadly, it appeared that we, not he and his thugs, would pay the ultimate price.

I was about to say something when the passenger door of his truck opened, then slammed shut, and I heard footsteps approaching. I turned my head and gasped in disbelief as the hulking figure of J. D. Potter approached. I was speechless and my mind searched for some reasonable explanation, but there was none that made any sense.

"You see, Mr. Harrison," Tall Horse said with a wide grin, "the authorities of whom you spoke are already here." He laughed from deep inside his chest and Evil-eye joined him. Even the guards had lost their nervousness and were grinning widely at our predicament. I knew then that any hope we might have had of getting out of this alive was now lost.

CHAPTER FORTY-FIVE

Potter approached with a leering, ugly grin on his meaty face. Hot bile rose in my throat and I felt like vomiting. His presence explained a lot. Now I knew how Lester Crow had managed to escape after attacking me while Potter was only a short distance away when the alarm was sounded. It also explained why the Sheriff's Department had been unable to produce any solid leads in the investigation of Ben Griffin's accident. It might even explain who had deliberately cut the brake lines on Ben Griffin's car. The pieces of the puzzle were finally fitting together.

A frightening thought flashed through my mind. Was Sheriff Jenkins also involved? It was too incredible to believe. The sheriff had a long history in law enforcement and had impressed me as a man of character and integrity. I found it hard to believe that he could be corrupted by someone like B. J. Tall Horse, but Potter was a different story. The corpulent deputy fit right into the picture.

Tall Horse looked at me, saw the shock in my eyes, and was visibly pleased at my reaction. "I believe you know Deputy Potter, Mr. Harrison?"

With a mock show of friendship, Tall Horse placed his arm around Potter's broad shoulders. "He has a keen interest in your intrusion into our operations. He was, of course, disappointed when you eluded his surveillance, but when I learned that you had finally been apprehended, I invited him to witness your going away party."

Evil-eye grinned at me and grunted in pleasure. Potter's beady eyes gleamed in delight. He stood with his hands on his bulging hips and looked at me as if I was his next meal. He just stared at me, and the hatred in his eyes said it all. I hadn't liked him from the first time we met, but I had no idea just how corrupt he really was. I was angry at myself for not figuring it out sooner.

I couldn't resist telling Potter what I thought of him. "I suppose I should be surprised to see you in cahoots with these guys, Potter, but it all makes sense. What will Sheriff Jenkins say when he finds out about your involvement?"

Potter didn't answer my question, but his ugly grin widened, and he squinted his bovine eyes at me. "You shoulda left town when you had the chance, Harrison! But no, you just hadda stick yer nose in where it don't belong. Now yer gonna get what's comin' t' ya!"

He spat something brown and ugly from his mouth, and it splattered on the ground next to my legs. Foul-looking saliva dribbled unnoticed down his chin. "Far as Sheriff Jenkins goes, neither you ner them injuns will be 'round to say nuthin' 'bout me." He hunched up the sagging gun belt imperiously and grinned at B. J. Tall Horse and Lester Crow, but they didn't return his smile. They were using Potter, but he was too dumb to know it. They'd discard him without a thought when he was no longer useful.

I was going to die anyway, so I figured it might as well have my say. "Don't kid yourself, Potter. Sheriff Jenkins is no fool. He'll put it all together one way or another, and eventually the lot of you will go to death row for what you're about to do here. My only regret is that I won't be around to watch them put the needle in your arm."

Potter merely snorted at this, and I knew nothing I could say would penetrate his thick skull. Potter believed he'd be allowed to walk away from all this. His fate was no better than ours, but he was too dense to know it. He could be the poster child for blissful ignorance. I almost felt sorry for him, but stupidity was no excuse for his connivance. I could only pray they'd all pay the ultimate penalty. This thought gave me some small comfort.

B. J. Tall Horse turned to me and said, "It seems, Mr. Harrison, that you have the situation all figured out." His voice was oily smooth. "The only thing you seem to have forgotten is that you and your comrades are about to disappear . . . without a trace. It is we who will be free. You should spend your last few minutes preparing to meet your Maker rather than boring us with your empty threats."

He was right. I was wasting my breath. In the end, it wouldn't change our fate, but it was important that I show my own defiance, if for no other reason than to bolster the spirits of Estelle and the others. I had to admire them. Even though they knew full well the hopelessness of our situation, they didn't show it.

Tall Horse looked at his wristwatch and said to Lester Crow, "We have wasted enough time here. There's work to be done." He stepped aside and motioned to Lester Crow to follow him. The two of them conferred in hushed tones, then Lester Crow told Harry and Joe to load the Indians into Tall Horse's truck. Lester looked at me with a smile on his face and said, "You're coming with me." I was initially shocked that B. J. Tall Horse would allow Lester Crow the pleasure of dealing with me. But when I thought about it, I came to the conclusion that Tall Horse – despite the evil in him – probably didn't have the stomach for seeing a man die at his own hands and would rather leave the dirty work to someone else. Lester Crow, on the other hand, no doubt relished the idea of ending my life.

I had no doubt about my own fate, but what about the Indians? I figured they'd be taken back into the mine to finish their work, after which they would be disposed of.

Harry and Joe loosened the ropes that bound us together, then untied our feet and ordered us to stand. The two of them shoved the Indians toward Tall Horse's pickup truck. Lester Crow ordered Potter to put me in the back of his truck, and Potter eagerly obeyed, pulling me roughly to my feet. But my legs were so numb from lack of circulation I nearly collapsed. Potter pushed me roughly toward the blue truck and I fell awkwardly, my hands still tied behind my back. When I got to my feet, I could tell that the knots holding my hands were much looser than before. Jacob had made more progress than I realized. It was up to me to parlay this one small opening to our advantage, but I wasn't sure how.

I watched the Indians being herded toward Tall Horse's truck and marveled at their courage. They didn't cry out or show any signs of fear. Potter threw me up against the side of Lester's truck and grinned at me with obvious satisfaction. I kept my hands busy on the remaining knot, hoping to free them.

While Potter's attention was on me, Joe and Harry had their hands full getting the six Indians to the red truck. Luther was conscious, but just barely. He fell to the ground, and Harry jerked him roughly to his feet. The blood began flowing from his wound again and Estelle sobbed loudly, pleading for mercy, but none was shown. Mona Dove said nothing but looked at the men with contempt and loathing. Little William was as brave as ever, taking his punishment without complaint.

If I was going to have any chance to make a break, it would be while the guards were occupied with loading the Indians onto the truck. Lester Crow and Tall Horse were deep in conversation, while Potter's attention was focused on me.

He started to grab me around the waist to hoist me onto the truck bed, but just as he did, I made my move. With one last twist, I freed my hands from behind my back, jabbed my right fist upward into Potter's larynx with the force of a sledgehammer, causing him to gag and go into paralyzing convulsions. Before he could react, I hit him a hard left to the mouth and heard the sound of broken teeth, causing him to roar out in pain. He slumped forward as blood spurted from his nose and mouth. I seized the Colt revolver from his holster, spun him around, twisted his right arm behind his back, and pulled him close in front of me. I used his body as a shield and trained the gun on the guards. Evil- eye and his men froze, staring open-mouthed at me. Lester Crow was the first to react, and had his revolver leveled at me in an instant. I knew he'd fire on me, even if it meant killing Potter, who suddenly realized what was about to happen and cried out in vain. He tried to free himself from my grip, but I held on desperately. Out of the corner of my eye, I spotted Jacob signaling the Indians to drop to the ground.

The roar of Crow's revolver sounded like a crack of thunder. Potter's body slowed the bullet, but I felt searing pain on my right side and nearly blacked out. The impact knocked me down and Potter's body fell free from my grasp, while a large red stain spread over the front of his shirt. I sat half-sat, half crouched and fired twice at Lester Crow. The first shot missed him completely, but the second found its mark. His legs buckled and down he went. He was not dead, though, and he struggled to a sitting position, trying to get a bead on me. Before he could get off another round, I fired again. The bullet caught him dead center in his forehead, and he went over backwards, his arms flaying outward.

I cracked off a round at B. J. Tall Horse but missed him as he ran to his truck and climbed inside. I thought he was going for a weapon. Instead, he fired up the engine, and sped away, throwing up a dense cloud of dust and gravel. The sight of him running like a coward brought me small comfort, but there was no time to celebrate.

When their boss made his getaway, Harry and Joe showed their true colors.

They ran to their horses and galloped off, leaving their rifles in their scabbards.

That left only Evil-eye. Just my luck – he was no coward and was determined to see me die if it was the last thing he did. He had dashed back to retrieve his rifle from its scabbard on his horse and in seconds, had his Winchester trained squarely on me.

He cackled crazily as he coldly took aim, but I got off one shot in his direction. It went wild, and he laughed even harder. His first shot missed me by a fraction of an inch – I'd ducked just as he pulled the trigger. I was getting weak from the loss of blood and could hardly hold the revolver steady. I got off one last shot that caught him in the thigh, but he didn't go down.

I pulled the trigger once more only to hear the hollow click of an empty cylinder. I was out of ammo, and he knew it. I looked for cover, but there was none. His next shot hit me in my left arm, tearing through bone and tissue. Blood spurted over me – I was done in, and I hoped the end would come quickly.

Evil-eye limped toward me, cackling insanely. He was coming in for the kill and there was nothing I could do to stop him. I had one last glimpse of the Indians, terror in their eyes, still flat on the ground where B. J.'s truck had been. They knew they'd be next, and they were helpless to defend themselves.

Evil-eye stood over me with a cruel smile on his lips. His rifle was pointed directly at my chest, and I waited for the impact even as my body weakened from the loss of blood. I was slipping into unconsciousness. The gun roared loudly, but I felt no pain as I fell into a dark, swirling vortex. I had at last reached the end of a very long journey.

CHAPTER FORTY-SIX

Somewhere in the deep recesses of my mind I heard fragmented sounds of guns blasting, people shouting, women crying, men cursing, horses screaming and engines roaring, but I couldn't comprehend their meaning.

Then the images slowly came into focus, and I was startled to find myself surrounded by masked faces, their voices hushed and unintelligible. This apparition was superseded by a white ball of light hovering directly over me, blinding me with its dazzling brilliance. I struggled to rise, but my muscles were numb and refused to respond. I tried to speak, but my throat was dry and parched like sandpaper – the best I could manage were a few guttural moans.

I didn't know if I was alive or had passed on to some afterlife. The masked faces continued to hover over me, their murmuring voices rising and falling with the irregular rhythm of the ocean tide. *Were they talking to me?* I couldn't understand what they were saying. The light grew more intense and radiant and drew me toward it, like a moth to a flame. Its glow was warm and comforting, and I surrendered to its beckoning embrace, floating along in a sea of soft clouds. The world was a kaleidoscope of sparkling colors, blurred shapes and shadowy images.

Then the bright light slowly faded, and the soft, fleecy clouds drifted away. I became aware of a dull, throbbing ache in my shoulder and right side, and a bandage around my head. Another image appeared, but this one was real, with a face and body and hands that were probing every part of my aching body. I knew I wasn't dreaming when I saw the oval face of Nurse Snyder come into focus, her large blue eyes staring down at me. In this instant, I realized that beauty is truly in the eyes of the beholder.

Her thick, pink lips twisted into what passed for a smile, and she dispelled any possibility that I might be dreaming when she said, "Well, Mr. Harrison, isn't this a nice surprise! Is it my good looks or our gourmet food that keeps you coming back?" Her meager excuse for humor sounded like the singing of an angel.

It hurt to talk, but I managed to grunt, "Just back for my two-week checkup, as ordered." I did my best to smile, but it hurt too much, so I settled for a weak frown.

She laughed heartily from deep inside her ample belly, adjusted the pillow beneath my head, checked the IV tube attached to my arm, and gave my shoulder a motherly pat.

"Dr. Bradford will be in to see you in a while. You know the drill. Push the button there by the bed if you need anything."

She placed a plastic container of ice water and a plastic cup and straw on the tray next to my bed. "Your throat will be dry from the intubation tube they had to use on you. Sip the ice water. You'll feel better soon."

Then she was gone, and I was left to contemplate my situation. I was amazed that I'd somehow survived what I recalled as a violent shoot-out with Lester Crow and Evil-eye. *How can this be? Evil-eye had the drop on me. What about Estelle and the others? Did they escape safely?* Lester Crow was certainly dead.

But what about B. J. Tall Horse? I was startled from my reverie when Sheriff Jenkins entered. He walked to my bedside holding his sweat-stained cowboy hat in his oversized hands. He looked tired and a little older than the last time I'd seen him, as if recent events had taken their toll on him. He looked grim, and a sense of dread came over me. Whatever he had to tell me was not going to be good, but I wanted to know. "What is it, Sheriff? What's happened?"

"It's nothing," he said, twisting the brim of his hat nervously. "It's just that I
. . . well, I feel kinda responsible for you bein' all busted up. If I'da known .
. ."

It still hurt me to talk, but the ice water I'd just sipped helped. I whispered hoarsely, "It's not your fault, Sheriff. I took on this job knowing that there were risks."

"Well, Harrison," he said, finally looking me in the eye, "I figured you'd say that. But it don't make me feel any better 'bout the shape yer in."
I knew he must be sickened at learning of Potter's involvement in the whole
sorry mess, but I wasn't going to bring that up.

"Well, anyway, Harrison," he said gruffly, a faint grin playing on his lips, "you did a hell of a job on this case, and I'm just glad it's all over."

He relaxed, and I invited him to sit in the only chair in the room and bring me up to date on what had happened after I blacked out. I sucked on the ice water and listened while he filled me in.

The key to our rescue, he said, was that military cell phone he'd given me. Even though the battery for sending and receiving messages was dead, the geo-positioning device was solar-powered. The signal it emitted allowed the sheriff to pinpoint our location.

"We had volunteers on horseback and in trucks all over those mountains lookin' for you, Harrison," the sheriff said, "plus the State Police loaned me one of their best sharpshooters. But without that homing signal that suddenly flicked on, our chances of finding you were slim and none."

A wave of relief swept over me when I thought about how I'd nearly discarded the cell phone when I realized I couldn't use it to make a call. It had been my dumb luck that Evil-eye clicked the phone on, activating the geo-positioning signal. Fortunately for me, God does sometimes take care of those who can't take care of themselves.

"I remember shooting Lester Crow and then being shot by the one I called Evil-eye just before I blacked out. What happened after that?"

The sheriff went on to tell me he and his men had been closing in on the signal when they heard the sound of gunfire. By the time they reached a vantage point, Lester Crow was dead and Evil-eye, whose real name was Gus Latrobe, and I had been trading rounds, each of us finding our mark at least once. The State Police sharpshooter took Latrobe out at 1,000 yards just as he was about to put a bullet between my eyes, just as I'd done to Lester Crow. The trooper's fatal shot found its mark just as Latrobe squeezed off his round, causing his bullet to only graze my skull, thus accounting for the bandage wrapped around my head.

"They don't come much closer than that," the sheriff observed, and I knew just how right he was.

"What about B. J. Tall Horse?" I said anxiously.

"Caught him goin' like hell down the trail as we were comin' up. Tried to run down two of my men and paid the price for it." The sheriff's voice turned somber.

"He's dead?" I asked, not caring one way or the other.

"No, 'fraid not," he said. "One of our shots blew out his front tire and he lost control and went crashing down a ravine. He rolled the truck over three times, got thrown out halfway down, lit on a huge boulder and broke his spine in two places. But we'll have the good fortune of bringing him to trial on a long list of felony charges. Plus, the federal authorities say they want a crack at him, but right now he belongs to us. He'll likely spend the rest of his life in a wheelchair behind prison walls."

The finality of his words hit home hard. Talk about a fall from grace! But then the memories of the pain and anguish Tall Horse and Crow and their men had inflicted on their own people registered with me, and I felt no pity for him. I wasn't sure any punishment he might receive could balance the scales. For a few moments I did not know what to say and the room was quiet.

Sheriff Jenkins informed me Harry and Joe had been rounded up quickly and surrendered without resistance.

"What about Estelle, Mona Dove and the rest of the Sequoias?" I mentally crossed my fingers. "Are they all right?"

Sheriff Jenkins nodded his head and exhaled slowly. "Yes, they're all safe and sound, thanks to you, Clint. The one called Luther is bunkin' right down the hall." He nodded toward the door. "He'll be fine after some mendin'. The rest were treated for dehydration, but they're a strong bunch. They're back on the reservation with their families."

I was relieved to hear the news and sighed heavily. A great weight had been lifted from my shoulders.

He paused for a moment, then said with a broad smile on his face, "There was quite a little commotion when they all showed up on the reservation. You're something of a celebrity out there!"

His words were comforting, but I knew it was more like good fortune, and just maybe Charles Bird's gods, that kept us alive.

The sheriff grew silent, and the smile faded from his lips. I worried that he'd been holding back some bad news. I wanted to ask him, but was afraid I wouldn't like the answer, so I said nothing.

He rose and stood stiffly by the bed and said, "I'd best be on my way 'fore they throw me out."

I had a feeling there was something else he wanted to tell me, but he seemed hesitant, and this made me even more uneasy.

"What is it, Sheriff? What's wrong?"

He started toward the door, then stopped, paused, and turned back to me. He was plainly nervous, and I began to get queasy. I wasn't even sure I wanted to know what he was afraid to tell me. "Clint, I know this is not the best time to be bringin' this up, but it's been on my mind a lot since all this happened, and I need to get it off my chest."

"What's that, Sheriff?" I braced myself for bad news.

"Well, I don't know what your future plans are, Clint, but I could use a man like you as my Chief Deputy. Truth is," he paused and fumbled nervously with the brim of his hat, "I've got two years left in my term but I'm thinkin' 'bout hangin' up my gun belt early and turnin' the place over to a younger man. I figure you'd be 'bout the best person I could have take over this job."

I was caught completely off guard by his offer. I had no definite plans for the future, it was true, but the idea of staying in Climax hadn't occurred to me. But I liked the people I'd met and the quality of life was far better than I'd known in L.A. The idea of getting back into law enforcement was intriguing, but I wasn't sure I was ready for that just yet.

"Can I have some time to think about it?" I said hopefully.

"You bet," he nodded. I think he was relieved I hadn't turned him down on the spot. "You go right ahead and think on it and get back to me whenever you make up your mind." He squared his shoulders, put on his hat, and patted my arm. As he walked out the door, he was whistling softly to himself, clearly in much better spirits than he'd been a few minutes before, and I realized I was feeling better too.

Sheriff Jenkins had just left when Nurse Snyder reappeared, grinning broadly. "There's someone here who wants to say hello."

I couldn't imagine who it could be and was surprised when Melanie came in pushing a grey-haired man in a wheelchair. Before I could speak, Melanie said, her face beaming like bright moonglow, "Daddy, this is Clint Harrison. He's the man who saved your life."

Ben Griffin looked feeble, but I could read energy and intensity of purpose in his steel-grey eyes. It was obvious where Melanie got her good looks. He smiled widely, showing off a set of even white teeth and a dimple on each side of his mouth. Warmth and goodwill flowed from his pores, and I liked him immediately.

Melanie pushed his wheelchair next to my bed and Mr. Griffin expended his hand to me. I took it, surprised at the strength of his grip.

"I owe a great deal to you, my boy. Not just for what you did on that mountain road, but for what you did for Melanie and the newspaper." He shook my hand fiercely and I tried my best to hold on.

I was speechless at first, not knowing what to say. Finally, I was able to form whole sentences. "I only did what anyone would do in the same circumstances. I'm just so relieved to see you've made such a marvelous recovery."

Melanie smiled broadly and said, "Daddy's doing just great. He'll be going home in a few days and can't wait to get back to work."

I couldn't resist the temptation to get in a tease. "And I know Sam Dooley can't wait to have you back, Mr. Griffin."

He looked at me sharply through squinted eyes and started to say something, then realized I was joking. He thought for a minute, then he said, "The problem with Dooley is he forgets who's the boss of this outfit, and there's not room for more than one boss." He shook his head in exaggerated exasperation.

Then his face broke into a wide grin. "But dammit, there's no one better on those presses than Sam." We all had a good laugh, and I felt even better than I had a few minutes earlier.

After some more small talk, Ben Griffin shook my hand again and told me to come by and see him when I was able. I said I would. Melanie wheeled him out and I drifted off to sleep almost instantly. When I awoke, the sweet face of Mary Alice was looking down at me.

There was something in her eyes that made me feel very warm and content, and I realized how much I'd missed her the last few days without even thinking about her. I started to rise, but she pushed me back down, brought her lips to mine, and kissed me ever so gently. The kiss was warm and full of promise, and once again I thought I heard angels singing.

Neither of us said anything for a while, but I knew we'd found something very special in each other. The hurt and anguish of the last few days was fading away, and I felt better than I had had for a very long time. The golden rays of the afternoon sun burst through my window, and I knew then that I had a great deal to look forward to in this pleasant little town called Climax.

ACKNOWLEDGEMENT

This is my first novel, but, like any author, I had a lot of help making this book a reality. First, and foremost, I'd like to thank my wife, Marlene, who encouraged me to continue the battle, and who gave me the space and time to get the job done. Without her inspiration, this book would still be an unread manuscript.

Second, I wish to acknowledge the craftsmanship and tutelage of Cliff Carle, who taught me what it means to be a good writer. While I alone am responsible for any errors or defects in the book, Cliff helped make it a much more polished final product, and I am eternally grateful for his generous assistance.

Third, I would like to thank Dan Fry, who did an excellent job of proofreading when it needed it badly.

Finally, I wish to recognize the talents of Deborah Ann Marshall, who helped me get the manuscript ready for publication.

I am humbled and appreciative of the assistance and encouragement I have received from all these kind people.

ABOUT THE AUTHOR

Charles Dennis Hale served six years in the U.S. Marine Corps, is a former police officer and, since 1972, has been a police consultant to several hundred cities, towns and villages across the United States. He owns his own consulting business, Resource Management Associates, which has provided technical assistance and consulting services to municipalities in more than thirty states. His company specializes in the field of public safety and conducts management studies and promotional emanations for all ranks in municipal police and fire departments. Mr. Hale has published numerous articles in public management and law enforcement publications and is the author of four textbooks on police-community relations, police administration, police patrol operations and the design and administration of assessment centers for police and fire departments. This is his first book-length work of fiction.